Outside Influence

by

Lucy Abelson

Lone Hare Press

A LONE HARE PRESS

First published in Great Britain by Lone Hare Press

ISBN 978-1-913663-14-8

Copyright Lucy Abelson

First Edition 2020

These days the ancient game of Golf aspires to be inclusive, approachable and welcoming to all…but..

Beware the

'**Outside Influence:** Any of these people or things that can affect what happens to your ball or *equipment* or to the *course*:

- Any person (including another player), **except** you or your *caddie* or your *partner* or *opponent* or any of their *caddies*:

- Any animal, and

- Any natural or artificial object, **except** natural forces.'

From
Player's Edition of the
Rules of Golf

"Friends, Romans and countrymen lend me your ears"
as Mark Anthony said in Shakespeare's
Julius Caesar.

"The evil that men do lives after them
The good is oft interred with their bones."

1. A Car in trouble

The noise was terrible.

Crystal's foot jammed on the brake to stop the car.

The crunch echoed so loudly she feared the car might explode. Was there a bomb under her car? The fear hit her. Jason, her partner was in the army, the Parachute Regiment, no less, until four years ago. One of his mates had even hinted he had a spell in the SAS. Still, they weren't together then, so why should someone tamper with her car, unless they thought it was his?

She clenched her fist round the steering wheel telling herself that fear was absurd. There must be stones or other debris beneath the car which she hadn't noticed when she parked.

Calm down. Crystal told herself as she re-started the car, but to her horror the moment she pressed her foot down on the accelerator to move forward, the horrific noise sounded again.

Gritting her teeth, she drove onward. There was nothing wrong with her car when she came here to the club from her home. It ran perfectly smoothly so there must be a simple cause like a tree branch caught up underneath which would loosen as she drove. Then all would soon be all right.

It wasn't. The racket worsened as the car moved. She must stop. This trouble was integral; something was definitely wrong with the car, except that was ridiculous. The car was nearly new, less than a year old, bought with a view to her driving here.

"If you're going to play golf seriously, you'll want a car to cart your stuff around in, a four by four," said Jason, when he insisted on buying her this sturdy vehicle.

More likely to ferry your children around was Crystal's unvoiced thought, unsure a bulky four by four presented the right image for a model, even if nearing forty these days, she displayed more middle-aged fashion. Only once she'd started driving this sky-blue silver vehicle did she start to like it, even felt it was her own beloved car because it hadn't given her a moment of trouble until now.

Shuddering again, she ground her teeth at the ghastly sound. Something had to be seriously wrong with this vehicle. Time to ring for someone mechanical to sort out the problem.

She jammed her foot on the brake, turned off the engine and, with a swift grab of her silver blue handbag, pulled out her silver mobile, as she jumped out of the car. A moment later she was about to press the number of the AA, which her partner Jason thoughtfully put onto speed dial on her phone, when the sight of the blank screen made her swear. She forgot to charge it.

Someone would have to lend her one. Crystal looked round the carpark where about a half a dozen empty saloon cars were parked. No sign of any owner though. The only other human being in view was a beggar seated by a fence at the carpark's entrance.

Jason's warning not to speak to him resounded in her ears. "I know you; you're too kind. Don't get involved. That wretch often hangs around the Visitors carpark."

Well maybe now he can do me a favour.

Crystal walked over to the entrance where the old man wearing check trousers of a plus four variety, which looked suspiciously like ancient golf gear, a polo shirt and a sweater with an emblem on it, reclined droopily against the fence. Near enough to drop a couple of coins into the bowl in front of him, which already contained a few envelopes and a little cash, the old guy was, Crystal reckoned, possibly older than she first thought, maybe nearer seventy than sixty. The wrinkles on his round face were deeper than she would expect in a younger man, despite the healthy sheen of his complexion. As someone in the business of appearances she recognised these signs.

"I suppose you couldn't do me a favour," she asked.

He shrugged. "Possibly. What do you want?" There was a note of suspicion in his voice, redolent to her ears of someone who'd been to a posh public school.

"Could I borrow your mobile phone?"

The throaty chuckle he gave made his round head jerk forward. "Do I look the sort of person who has a mobile?" This time he croaked.

"Most people do these days."

"Well I 'aint." There was a touch of sarcasm in the way he said "'aint".

"Oh, Oh, I do understand." Embarrassed, Crystal turned away, took a couple of steps then turned back. "I don't suppose you saw anyone around my car, the Suzuki over there." She pointed to where her car was now parked out of line.

"See no evil, hear no evil, speak no evil," the beggar muttered.

Crystal's lower lip dropped. Under her breath she swore before she said, "So you did see something."

"Nah. I'm not here to watch the cars and I don't see that well anyway stuck here."

"Well I'm stuck here too if I can't move my car."

"Nah, you can go to the clubhouse and get that fat arse manager to ring up a garage to come and help, sort out that damn awful noise."

So you heard that, thought Crystal as she strode back towards the Elmsleigh clubhouse. How embarrassing this was. She had come here today for a playing interview to move forward her application to join the golf club where Jason belonged.

Glancing at the form she'd submitted a woman in the office had already turned up her nose at the word Model which Crystal had written in the slot for occupation. She should have written Designer, which she aspired to be, or maybe Beautician since she did sometimes help people with their appearances. When she'd feared diversity in the fashion industry meant tall slim girls with shoulder length blonde hair were passé, she'd done a quick training as a stopgap, which turned out unnecessary as she was still booked for modelling work.

It was a short walk from the Visitors carpark through the main Members Carpark to the clubhouse, giving her enough time to recall someone once making a joke about the manager's wandering eye for girls, which had upset Jason. Still that might have been a different man. Hopefully this guy would be more helpful that his snooty assistant.

8

The alternative was to go back into the lounge and seek out the woman who had played the course with her, to ask to borrow her phone, but that did not appeal. Sitting in the lounge was Oggi, the Ogre, a man renowned in the fashion world for seduction, but a man with such influence that girls who threatened to expose him suddenly found their work disappearing. Crystal's own career had survived the slap she'd administered to his oval fleshy face; she'd swung round to hit him after he'd stroked her behind once on a shoot, but the nostrils that flared on his prominent nose suggested one day in a less public place, he would get revenge for the insult.

Here the Ogre was a powerful man. That was according to Tabby, who had played with Crystal. Since her husband Hector was the Vice-Captain she should know; she said the men sitting with him were "movers and shakers in the club". Crystal could not remember their names, other than Oggi whom Tabby referred to as Ozzie, but she picked up that a couple were on the committee.

Crystal shuddered at the thought of going back into the lounge if he was still there, for she doubted she could enter the room inconspicuously. Her five foot eleven inches of height along with the way she slung her slim body as she walked always attracted eyes. Admirable though this was on the catwalk, it had the disadvantage she could not easily hide from unwanted attention.

As she walked from the Visitors carpark through the Members carpark to the large clubhouse, she reflected on the difference between the dignity of the clubhouse with its old-world grace and the vulgarity of some movers and shakers in the fashion world. The large brick building, evidently a converted and sympathetically extended former country house, exuded a welcome calm. The entrance through a stone pillared porch suggested that only the right people should walk through it, although there was no indication visitors should ring or somehow announce themselves.

The manager's office, as Crystal knew from her previous visit, was immediately on the right of the entrance, fortuitously, since Crystal had forgotten it, labelled with his name Simon Duckworth. She knocked at the door apprehensively, noting with irritation her blue nail varnish was chipped. Lucky in more ways than one that she had no model assignments today.

"Come in. What can I do for you?" Asked a broad-shouldered athletic looking man seated behind a large old-fashioned wooden desk, steering his head and shoulders round a big antiquated computer with a large monitor.

While Crystal explained her car problem, the manager's muscular chest heaved up and down as he breathed out through his slightly parted lips in what looked like exasperation.

"So please could you lend me a mobile or let me ring the AA from here. Or is there a pay phone I could use?"

"No, we dispensed with those long ago, now everyone has mobiles. No use anyway. The AA won't be able to do anything."

"What do you mean?" Asked Crystal perplexed. Would the AA not come out to a private club because it counted as a home call or something similar?

"If it's what I think it is, they won't have the part. We'll have to call a garage." As he rose from behind the desk, his dark haired large square head towering above the computer, he reached for the cream telephone sitting on his desk. "I'll call the garage we use. That'll save wasting time with any of the AA, RAC or anyone like that."

"Won't that be expensive?"

Simon Duckworth waved his left hand airily whilst using one finger he pressed a couple of keys to dial what must be a number, recorded by speed dial, on the phone he held in his right hand. "Insurance will pay."

Crystal wanted to ask whose insurance that would be, but decided that would be something for Jason to argue about later. He dealt with car things.

"'Fraid they won't be here for a while," Simon told her after a short conversation mentioning some obscure part of the car Crystal had never heard of. "They may have to do it tomorrow morning."

"How am I going to get home?" Wailed Crystal. Fortunately the children were being given a lift home from school, but they lived with Jason and her which meant she would have to cook them tea in less than an hour.

Simon looked at his watch. "Where do you live?"

"Petersfield, or at least near there."

"I'll run you back," said Simon. "It's on my way home. Hang about for quarter of an hour whilst I pack up here." He waved his stubby hand at her in dismissal.

Outside his door Crystal wondered whether she'd been mad to accept his offer. Without a phone she could hardly ring Jason to ask his advice. No, that would be ridiculous - like asking his permission. Simon was hardly likely to attack her on the way home. A man in his position shouldn't do that. Besides Jason had taught her all sorts of self-defence manoeuvres. It was ridiculous to be frightened when Simon had made his offer so kindly. That was the spirit in which she should accept it.

She did wonder about this club though. Clearly her problem with the car was not the first time such a thing had arisen here. The few members she had met seemed nice fun people, not the sort to tamper with cars, but from the way the manager reacted it sounded as though they might not care about their visitors' vehicles.

Jason had been a member of this club for ten years, which he said was a "Forces friendly place". He was now on the ruling committee. Yet was he really aware what some other people were like in this place where he wanted his children as well as his partner to belong to, as he put it, a family?

While she fed Jason's children their tea, she shuddered at the thought of his ten year old daughter Maisie having to cope with some of the men she met in the modelling industry. Yet could the golf club be much better if Oggi the Ogre belonged? There was also the man he was talking to, whom she thought she recognised. Yes, she recalled that face as she stacked plates into the dish washer. He was the Russian, who always looked bored, even went to sleep at fashion shows. Must have been dragged along there by his loud out-spoken wife.

With people like this around, Elmsleigh Park was not a place Crystal wanted to join, despite the entreaties of her partner and best friend, the Lady Captain.

2. Another Theft

Samantha, or Sam as everyone called her, did not want to hear this.

"I don't want to join here," said Crystal as they sat opposite each other in the Elmsleigh Park clubhouse lounge drinking mocha coffee.

This remark was disappointing, but not entirely unexpected after last week's troublesome theft of Crystal's catalyst converter from her car, parked here at the golf club. Nonetheless Simon the club's manager sorted out the problem deftly with the crucial discretion needed for the club's reputation. People who paid good money to play here would cancel their bookings if they learnt about the alarming spate of catalyst thefts from cars parked in the Visitors carpark.

Guessing the worst when he heard about the noise Crystal's car made, Simon had advised Crystal the AA would be unable to help because they did not carry the right parts. He then organised with Matthew Borden, a helpful committee member who ran a local garage to get the converter replaced after Simon himself gave Crystal a lift home. She shouldn't be able to fault that.

Prior to Crystal's negative words, Sam felt today was going well. After playing an enjoyable few hole of golf, she made the coup of enticing her friend to drink of mocha coffee with fattening chocolate in it.

"What's not to like?" asked Sam, in as cheerful a tone as she could muster. "Jason's keen for you to be a member and he's on the club committee. This club has got everything going for it, especially this year when I'm Lady

Captain." As she spoke the words the thought reverberated in her mind, *Maybe that's why.*

Perhaps Crystal thought it would distort their friendship. Maybe she feared it would take them back to their school days when Sam had been the cleverer one who helped Crystal with her homework. Still it wasn't as though lack of educational attainments held her back these days. No one in the media cared a rap what Crystal had or hadn't done with her education as long as she could show off clothes or cars.

No doubt about that. She'd maintained her enviable slim figure over the twenty years since they had left school. Yet, to Sam's surprise, she now crumbled up the small shortbread biscuit which the club served with coffee. It made Sam wonder whether the pout on Crystal's mouth men found so kissable, was about calories in shortbread or the club's ambience.

"I'm not sure it's for me." Crystal's nose wrinkled as she popped the biscuit into her mouth.

This was bad news. Crystal would be good for the club. She was a trendsetter, someone people copied. Years ago, as a teenager, the way she hitched up her skirt, clipped up her hair, tucked or tied up the ends of her shirt became a fashion amongst their school fellows. Now in her late thirties, she had a following as a celebrity. Her presence here at Elmsleigh Park would inspire girls to join, instead of going to other rival clubs.

Alarmingly important too, Crystal would appeal to the male membership. Her athleticism as well as her looks would rebut their jokes about frumpy old lady golfers.

Sam knew she was chosen to be Lady Captain, partly out of respect for Dougie, her late, or rather missing, presumed dead, husband's family; they'd provided three captains, two men and a woman, her mother-in-law, for Elmsleigh Park. She was also wanted because she was a journalist who wrote about golf for leading magazines, even the odd newspaper article.

Useful these attributes might be to the club as her strong athletic figure was to the game, Sam was aware they were not qualities which would necessarily attract glamorous young female players. The club needed them to balance the aged dignitaries from the Foreign office or industry mandarins who abounded here as well as the many younger men of all trades. She must persuade her friend to see the club's advantages.

Elmsleigh Park wasn't the smartest or most prestigious club in Hampshire, but the place was beautiful. Crafted sympathetically out of the grounds of an old country house, the course followed the natural contours of the land. A wonderful avenue of elm trees had survived the onslaught of Dutch elm disease. Now in late summer with the trees abundantly in leaf, their green foliage was a joy to behold. Willow trees with silvery bark stood alongside a couple of lakes. Even the annoyance when you hit a ball into them was mitigated by their tranquil atmosphere, with ducks and swans gliding over the water.

Crystal chewed thoughtfully as though gathering the appropriate words before she said, "I don't like the look of some of your members."

Sam opened her hands in a gesture of acceptance as she said. "But you'd find that anywhere"

"You don't find Oggi Reynolds necessarily."
Crystal wrinkled her nose as though the man in question
had a particularly bad scent.

"Who's He?" Sam's own face crinkled. "I don't
know him, but then I don't know all the members. She
bent over the pale wooden arm of her green and blue
tweed upholstered chair to delve down to pick up her large
floppy cream handbag. Inside was her diary with a list of
members at the back. "I can't find his name here."

"Actually, that woman I played with called him
Ozzie, but he's probably ex-directory; he's that sort of
person, too important to be listed."

"That's not likely. Members' names are printed in
the diary so others can contact them to play."

Was she being naïve? Sam wondered as she
recalled some members requested their names should not
be published on the club's website. Yet having belonged
to Elmsleigh for fifteen years, she should recognise Ozzie
Reynolds' name if he were a regular player."

"I tell you he was sitting in the lounge when I
finished playing talking in a very chummy way with some
blokes." Crystal told her.

"They might have been from a visiting society."

"Frankly I wouldn't want him even visiting."

"What's wrong with him."

"Ask any model who's had the horror of working
for him as a client. He's known as The Ogre. Don't know
how he gets away with things but somehow he does."

"What does he do?"

"Some sort of jewellery business, I think, which
gives him the excuse to turn up regularly at modelling

sessions. He likes bodies, long necklaces dangling between boobs in ultra low cut dresses, high thigh bracelets and vast brooches stuck into your belly button."

"I appreciate..." Sam hesitated, her apprehension deepening as Crystal, turning her head slightly, rolled her eyes towards a couple of sturdy middle-aged ladies sitting the other side of the lounge for she knew the jolly blonde Tabitha, or Tabby as she was called, had played an interview round of golf with Crystal.

"And I couldn't get on with her."

"What do you mean?" Sam lowered her voice. Wonderful though the conversion of the clubhouse had been, taking down old walls to make this huge open plan seating area with minimal soft furnishing to help the acoustics, it meant voices carried when there were not many occupants in the lounge. "Tabby is lovely person, a wonderful golfer but happy to play with anyone."

"Yeah, I get golf's more important than people."

"How did you arrive at that idea?"

"'Cos when she asked me why I wanted to join Elmsleigh Park, I said something about wanting to make friends and meet the right sort of people and she went bonkers. She said golf clubs were not snobby these days. What mattered was golf and enjoying the game."

"That's right," protested Sam. Golf clubs might be tarnished with a silly image but golf was historically an all-comers game. Okay, Prince Andrew played now, but the feminist Mary Queen of Scots was castigated for "lack of decent feeling" because she went out to play to console herself within days of her husband Lord Darnley's murder.

And the first ladies golf society was actually the Musselburgh Fish wives who played golf on their days off.

Then Samantha remembered years ago Crystal confiding in her that the reason she'd been sent to private school was to meet the "right sort" of people. No one else knew her father, a dustman, or rather a *refuse collector,* as Crystal insisted he was termed, paid her school fees out of a huge sum of money he had won on football pools.

"But you must have met all sorts of people in the modelling industry," added Sam in a cheerful tone.

"Precisely. That's why when I'm not working, I don't want to meet them, especially rich trash like Ozzie Reynolds. I've told you about some of the clients I've had to work for, their deceit not just about money but what they expect models to do, getting us into compromising situations. You know you wrote that article."

Sam rolled her eyes as she shook her large head, her thick chin length sandy brown hair waving. She did not want to talk about the work that particular article, based on Crystal's experiences, led her into doing. Nor did she want to discuss, especially here in the clubhouse, her job as a private detective.

"You can't compare corrupt model agencies forcing anorexia on women or cheating them out of money with golf clubs. Things that might go on there are a far cry from anything that happens here in a golf club. Elmsleigh Park is a place for friends for goodness sake."

"And a business that discriminates against visitors."

"Hardly," Sam laughed, "we need the income from them. Anyway as member you'd be protected." The moment she said those unfortunate words Sam could predict Crystal's response.

"Protected? You make it sound like the Mafia."

"No way. The game of Golf is against any corrupt behaviour. Integrity and trust are an integral part of play."

"Oh, come on! That's what Jason says." She shrugged her narrow shoulders. "It applies to lots of sport, but it doesn't have to be true of companies that run them."

"I admit that's right about some sports organisations but golf clubs owned by members are different. Don't you trust your man? Jason's part of the management. He was voted on the committee. Don't you want to join the club for his sake?"

"Oh come on Sam – that's such a granny outlook. I may live with Jason, but I'm my own person. I don't have to follow him around everywhere. I do quite enough looking after his children."

"Yes, I get that, but being members of the same club means having the same friends; it's good socially."

"I wouldn't want a friend like Oggie Reynolds. Anyway I got the impression from your mate Tabby, that Elmsleigh Park is more of a business than anything else."

Sam sighed. She'd thought well-dressed blonde, bubbly Tabby, who was in her mid-forties, marginally older than she and Crystal were, made an ideal person for Crystal to meet, especially as Tabby was the second, albeit much younger second wife of Hector Bravo; this bright modern lady was also savvy enough to cope with being the spouse of the strong-viewed Vice-Captain. Sam sighed again as she then recalled that though an apparently high-powered civil servant himself, Hector had mentioned the club must become more business like to survive. If Tabby quoted her husband to Crystal, she hit the wrong ball.

"A golf club has to be more money orientated these days." Sam tried to explain. "Don't ask me about management details because I don't understand them, but because the committee who run the club are all playing members, it means making money isn't the main priority."

Crystal hummed suspiciously.

"Honestly," said Sam, "Sticking at golf which can be such a frustrating game improves people, makes us sweeter natured." She pulled an ironic face since she was not entirely sure she herself liked sweet-natured people.

"Like the charming manager here?"

"Simon? Oh, he's harmless." Sam tried to speak reassuringly. "Really he is. Another coffee?" Persuading Crystal to hang in might take some time. Without waiting for acquiescence Sam swept up their cups and took them back to the bar where she asked for another couple of coffees, which Misty, the slim brown-haired woman behind the bar obligingly offered to bring to them. "At least he got you home in one piece." Sam looked at her friend's dubious face. "Don't tell me he tried something on with you?"

Since the corollary of Crystal's suffering from all too many men making passes at her, was that she tended to be suspicious of any man doing her a favour, she was not surprised at Crystal's next onslaught against the manager.

"Not physically, but he had this sleazy music playing with some man singing 'The very thought of you'." Crystal gave a dramatic shudder as she blew out through her petal pink lip-sticked rosebud mouth.

What could Sam say? Best to change the subject. "Anyway, he did a good job in sorting out your car out."

"That's because of his previous experience. I hate to say it, but there seem to be troubles here at your club."

"Having your catalyst converter stolen could happen anywhere," said Sam.

Crystal's blue eyes widened in protest as she raised her eyebrows. "Yes, but why was Elmsleigh picked? Pretty odd Simon guessed exactly what must have happened the moment I spoke to him about my car."

"He's a bright efficient chap," protested Sam.

No. Crystal insisted. Simon was driven by the need not to draw attention to the damage done to her car as it would alert other people to the club's pathetic security. "That creepy beggar too," she added, "obviously knew something about what happened, but only muttered about evil goings on when I asked him if he'd seen anything."

Sam pursed her lips. Hard to know what to say about the beggar. She'd hardly seen him when she drove through the Visitors Carpark, but she'd heard about him. There was a suggestion he was once a member which made people reluctant to confront him. At the last joint Captains' committee meeting it was proposed he should be investigated, but though agreed in principle, rejected since everyone was worried about adverse publicity owing to the beggar choosing to sit on a public right of way.

"He's being looked into." Sam spoke in as reassuring voice as she could muster, "by management."

"More efficiently than our coffee," laughed Crystal as their cups had yet to arrive. "Is that bar lady called Misty because she forgets or can't find her way about?"

"No, it's her real name for Heaven's sake." Sam began to feel the effort with Crystal was more trouble than it was worth. The downside to her celebrity status was that Crystal was encouraged to be opinionated over small matters. It was the fault of newspaper and magazine reporters like Sam herself, who asked her to pontificate.

Misty had some connection with Simon, the secretary, who was lurking around near them. She beckoned him over to ask what it was. It would be good to know the origin of Misty's name in case anyone else drew the same unfortunate conclusion as Crystal.

"It's from a song," explained Simon, as he sat down to join them at the table. The large mouth on his round friendly face creasing into a smile, indicating that this was not the first time he'd been asked the question. "Misty's a trad jazz song that got popular in the 1980s."

Obviously realising what inspired the question of her name, he beckoned to Misty to bring over the tray with coffees which she was carrying around with a puzzled demeanour.

With surprising speed, the slim energetic lady rushed to them, apologised for the delay and put their coffee down on the table in front of them.

Good. Now Crystal will see how fast he sorts anything out.

"How do you know our Misty was called after the song?" Sam asked once the lady in question had departed.

"Because by a strange coincidence our fathers were in the same jazz band for a while." He turned to grin at Crystal. "I've got loads of the old recordings our fathers made together. Most people like them although I know they don't appeal to you Miss Sears."

Crystal gave him a charming smile, "No, quite right, not exactly my style. I prefer something with a bit more beat and humour."

Ah, this is promising, thought Sam, as Simon replied "Yes, they did that too."

Balls. No. For Simon continued, "My grandfather did a great rendering of that Lonnie Donegan song of the seventies, "My old man's a dustman". He almost sang himself as he rocked to the next line, "He wears a dustman's hat."

"Actually, my father was a refuse collector," said Crystal through pursed wrinkled lips.

"Great job," nodded Simon.

"Yes, and I don't like it made fun of."

"Shame you feel like that, but I can appreciate you feel sensitive where club management's concerned at the moment." His mouth dropped at the corners into a rueful smile. "You're not the only one."

Surely he's not apologising for making a play for her? That's what Crystal thinks judging from her face. Or is he going to tell her lots of our members collect refuse? That could backfire too.

Sam stood up before Crystal, whose expression suggested he'd implied the club was full of beautiful women men might accost, could launch into any protest or correction. "I'm afraid we really should make a move."

"That's a shame. I hope you've enjoyed your visit," he smiled at Crystal.

"What's happened?" Sam asked Simon in a low tone over her shoulder as she passed him.

"Those damn thieves have had a go at another car."

"Oh no." Sam groaned. "Anyone I know?"

Nicholas Roman, a member's guest, had his catalyst converter stolen in broad daylight."

Sam frowned. "Nicholas Roman? Where've I heard that name before?"

"From his friend Yuri Leonov probably. Or, since Nicholas Roman's actually a Romanov, one of the former Russian royal family, you might have read about him."

"I thought they were all murdered."

"This guy's branch must have survived. I'm told he's a distant cousin of the Queen."

"That rings a bell. What club does he belong to?"

"Need you ask? Royal Winchester."

"Where Prince Andrew is or used to be the esteemed patron?" Asked Sam praying Crystal wasn't listening. Sam could guess what her views on Prince Andrew might be, but as Crystal was standing a few feet in front of her almost pawing the ground like a horse ready to move, Sam whispered, "Are they friends?"

Simon's head quivered as he said, "I should imagine so. They're related and belong to the same club, but his great friend here, Yuri Leonov, you know our Russian member, is absolutely furious and thinks he's been personally targeted."

3. Detective work calls

Laurie's summons was not unexpected.

At the Elmsleigh Park Captains' last night's committee meeting, Cabinet as they called themselves, the main topic concerned the attacks on cars parked at the club. Besides the President, Captains, and Vice-Captains, all those present in their various roles as organisers of matches, social events or managers of the house and course supported Simon, present in his role as manager. Even Chris Pearce, the treasurer, agreed when Simon had suggested the club needed to employ a detective agency to assist the police with their enquiries.

What none of those sitting in the old library knew was the presence amongst them of a private detective. Whilst they discussed whether, in the club's penurious state, such employment would be an appropriate use of its funds, Sam kept quiet. After all she was not a full time employee of the Old Alresford Investigators. Her profession as far as Elmsleigh Park was concerned was journalism with an emphasis on leisure.

With the old town of Alresford being so near Elmsleigh Park, Sam supposed it was likely Old Alresford Investigators would be approached. Since she also guessed Laurie, knowing she played golf, might ask her to do the job, she'd been wondering how to refuse the commission. Her contract with the Investigators did not specify she must take every assignment offered, merely that she should do ten cases a year plus the assurance she would not work for any other agency employed in similar business. In return the company paid her a small retainer, plus all expenses needed for the maintenance of Monty the black Labrador dog Laurie gave her, supposedly to help with any of her assignments.

Only later did Sam discover Monty was provided by one of Laurie's friends in the police force because he failed in some or other training course. That did not matter to Sam, most of whose assignments were tracking down regular shoplifters, whose cunning ways enabled them to avoid security cameras. Sam herself was of average height and build, an appearance which gave her the capacity to bumble about incognito around shops or stores. Even her mid-brown hair, which she never tinted because Dougie, her lost husband, liked it raw, as he called it, once describing it, to her chagrin then, as "rich mouse", she now saw as an advantage.

Whilst pretending to be engaged in conversation, or looking at goods herself, with her hidden mobile phone ready to snap the perpetrators secretly, she succeeded in identifying culprits. Her skill, developed from a fascination with conjuring tricks as a child, also helped her understand how shoplifters could use sleight of hand to whisk away a desired item whilst engaging onlookers to cast their eyes elsewhere.

Now as she approached the Victorian three-storey terraced town house in Old Alresford she wondered how to explain to Laurie Moorland, proprietor, chief and good friend of Sam's late or missing partner, it would be inappropriate for her to be involved in this investigation. She wanted to tell Laurie that if her man could be here, have returned from being lost Afghanistan, he would agree with her.

As usual she did not enter the building from the front door in the High Street but a backdoor entrance into a room, which had once been a kitchen, to get to stairs to reach his first-floor consulting room. The only window faced a small garden rather than the street. Although local gossip ensured the building was known to house a detective agency, Laurie tried to guard its privacy, so important for his clients.

Though Monty leapt eagerly into the room wagging his tail, Sam felt her body stiffen as the stocky man stood up to welcome her with his arms out-stretched to clasp her hand with both his in a welcoming gesture. He leant forward as though he might kiss her but she backed away. She wanted to keep their relationship strictly on a formal business footing, especially now he had grown a fashionable stubbly beard.

"Couldn't you get someone from Alresford golf club, if you really think it's a golf club thing?" She asked once the preliminaries were over and they were sitting down on opposite sides of his desk. "Or there are a couple of clubs in Winchester which probably attract people from a much wider catchment area, especially Royal Winchester. I gather our last important guest who had his thing stolen belongs there."

Laurie's large brown eyes widened as he looked straight into Sam's blue ones, but his mouth twitched in a smirk as he spoke. "Yes, and Peter the Great's descendant says such thefts would never happen at his club."

"Do you actually know Nicholas Roman then? I wonder if I've seen him. What does he look like?"

"Like Peter the Great's famous portrait, round face, lots of black hair and a black curly moustache. Lots of people round here know him, but the point concerned here is your inside knowledge of Elmsleigh Park and the personnel involved. That's what's needed in this case."

Sitting beside her Monty's head rubbed her legs in sympathy as Sam repressed an embarrassed shudder.

"Yes." Sam drew out the word in a plaintive note, "but I don't know anything about cars or the parts that might be purloined from them. Surely these thefts must concern people's vehicles, not their owners."

"Absolutely." Laurie nodded in a way with his head poking forward that his long nose almost seemed to be pointed at her. "It's additionally about retail, your subject. That's your entry point, the selling of the parts."

"But Laurie I keep telling you I don't understand anything about cars, other than the obvious fact they have," she laughed as she corrected herself, "usually have four wheels. I don't know a thing about converters, except they stop the car making a dreadful noise when you drive, and I don't know any second-hand car dealers to start asking who would buy second hand converters. I wouldn't even know what to look for if I could penetrate a second hand car dealer's workshop."

"Not asking you to Darling. My hunch is this is about jewellery. The precious metals found in converters, platinum, palladium and rhodium can all be used in priceless jewellery. That's where you come in, finding who might receive the stuff."

"I don't think we've got any of that sort of jeweller at Elmsleigh Park," protested Sam, getting to her feet.

28

Laurie smiled at her. "You could be surprised."

"I suppose I could.," she agreed, thinking of the five hundred members, many of whom she had never met. "Anyway, if we have, that would make the job a real conflict of interest. The last thing we would want is publicity if we have to ask someone to leave because we discover they've inadvertently accepted stolen property."

"I doubt it would be inadvertent." Laurie stood up and leant over his desk whilst he continued in what Sam knew as his winning voice, "Anyway, this is what makes you such a suitable person to take this on. You can make enquiries discreetly. It's your forte; you can work in a way that no-one will guess what you're investigating."

Sam chewed her top lip ruminatively before she asked, "Did you tell Simon Duckworth you were going to ask me to do this. Does he know I work for you?"

"No." Laurie shook his head. "Our brief is to support the police with their enquiries, to do stuff the police won't have time for. We could set up some hidden cameras but Mr Duckworth's not keen for us to do that."

"Why not?"

"Because he'll have to go through them and he's not keen to point a finger at a member, should a member be involved."

"I'm not either."

"You wouldn't be named. You'd simply inform us and then we'd tell the police when we got more evidence, a sequence if you like and for that we need a discreet observer who can put the jigsaw together, make the dominoes line up."

"I'll think about it," Sam promised.

"Don't take too long. There are other girls who'd love to have this job. Plenty of Hampshire ladies fancy themselves as potential sleuths."

"Okay." The response jerked out of Sam's mouth. She did not want to lose her useful retainer income from Laurie's detective agency, let alone the money to pay the dog-sitter when she played serious golf as well as when she worked. "But promise me I won't be identified as your agent to anyone in the club. And I really mean that."

"Agreed." His oblong face broke into a grin with his eyebrows raised, but they fell again at Sam's stern expression.

"It would be social death for me and not too good for you if it became known I am involved," she said. "I must insist you take me seriously Laurie."

"Okay." He acquiesced with a slight nod which suggested that though he heeded Sam's concerns he could not make them the priority she wanted.

"It isn't that straightforward." Sam tried to explain that as a single woman she would have to take care enquiring about the work and lives of men in the club or people might think she was on the search for a partner. She could see a joke trembling on Laurie's lips that maybe this investigation could serve a dual purpose for her.

"Couldn't it be useful in more ways than one?"

"No." Sam said through clenched teeth. "I can't question the men about their work, especially whilst they're playing golf."

"What about the nineteenth hole? Isn't that the time when you're all sitting around in the clubhouse drinking and exchanging jokes? Couldn't you manage subtle enquiries then?"

"Easily enough with the girls, but not the men. Goes back to what I said about cars – I'm too ignorant about them – unless…" she hesitated.

"Go on."

"I take a sudden interest in jewellery, precious metals as an investment. Didn't you say that stealing converters was all about, taking the elements out?"

"Something like that." He said. "Boils down to retail like a lot of things."

"Problem is I don't know where to start. There are over four hundred members listed in the diary, but I've a feeling," she wrinkled her retroussé nose, remembering her conversation with Crystal, "there may be more, possibly with something to hide, left out of the diary."

Laurie smiled. Without a word he switched a key in the drawer of his desk in front of him and pulled out half a dozen sheets of A4 paper stapled together. "Guard this with your life. It's a full list of members' details with their occupations, or at least the jobs they had when they signed up to join Elmsleigh Park."

"Thanks." Sam glanced at it as she stood up to leave. A name at the bottom of the top page glared out at her. "Ozzie Reynolds". His occupation was listed as "Company director."

"Goodness," she exclaimed as she perused the list more. "You've even got a profession for Yuri Leonov. We've always wondered what he did. – Not that this is much help since it's another 'company director'."

That just shows how ludicrously difficult this project's going to be. The mystery about what Yuri did led some members to talk in hushed tones about the possibility that Yuri with his Russian accent could be a spy, which she had previously dismissed as silly fantasy. Yuri was an excellent golfer and good company with a great sense of humour, she'd found when she played with him in mixed foursomes' competitions. Now she saw he lived west of the golf club in the direction of Salisbury she wondered if there might be a grain of truth in their suspicions. Many diplomats, army and ex-army officers were members, including Dick Norton, the President.

Owing to the way prospective Elmsleigh members had to be proposed and seconded by existing members, golf clubs should be safe places. Yet she recalled with horror the terrible incident in Ireland when a bomb was put under a police officer's car parked at a Belfast golf club where that police officer was a member. The head of terrorism said it was clearly intended to kill the officer, but anyone else around at the time could have been injured.

No that's ridiculous. Bombs were not involved here. Besides now she recalled she had heard it on good authority some time ago, that Yuri's money came from mining. Not that she could remember what they dug up in Russia to sell here. Nonetheless, their wealth, it was rumoured, allowed the invariably beautifully dressed Mrs Leonov to take a suitcase full of cash to a famous boys' public school to pay for her son's school fees. The Leonovs were rich anglophiles with no need to engage in stealing bits of cars, unless what they were mining coincided with bits found in catalyst converters.

Maybe that wealth aroused envy. Perhaps Yuri was right about his royal Romanov guest being targeted when his converter was pinched. After all, his friend Nicholas Roman did belong to the grand Royal Winchester golf club where his relative Prince Andrew was the Patron and they were all roughly the same age.

She shook herself. Sensible Elmsleigh Park members were grateful to the people Tabby had pointed out as the club's benefactors after she had played that introductory round with Crystal. She had definitely mentioned one of the group sitting with Ozzie Reynolds was Yuri Leonov.

Yet Crystal, Sam reflected, was not the only person who had recently castigated the rich. Last night in the meeting, Dick Norton the President had turned on Neil Lavant, the course manager, because he'd suggested perhaps one of the great rich members might get a consortium together to buy the club to run it more as a business. Dick had been horrified. "This is a members club," the venerable old man had roared. "We own the club and that's the way we want it to stay. Don't want Russians taking over."

"Money is a problem." Chris Pearce, the treasurer, shrugged his shoulders. He held up his hands helplessly, as, in his light tenor voice, he'd continued in an ostensibly reasonable tone. "We're too short of cash to keep the course up to the standard needed for our members as well as to attract visitors to pay to play here."

"Members don't want their subscriptions raised," agreed Captain Roger Turpin.

"Tough," Dick Norton had snorted, "we'll have to raise money some other way." He turned to Matthew, responsible for social events. "Can't you do something?"

To Sam's alarm, she found herself drawn into the argument, and trying to help matters, agreed to organise an entertainment for a social evening, which became a more alarming prospect as the evening progressed. After the meeting had ended in some disarray, only partially soothed by drinks in the lounge afterwards, what improved the men's moods was talking about prospects in some or other world cup. Though Amy, the ladies Vice-Captain was able to hold her own, joining in animatedly, Sam wondered how she could arrange any money raising social event that would arouse the same enthusiasm. Also plaguing her as she drank her Sauvignon blanc was the possibility of being dragged into the car investigation.

Now it was happening.

Laurie insisted she was the ideal person to discover what was going on.

"Provided there is something to find relevant to the club." She'd retorted. It would be dangerous to suggest President Dick Norton might be as paranoid about the rich as Crystal. Were other golf clubs being targeted, she wondered, Royal Winchester in particular.

There was rather an odd look on Laurie's face as he told her, that was an aspect she ought to discover.

It could end this wretched investigation if that were the case. So that would be worth doing. Hardly believing what she was agreeing, she found herself say, "Okay, I'll look into the retail side, see if I can find where these things are being sold."

"There is a personal side too," admitted Laurie, "which you would be rather good at."

"No, I don't want to investigate members."

"This isn't about a member." Laurie wrinkled up the long nose on his oblong face in his customary way when he had a job he evidently felt insignificant. "Apparently there's a beggar who's regularly in a nearby carpark, something about visitors' premises, which has a public right of way through it so he can't be turfed off. Anyway, this old guy's saying to anyone who'll listen, that he's descended from a previous owner of the property. That's causing a bit of trouble. Your gang want us to find out, and preferably prove it's rubbish."

"When this was discussed in committee, the consensus was not to bother about him," said Sam, feeling rather guilty she'd implied the opposite to Crystal.

"Yes, it's a side-line. Comes specifically from Sir Hector Bravo who I believe is your Vice-Captain. He's insistent it's done, discreetly of course."

"Surely it's something better done by lawyers."

Laurie laughed. "Your management know all too well lawyers would charge a fortune for getting people like us to do the leg work for them. You probably won't have to do much work, just chat up the old fellow. You might even get him to help you get to the bottom of what the hell's going on at Elmsleigh Park

4. Planning the game

What a nightmare. How on earth did Laurie think Sam could question members about their activities on the days of the thefts from cars parked in the club's Visitors carpark? She would have to approach the investigation from a different angle. She looked down at the sheets of paper listing the members' names with their occupations alongside, that lay on the table in what the estate agents called her "Breakfast room".

They meant a room in which you eat, but for Sam the room was also her work room, housing her computer, printer and shelves full of books. Eating alone or with guests was always done sitting on benches by the pine table in her kitchen. As Sam gazed around running her full top lip over her bottom front teeth she reflected, *socialising over food is out.* Even if the cocktail set at Elmsleigh Park ate in kitchens, their places were likely to be far grander than hers. Any of the members might be agreeable to slum it with Sam because she was Lady Captain, but they would be unlikely to betray themselves whilst she hosted them to lunch or dinner.

Yet socialising somehow had to be the answer. She clapped the long fingers of her right hand against the palm of her left hand. The club must be the venue. She had the perfect excuse to approach people about an event there. What seemed like madness when she agreed to organise the next club social was now an opportunity. She would set up a game that entailed people talking about themselves.

A quote from Shakespeare's Hamlet rang in her mind, "The play's the thing wherein I'll catch the conscience of the king."

It wouldn't be as grand as that but in a flash, it came to her. *Ancestry can be the topic.* She could approach any number of people to ask if they would take part. How they reacted to talking about their lives would tell her a lot. Their ancestors did not have to be grand as long as they were interesting. Furthermore, they did not have to be actual ancestors. Family Tree would be the theme of the game, but what they claimed could be True or False.

Players would describe a great grandfather, grandmother or maybe an uncle, or even cousin once removed, who was a famous or infamous person for audience then to decide whether their claims were true. The President himself could play, even start the game for she had heard him once say jokily that he was a descendant from the wrong side of the blanket, of his namesake, "Mad Dick Norton of Southwick", the man who owned and lost Southwick village. He was a famous Hampshire man. Some club members must have heard of him. If not, they might have visited the village of Southwick which was not far away.

Captain Roger Turpin would have to join in too. Though she had never heard him suggest he might be descended from that famous outlaw highway man Dick Turpin, he could suggest he was. Who could guess what it might lead to people telling her about themselves or others? Even if they were not exactly going to confess to any crimes, it could start members talking.

It would give her a chance to speak to Yuri Leonov. Since more than once she had been drawn to play with him in mixed foursomes competitions approaching him would not be awkward. Also, as he liked to bring his glamourous wife Ekaterina to lunches and dinners at the club, he might be persuaded to take part. He did not need pretend to have connections with the executed royal family of his friend Nicholas Roman, whose converter was stolen. There were enough famous Russian authors or composers, even musicians with whom he could surely find it acceptable to claim kinship.

Put to him simply as an entertaining after-dinner game, the President agreed eagerly. Despite the mad appellation of his famous seventeenth century namesake, he was happy to lead the participants in their claims of famous or infamous ancestors. He liked the idea people should be encouraged perhaps to claim a pirate or some other scoundrel as a forebear, although he doubted anyone would believe the club Captain, Dr Roger Turpin, a highly respected orthopaedic surgeon could be a descendant of a notorious highway man.

"Not sure about that," laughed Roger Turpin when Sam approached him in the clubhouse foyer, "if they hear Dick Turpin's father was a butcher."

"Then he was one of your ancestors. That's amazing," lied Sam with a laugh, since she knew about the butchering having already researched Dick Turpin the highway man.

"Not an ancestor." The denial came out with an awkward one-sided smile on the Elmsleigh Captain's face.

"That doesn't matter. What I'm calling the game is 'On My Family Tree'. Dick Turpin could be a brother of one of your ancestors.

"You will play, won't you? It would be such a wonderful bluff. You could say cutting up creatures ran in the family." She wanted to laugh at the dismal expression on the Captain's long face, but having got him literally with his back against the wall of the clubhouse foyer, so that he would have to push her out of his way to escape, she pursued with the exaggerated claim, "The President, Dick Norton, thinks it's a frightfully good idea. He's happy to claim he's actually descended from Mad Dick Norton, whilst all I'm asked you to do is suggest Dick Turpin is on your family tree somewhere."

"Do we really want our members and their guests to pay good money to hear we, the club's hierarchy have got a lot of Dicks in our backgrounds," asked the tall handsome Captain jovially, shuffling his large feet towards her.

"Absolutely," Sam spoke in her most confident reassuring voice. "It's very respectable these days to have a gangster hovering in your family background. Remember that acclaimed television series Peaky Blinders which was so popular?"

Roger nodded.

"There's an eminent university professor Carl Chinn who's written a best-selling book about the real working-class gang in Birmingham which inspired the series; he sells the book with the claim he's descended from one of the gangsters." She lowered her voice noting a couple of the much older ladies standing nearby who might not share this opinion.

"Okay." Roger agreed with a twinge of a smile, speaking loudly enough for anyone to hear. "It's certainly a far cry from the way golfers traditionally present themselves, but chaps do bang on about our need to change the image of the class-ridden golfer."

"Absolutely right; you'll do a great job." Sam agreed with delight. She knew Roger was keen on amateur dramatics and spoke well. His participation gave her a starting point for questioning other members about their potential villainous ancestors or simply making conversation about criminal activity, a topic which could lead on to those wretched car thefts.

As she left the club, she suddenly remembered she was also supposed to be checking out the beggar who sat regularly in the Visitors carpark, the man who so disturbed Chris Pearce, the treasurer, because he was off-putting to visitors. Nonetheless, since the beggar claimed to be descended from the family who owned the Elmsleigh Park grounds, she might even include him, especially as Crystal was convinced he knew something about the car thefts.

The ragged old man looked up eagerly as she drove into the Visitors carpark, but to her chagrin, she realised he was not looking at her car. Behind her was the smart BMW saloon car belonging to the general manager Simon Duckworth. He was a nice enough guy, but not someone she wanted to view her chatting up the beggar. She might be Lady Captain, but that made it even more important to be correct. She dismissed the thought of speaking to the beggar now; she must not be seen to encourage him.

All the same it struck her what a good place the carpark was to waylay people. So, a couple of days later, when she saw Yuri Leonov unloading his clubs from his car in the Members carpark, she waylaid him. She began by implying how much Ekaterina, his wife would enjoy the social event to take place in three weeks' time. It might even encourage her to become a social member.

The thickset man put his large golf bag back on the tarmac, resting on its stand, to shake his large head. "We haf not thought about that." He said in his deep gravelly voice. "I am not sure she will like a golf entertainment. She does not play you know."

"Ah yes, I did know," said Sam. "But this is going to be a general fun entertainment, not focussed on golf. This show is about people so it will help her get to know and understand our members as individuals outside golf."

"Vat do you mean?" Though Yuri's English was perfect, sometimes his intonation was a little strange, making him sound a mite suspicious.

But that could be my imagination. So Sam continued. "Ekaterina would see you play a part."

"I do not act. I am myself."

"Yes, that's it. You would be playing yourself; you would need to sound like yourself. That would be the point of it. Because you're known as a straightforward guy, you would be all the more convincing."

"I am not viv you."

"Well it's like this. – Oh before I go on I must tell you that the President Dick Norton is taking part and our

41

Captain, Roger Turpin the Orthopaedic surgeon who I believe operated on Ekaterina?"

"Yes, when she broke her elbow. He did a good job."

Sam went on to explain the parts that could be played, suggesting to start with a that he might be descended from a famous author like Solzhenitsyn."

The Russian shook his head. "Nah nah. Too dangerous. Give FSB here the wrong idea."

At Sam's puzzled expression, he explained, "FSB is secret service. Not good for me to have grandfather who boasts his books show pains and ills of Russian society."

"But there aren't any Russian police here," protested Sam. She choked back a laugh at the very idea a member of a golf club like Elmsleigh Park might belong to the Russian secret police force.

In response Yuri raised his eyebrows as if to say *You simply never really know.* When he then showed no more enthusiasm for Tolstoy or Pushkin, whom he denigrated as "tortured souls," Sam moved on swiftly to suggest he might boast a famous musician or composer for a relative.

"Same difference," Yuri shrugged, his hand reaching out to pick up his golf bag. "Shostakovich, he ran away from Russia to America, not a popular move."

"You could go further back to Tchaikovsky," suggested Sam, beginning to wonder whether she was learning anything useful, until Yuri replied.

"Absolutely not," he retorted, recoiling backwards. "That dreadful woman."

"But I meant a man, the wonderful composer."

"Yes but you cannot put the name Tchaikovsky with a family tree with a Russian like me."

"Why ever not?"

"I told you, that dreadful woman who claimed to be the poor murdered princess Anastasia Romanov – her surname was Tchaikovsky. She caused trouble."

"Sorry, I did not know that."

"I am surprised," said Yuri. His voice rose as though in shock as he explained there was no way he could mention the name Tchaikovsky when his very good friend Nicholas Roman was a real descendant of the erstwhile Russian royal family though he was too well-bred to boast about it.

Then suddenly his mouth widened into a broad smile as his eyes lit up. "I have good idea, good for me too. I will play a real man I am related to, Alexei Leonov."

"Who?" The name was familiar, but Sam could not remember why.

"You do not know Alexei Leonov? He is the first man who walks in space."

"Well you'll certainly want to remind us all at Elmsleigh Park about him."

"Yes, yes. He was a great man. And he only died last year."

"Wow! You're actually related to him?"

"A little. As you might say, by a long shot."

"That doesn't matter. It's about being on your family tree. It's great that you'd be telling the truth. The whole idea is that people have to judge whether you are lying or telling the truth about your relationship. Obviously if Alexei was an astronaut, he'd have been a very fit man so you could claim he played golf. It's the relationship to you that's important."

Success. Yuri's smile embraced his whole face, his eyes widening as his left hand let go of his golf bag's handle to rise into the air with his fist clenched as he exclaimed, "Yes, yes, I relate to him. Space ships, they are good. They use my stuff."

"Your stuff?" Sam queried.

"Antimony. You have heard of antimony."

"No." Sam frowned, realising the word was familiar, but she could not think why. "What is it?"

"A mineral. My family we mine it in Russia. We give antimony for space ships as well as many other things. Yes, that is what I can tell your members. Antimony is used for batteries and flame retardants. It helps stop fires. That is important in space ships."

"That's good. I'm sure some of our members will be interested in spaceships." Sam said glibly with a nod.

"Maybe they don't have a spaceship in their garages," chuckled Yuri, picking up her tone, "but they do have cars and they have antimony."

"Really," gasped Sam.

"Certainly." Yuri nodded. "Yes, yes, but I must go now." He hoisted his clubs on to his back and strode off across the car park towards the first hole where three men were waiting for him, one of whom was the stocky Ozzie Reynolds. He, like the other two players, had their golf clubs strapped on to a battery-operated trolleys. Beside them Yuri, with his clubs carried on his back by a strap over his left shoulder, looked rather more muscular and athletic, despite his paunch. Yes, she had forgotten that aspect of him when she had played with him. Unlike most men over forty, he still carried his golf clubs.

Antimony? Where have I heard that word before? Of course. How dumb I am. That's one of the elements in the catalyst converters, a reason why they are stolen. Sam reflected how lucky it was she had not blurted out that connection when Yuri mentioned antimony.

But there was another connection beating about her brain, something to do with her recent research on the internet. *Bravo.* She had it. That was it. *Charles Bravo,* the man who was poisoned, accidentally poisoned himself when he wanted to kill his wife was the theory in the nineteenth century. He had died from ingesting antimony.

She need not mention the antimony to Sir Hector Bravo, the Vice-Captain when she asked him to partake in the entertainment, but at least she had an idea to put to him. He was a blokey sort of man who tended to congregate with similar types in the spike bar, which at one time did not admit women, so he might be amused to suggest he had such a famous, or perhaps infamous man on his family tree. It could heighten his profile.

Anyway, with regard to her job, at least she had something to report back to Laurie.

"Great," was Laurie's enthusiastic reaction when she rang him with an update that night. "Leonov must see it as a sales opportunity."

"Yes, he virtually admitted that," groaned Sam, "only it's investors he's looking for as far as I could tell, not people who might buy the sort of antimony, whatever that might be, which comes out of a car part."

"Never mind." Laurie continued to enthuse about the project which gave Sam an opening to find out where precious metals were sold and to whom. It was a promising start as Yuri, knowing about mining, might also know where rhodium, platinum, nickel and palladium amongst other metals which could be sold.

Sam wanted to protest again that she knew nothing about metals but Laurie forestalled her. She must know about jewellery and some of these metals such as platinum and rhodium were used to make jewellery. These days they were apparently two of the most valuable metals in the world, out-classing gold and silver.

Jewellery? Why did that ring a bell Sam asked herself as she replaced her house phone back on its hook on the wall of her kitchen. Why was it she had talked to recently who'd mentioned jewellery in less than appreciative terms. *Of course. Crystal talked about Ozzie Reynolds.* And who was playing with Yuri Leonov? None other than Ozzie Reynolds.

Knowing his name was not in the regular diary was a nuisance. It meant he was selective about the Elmsleigh Park members he mixed with so he was unlikely to want to participate in social event organised by the Lady Captain. He was not a man who joined in mixed events and he certainly did not have a wife or partner who played golf at Elmsleigh Park. Also, if he was the type of man who liked tall willowy girls to finger, he was unlikely to respond well to Sam whose talent was not presenting herself as desirable, but finding a wavelength with anybody to get them talking about themselves.

She smiled to herself as she thought of Maud West, that famous early twentieth century detective; she was renowned for her disguises. Sam brushed the notion away. Her photograph as Lady Captain was on the wall of the clubhouse foyer. She had been on a platform at the annual general meeting with her photograph on the news sheet. Ozzie Reynolds was an astute man interested in women's appearances. No, she would have to get someone to help her, someone whom Ozzie would not recognise as a club member and she knew who that someone should be.

It would have to be Crystal.

Men like Ozzie would not remember one of the multitude of women he had mishandled even if she slapped him ten years ago. He had not, as he threatened, sued her for assault because his threat stopped her filing any complaint about him.

Crystal could disguise herself. It was part of her trade. She could make herself look like anyone. What's more it would be a useful start for the new career she wanted to embark on, designing sports apparel. She could have a jewellery interest in making ornate ball marker brooches. Other logos might be a possibility too. Crystal had to help her. She would surely want to expose Ozzie, not bodily, Sam grinned to herself but morally.

It was a long chance that he might be involved in the catalyst converter robberies, but if he could tell them who might buy precious metals involved that help.

5. At Home with Ozzie

The cheek of it. Typical Sam to involve me in her detective problems. She says it's journalism, but I have my doubts about that. Anyway, it'll be useful to me if I go forward with the clothes accessory design business I've planned. Modelling can't last forever and being at an agency's command is a pain. Besides Jason's still desperate for me to join Elmsleigh Park.

He can't see the problem with Ozzie Reynolds. Funny how he could be so possessive one moment, someone chatted her up, then insouciant the next over her telling him about Ozzie Reynolds wandering paws. Jason's reaction was that was trivial compared with a chum of his falsely accused of rape. Besides, he'd heard Ozzie played a good game of golf.

Crystal hummed to herself as she looked at the ten-foot wall length wardrobe she'd paid to install in the spare room. Even at that size she'd needed to hide a trunk full of clothes she could not bear to part with, in the loft.

With the presence of tough Sam alongside there should be no danger from the Ogre's wandering hands. He understood the power of the pen and would not want to get written about as a sex pest these days. Nonetheless what to wear was a problem. She slid back the door of her wall long wardrobe. Leggings or tight trousers were out: men like Ozzie would always find a way to stroke a bum if its shape was revealed to them.

There was however her funeral skirt, a mid-calf flowing black garment which she'd bought to wear for Jason's first wife's funeral. He'd told her without any doubt in his voice that though he wanted her present at the event, he did not want her to be a "spectacle". She must "fold in" with the other mourners. He might be proud of her looks but he did not like "cat walk style" dressing.

She had not got rid of the outfit in case it came in useful one day. Once she had put it on, she wondered why she'd ever doubted it. The skirt was elegant and graceful when she walked. She had a light brocade jacket with gold in it which worked well not only with her hair but the accessories she designed.

Inevitably, before she finished dressing herself, the doorbell rang. Sam must be there to pick her up, and make sure she did not back out of going to see that man whose face she once slapped. It was a long time ago but could she truly believe Sam's insistent, "He's most unlikely to remember it, or even recognise you in such a different context."

It sounded faintly insulting, but she told herself sternly, it was what she wanted. Without further ado, she withdrew the hand which reached out for rouge to pat on her cheeks. The makeup she had on would suffice.

"Coming down," she shouted out of the open window of the spare room which privately she regarded as her dressing room despite its unsuitability because the window opened out to look on to the private road beside which their house stood.

Sam looked in surprise at her appearance when she stepped into the Mini. Her expression added to the irritation of hoisting her long full skirt into the confined space of the front passenger seat.

Crystal slung her capacious handbag with her designs and a couple of samples of material to use for pashminas on to the back seat. She did not want to work with Ozzie Reynolds. Nor did she want him stealing her ideas. The best that could come out of this meeting would be for him to point her in the direction of someone else. Her worst worry, that he might recognise her, was again poo pooed by Sam.

"I'll bet he's had a lot of worse things to worry about," she said as she took the car off at a brisk pace towards Winchester. "Anyway, he'll be thinking golf, not business".

"But presumably if you're interviewing him, he'll see it as business."

"Yes, but in a golf magazine, it'll be golf business. Anything significant to his other work and we'd be seeing him in his office, although he often works at home anyway. I've explained this is useful publicity for the club, something to help increase our membership, get us a higher profile in the golf world. He's keen on that because he's put money into Elmsleigh."

"I really don't see what you need me for."

"As an enthusiastic new face in the club who'll show golf girls today are not dowdy old-fashioned ladies. You've brought some designs with you, haven't you?"

Crystal nodded.

"Good, I… Help." Sam screeched. "No don't worry, only missed the turning, stupid bally satnav."

She swivelled the car round and, in a few moments, whilst Crystal held her breath, they were back on the main road and had turned into a road off which they turned again into a small winding lane. There at the end on the left, as a diagram on Sam's phone stuck to the dashboard showed, were large ornate wrought iron gates.

"Wow, look at that," Sam exclaimed, turning to Crystal. "Still I suppose you see plenty of stuff like this."

"Not recently. Jason doesn't have flashy friends."

Sam drove up a short gravel drive to a mellow brick house which was rather less imposing than the tree-lined avenue to reach it. Only the entrance porch with a security pad on the wall plus a spyhole in the door told of wealth. She pressed a knob that looked like a bell.

Within seconds a large matronly middle-aged woman, her slim legs encased in tight black trousers came to the door. Her hefty bust under a loose pink smock top swayed as she ushered them into the hall.

Mrs Reynolds smiled as she greeted them with, "You must be the golfing girls. Ozzie's waiting for you in the garden room." She led the way to a large room full of classy antique furniture, with many gilt framed works of art hanging on the walls, through to an attached glass conservatory where Ozzie Reynolds sat lounging in a basket chair.

An athletic looking man with a fleshy oval face, wearing dark chino trousers teamed with a long sleeved open-necked sports shirt, rose to greet them. He eyed them up and down without appearing to recognise Crystal, who stood a couple of inches above him in her high heels. She could easily have patted him on the head, the view of which made her wonder whether the thick dark curly thatch, a more vivid deep brown than she recalled, truly grew there, or whether he had a good quality toupee.

Surely a man in late middle age, probably well over fifty, could not have those dark curls. Then, as she scrutinised the hairs, she noticed the grey on the roots and realised the thickness might be true but the colour was a realistic dye.

As he held out his hand, Crystal found herself putting out her own rather limply to shake it after which Sam grasped the possibly offending paw firmly. "So kind of you to see us at such short notice," said Sam

Relieved Sam was taking over, Crystal glanced outside at the large garden where a large younger looking man was working on his hands and knees. Judging from the length of his brown hair tied to the back of his head with a knotted black ribbon, he looked much more fun.

Her attention drifted back to present company to hear Ozzie speak in a totally different vein from the arrogant commanding tycoon at a model shoot. He purred sympathetically about, "Always wanting to be of use to the Lady Captain." He called to his wife Cynthia to bring them coffee, after ascertaining how they liked their brew, making a joke about his own liking for nothing but a good strong Americano made with freshly ground beans from Brazil. He claimed he could even recognise a coffee's country of origin.

"Such a sophisticate" joked Sam. "That's why we want to tap your knowledge of the fashion industry."

This clearly was not popular with Ozzie who muttered disparagingly, "Just one of my interests." He gave a cursory look at Crystal's designs about which he made some polite appreciative remarks but said he was not in a position to commission any work, his interest in clothing accessories was limited to golf these days.

"I thought your main interest was jewellery?" Said Sam, raising her eyebrows in an enquiring expression.

"Yes," he agreed with a casual shrug of his shoulders. "I sponsor some designers, help them get their stuff in stores, that sort of thing."

"We thought so," said Sam, "that's why Crystal's come along with me. She's done some designs for golf accessory jewellery we thought might be interest you."

"A possibility," he agreed again, the thick lower lip of his large mouth drooping with a note of polite boredom. He proffered his right hand. "Let's have a look."

Crystal opened her large briefcase-handbag and propped it against the legs of dark wood veneered coffee table with raised edges. She took out a sheath of papers with her drawings and placed them on the table.

With a broad finger Ozzie flicked the papers over giving them a cursory glance. "Yeah, yeah, some promising stuff here. Reminds me a bit of the work my wife Cynthia used to do when we first met. He turned his head to smile at her as the plump middle-aged lady placed a coffee jug along with a plate of shortbread biscuits on the pretty mahogany side table.

I'll bet she didn't do baubles for belly buttons. Crystal managed to restrain herself from saying as Ozzie's face got all too near hers whilst they bent over the designs for her to point out which brooches and wrist straps could be used to measure distance or act as ball markers.

"Yeah, yeah, I'll bear them in mind. Now what else did you want to ask me about." He straightened up to turn to look at Sam, then frowned giving a cursory glance back at Crystal. "Haven't I seen you somewhere before?"

Crystal's mouth dropped open in horror but before she could think how to respond, Sam said, "In the clubhouse possibly. As I mentioned, Crystal's a new member, but you may have been in the lounge on that match day when Crystal visited, a terrible time for her because she had her catalyst converter stolen. You probably heard about that."

"Ah yes," Ozzie nodded as he sighed. "Dreadful business. Unfortunate introduction for you into the club. Hope it hasn't put you off."

"Happening all too often," said Sam. "You've heard I suppose that they took one from Nicholas Roman who's a regular guest of Yuri Leonov. Dreadfully embarrassing for the club. Strange he only drove an old Ford. Why didn't they go for something smarter like a Lamborghini or a Mercedes?"

"Don't know," said Ozzie. "Better ask Greg. It's time he came in for a cup of coffee anyway."

To his visitors' surprise, he stood up to pull open the long conservatory doors so he could shout to the man weeding in his front garden, to come in and join them.

A few minutes later, Greg, the gardener, with his gardening boots removed at the conservatory door, so that he would not soil its marble floor, sat down alongside Sam, giving her a warm smile after a cursory nod at Crystal. Not that Crystal minded, but it was surprising since she was used to being the most admired woman in any room. Pity though since he was such a good height, must be well over six foot, so he would be taller than her if she stood next him wearing four-inch-high heels, unlike

Jason her current partner. Alongside him she had to be careful not to wear anything more than a couple of inches.

Greg's choice of seat obviously pleased Sam whose mouth stretched out into a welcoming smile. Did she non-verbally invite him? Or was his choice due to Ozzie having introduced Sam as the one who wanted to ask about metals? Clearly he was qualified to answer as he explained better quality metals could be found in the catalyst converters of a Ford Mustang or a Ford Galaxy.

Crystal repressed a smile. That was it: Sam was investigating those robberies. Here was her chance to help. "I understand when it comes to making jewellery these days, something called rhodium is more valuable than gold, silver or even platinum. Is that involved?"

Ozzie turned to Greg the gardener. "You tell them; you're the one who knows about metal."

"Forgotten most of it," said the big man with a grin on his long face, as he lounged in a floral covered deck chair, "Now I'm a gardener, but yes, it's fairly generally known that platinum and antimony, stuff mined by your chum, is in catalyst converters."

"Don't know about that," said Ozzie, his thick lower lip dropped in a pout, "but I'm sure that's not why you want to see me to talk about cars undersides." He turned to face them. "We've got so many great plans for Elmsleigh which you should hear about. The great thing is we've got the land and a good-sized club house already standing. We could make it a major entertainment centre, something any great hotel group who run golf courses would envy."

"Do you think that would benefit the club members?" asked Sam in an unsuccessful attempt to disguise the disgust in her voice. "Clubs should be about friendship not money."

"Of course it's the game that matters and we would work on that by improving the course, expanding it by putting in another nine holes so there's more room for an increased membership and income from additional visitors."

"But one side of the course is bounded by the elm avenue," said Sam, "after which the club is named. When Charles Elmhurst sold his estate to the members, didn't he hope the elms would be there in perpetuity?"

"Some might have to come down, but we could plant others elsewhere. People have to accept it's for the greater good of the place."

Sam swallowed. "That wouldn't work best for the club's profile. Our elms are some of the few surviving after the devastation of Dutch elm disease. We should be planting more if anything. That's what will make our club memorable and attract visitors to support the club."

"Looking at trees isn't enough; it hasn't worked so far," commented Ozzie, shrugging his shoulders. "We've got to make the club a more entertaining place."

"Absolutely," enthused Sam, feeling the moment had come to make her pitch. "Actually, I wonder whether you might like to take part, a leading part in an entertainment I'm organising."

Ozzie's wide mouth spread out into a grin as if to say this was more like it. "What do you have in mind?"

"He's done some conjuring," said his wife Cynthia eagerly. "He could do magic." She had silently entered with another percolator full of coffee. Waving it around she asked if anyone wanted a refill or one of her homemade biscuits. Whilst Sam and Crystal shook their heads politely, the gardener nodded eagerly, holding out his mug for Cynthia to come over to his chair, rather as if he were also a guest, Crystal noted.

Sam continued, "Actually our game's going to be like the TV programme true or false with an appropriate tree theme, family tree that is."

"Imaginative," said Ozzie, his grin widening with a sceptical downward turn.

"Yes, that's the point. It would have a great fictional touch. Your name would be a huge asset which is what would bring you prominence amongst the members."

That made Ozzie beam, "Oh, why's that?"

"Because we're making it naughty"

"How's that?" His smile faded.

"We're focussing on Baddies. We're lucky enough to have a Captain with the name Roger Turpin, which means he's possibly got Dick Turpin the highway robber on his family tree. You could say you've got Bruce Reynolds on your family tree."

There was a stunned silence before Ozzie asked "Who?"

"You know, the great train robber," Greg laughed.

Ozzie gaped momentarily before he shook his round head. "Absolutely not."

"Oh come on." Sam spoke in her most persuasive voice. "Remember the film about him which lots of people will have seen. Stories about him and his exploits would bring lots of attention to any business activities you have."

"Maybe not the right sort of attention. I don't want Elmsleigh members to think my ancestors are criminals."

Even if they are, thought Crystal, rolling her eyes at Sam's response, "Ah but Bruce Reynolds was the typical British loveable rogue. Anyway, you would say it was false."

"Much rather I said something true."

"Such as?"

"The artist Joshua Reynolds."

"Golly. Are you descended from him?"

"Certainly." Ozzie gestured through the door of the conservatory to the living room. "See that portrait; that's Joshua's self-portrait."

Whilst both Sam and Crystal gasped in astonishment, Greg remarked. "I thought that hung in the National Gallery. Did you steal it?"

Sam suppressed a laugh as Ozzie answered with a note of irritation in his voice. "Of course not; it's a copy, but a good one."

"Are you really related to him?" Gasped Sam. "That's amazing."

"Maybe not exactly a descendant," said Ozzie with a smile, "but he's on my family tree. Artistry runs in my family. That's what took me into the world of gems. A jewel should be a thing of beauty that lasts forever to show off a woman's looks. Some people have said I look rather like Joshua too." He patted his dark curly hair and raised his thick dark eyebrows. "Joshua wasn't a big man but his body was packed with talent."

"That's great. You've obviously got the patter. We don't have to have everyone as a rogue. It's an interesting point though, that Bruce Reynolds' son is a respectable sculptor, so you could always use that if it's the artistic thing that gets you."

Cynthia, Ozzie's voluptuous wife smiled eagerly. "Since it doesn't have to be true, what about Fabergé the amazing jewellery designer. That would be great publicity for us. He designed wonderful gems not just eggs."

Greg the gardener stretched up his long body eagerly, his eyes glinting as he spoke, "Fabergé, the famous Russian jeweller? That could create interesting speculation at the club. I'd like to hear that."

"I thought Fabergé was French," said Crystal, "and his jewellery is worn by the royal family."

"Definitely Russian," said Greg, "and worn by the Russian royal family who passed the jewels on to ours."

Ozzie shook his head, almost scowling as he said, "That's as maybe but it's not appropriate."

"Pity." Cynthia pursed her lips whilst her forehead creased in a frown. "I know dear," she threw out her hand out towards Greg, making the flesh on her upper arm wobble. "You could do it; you could be a spy. You've got the name for it; you could say you had a spy in the family. That would be of local interest too."

The big gardener visibly shuddered, making the insubstantial garden chair creak. "No my name's Greg."

"But your surname," started Cynthia, then stopped speaking at the frown on Greg's face before finishing, "Maybe you should be a saint with a name like Gregory.

You've got the locks for it." She eyed his hair. "Isn't there a saint Gregory?"

"With a father who was a vicar round here, probably I should know that, but I'm afraid I don't. Anyway, I'm not a member of Elmsleigh Park."

"Yet," said Ozzie enthusiastically. "But you want to become one," You told me you played golf. And you should know, this lady here is our current Lady Captain."

"Good for you." Greg turned towards her with a little inclination of his head and an ironic smile with his mouth turning down at the corners, which irritated Crystal.

Why hadn't he said *Pleased to meet you?* Then she remembered Sam once advised her that was a really lower class greeting. What a conceited brat this gardener was, a real posh boy. That was obvious from his voice although she could hear he tried to disguise the old public school accent. She wondered how come he was a gardener now, or messing with scrap metal?

Sam obviously picked up that anomaly, although she smiled at Greg as though she fancied him. "You're the opposite of Seamus Heaney then," she said. How did she come out with these things? Must be her university education. At least it meant she got more from Greg.

"The poet?" He queried.

"Yes," said Sam. "He wrote that poem about being different from his father and grandfather who were gardeners because whereas they dug the earth, he dug a pen into paper."

"You're saying I'm the opposite? "Actually lots of people like me feel working with ones hands, doing the land is going upwards rather than downwards these days."

Greg's response must have appealed to Sam since she smiled even more welcomingly at him as she said something along the lines of if he wished to come to the Elmsleigh Park party, she was sure it could be arranged. She even added he should be sure to get in touch with her if he decided he did want to join Elmsleigh Park.

Crystal had had enough. She glanced at her watch. "Goodness, we mustn't keep you any longer. I've got children to look after. She stood up and started making her way to the door, hoping Sam would follow her. To her relief as she passed into the hall, she felt Sam behind her.

Less welcome was Ozzie's presence. In the hall he moved neatly ahead of them, his thick lips in a wide smile as he opened the front door for them.

"Did you get anything useful?" Asked Crystal once they were outside. "I might have guessed you were on a detecting mission not out to help sell my stuff.,"

"Yes, but it was very helpful having you with me and of course you're right about him."

"What do you mean?"

"Wandering hands; he stroked my bum as I went through the doorway and I don't think that was because he's got artistry in his genes."

"I did warn you; I have instincts about people you know." Crystal looked at her friend, "and I think you should watch it with that gardener fellow Greg."

"Oh why?" Sam's face knitted in a frown. "I thought he was rather fun."

"Maybe, but fun can be dangerous. I'm sure saw him mooching around Elmsleigh Park with some red-headed fellow the day my converter thing was stolen.

6. The Coffee Morning

Golf club Manager Simon Duckworth regretted the open-door policy instigated by the Vice Captain, Hector Bravo. There were phone calls he did not wish to share with any stray member who might happen to pass his door. He felt sorry for lonely people, especially the older members, but he had work to do and being a counsellor to some old chap with a query about current etiquette because he was organising a society game, was not a matter he wanted to spend time discussing.

Nor did he wish to be harangued as he had been already this morning by Ladies Vice-Captain Amy Hart, or "No Heart", as some of the old boys, "Codgers" in Amy's lingo, called her. She said, and he had some sympathy with this, that the Venerables, the older men's golf squad, who had regular Tuesday morning matches should include ladies. She had not liked it when he tried to explain he had sounded out this proposition to various of the more sympathetic older men involved, but they had adamantly refused to agree to any female participation.

Amy was further enraged when he explained his reasonable guy's point of view, that ladies would not enjoy the food. To this year's captain, Sam's ears the sensible guys made the valid point that women didn't want big lunches. They were known to peck away at salads or skimpy sandwiches. Only a few drank alcohol at midday meals which meant bar takings from the ladies would be minimal, but crucially they would spoil the occasions by finding the after meal jokes unpalatable.

He did not wish to make an enemy of the Ladies Vice-Captain but all he could do was to stall, tell her he would put it on the appropriate committee's agenda, but as she knew all too well, with this year's programme in place, that committee would not meet for months.

"When you will be in power," he'd tried to smile rather than shudder as he spoke.

Amy's smirk at this remark spurred him on to say reproachfully, "You must remember that the Venerables, our older men, are the strong backbone of the club."

"More like the floppy front paunch," was Amy's whispered retort, which he was not sure whether he was meant to hear, as she stalked out.

Simon's relief he could now get on with the real business of running the club was short lived. Before midday his work was interrupted by the entrance of the tall florid-faced Vice-Captain Hector Bravo. His powerful physique was accentuated with his usual stance of his left hand on his hip as he glowered at what felt like his prey.

Hector wanted to know how it happened rumours were flying round the club about the thefts of catalyst converters from the club premises. After the first theft from a visitor's car some months ago, they agreed they must keep this quiet so as not to alarm either members or worse potential visitors. Now he heard people gossiping about "those wretched car thefts" wherever he went in the club. The club's reputation was at stake.

Simon retorted that news of the thefts was bound to spread. It was inevitable players chatted during the five hours it might take four players to play a round of golf.

"Five hours," Hector snorted through his beaky nose. "No wonder people gossip if they take that long to play the course. This chit chat needs to be stopped or societies will cancel; we need their income or we'll never be able to keep the course up to standard. God forbid we'll have to end up letting those greedy fiends buy the club and turn it into the hotel complex they want." His strong body convulsed in a shudder.

"We do have some upstairs rooms standing idle," said Simon. "Letting them out could bring income."

"Perish the thought. I've had an idea about that too. We should move the committee room upstairs into a stronger office environment with sound proofing. Where we sit now in the former servants' sitting room is inappropriate for the company's decision makers."

"I thought the committee room used to be the library."

"That was the start, to get it altered from the servants' quarters. What we need now is somewhere with more prestige to meet, particularly when we have people who matter from the golf world."

"That will cost. To get a large enough room we might have to knock a couple of bedrooms together."

"Not a lot. I've got builder chums who'll sort it out reasonably. I'll get them to send you estimates we can put to the next meeting."

Scarcely was he out of the room before his visit was followed by another couple of complainers.

Red-headed Helen McTavish pranced in with a bright smile on her heart-shaped face suggesting that she was going to make some positive suggestion. A strong-looking woman of medium height, probably in her early thirties, the Scottish lass had joined the club only a couple of years ago, but a promising player to be taken seriously.

Simon's relief that she was not going to talk about car security changed to despair as she said she had an idea which could sort out the club's financial problems.

"Rewilding," said Helen rolling the r with relish, "that's what this club needs. We're too park-like but the changes we should make are not all these expensive improvements these lily-livered home counties scratch players want. We need to take golf back to its origins, a game against nature. We've got to stop chopping trees down and start getting the rough grass more meadow like. People would love it once they got used to the idea. I've actually met someone whose family used to own the Elmsleigh grounds and he's all for getting the place back to what it should be."

Simon could guess who that was, but he would not go there. Gossiping about past customs at the club would not be wise. He had been warned by one of the club's chatty older ladies that Helen's current squeeze was Greg Burgess, a single figure handicapper and former county player who had some years ago been turned down for membership at Elmsleigh Park. Worse still, Simon understood one of the men who rejected him was the current President Dick Norton.

As calmly as he could Simon replied, "Yes, but the game has developed and we must keep pace with it."

"Not the way it's happening here. Honestly, it's our social duty not to use so much weed killer and fertiliser. Do you know how poisonous weed killer is?"

Simon held up his hand. "I appreciate your concern, but this is something you should put to the club's course manager on the club's committee. Really the best place to put this forward is the club's Suggestion Book."

She opened her mouth to protest but stopped as Yuri Leonov entered the room. The disparaging look she gave him puzzled Simon. Surely Yuri could have dealings with Helen's man Greg Burgess? Wasn't he something to do with metal, possibly a scrap metal dealer? Then it hit him that Helen was opposed to Yuri's part in the group wanting to buy the club and develop the site, especially as she walked out, she muttered "Fffing cuckoo".

Her distaste was not lost on Yuri who scowled at her departing back. The moment she was through the door, he slammed it behind her. With a sigh he slouched up to Simon's desk, put out a hand to steady himself against his desk as he asked, "Mind if I sit down?"

Much as Simon would have liked to say *Get the hell out as I have work to do,* he nodded. "What's the matter?"

"There are problems here." Yuri's large head bobbed up and down.

"Problems everywhere." Simon tried to sound sympathetic, but his words did not improve Yuri's mood.

"Our space is being used. You say this is for club use only but I know it is not."

"You mean the shed?" asked Simon recollecting that in the club's desperate financial straits he had made a deal on Yuri's behalf with Chris Pearce the long-term treasurer, that Yuri could store some non-dangerous industrial equipment in a shed on the Elmsleigh Park estate. Chris was pleased because the club needed the income and he readily agreed to Yuri's request that the information should not be spread around, muttering something about burying it in the club's accounts.

"Yes, and now people are saying bad things about me," complained Yuri. "I know people have joked I am a spy and I take that in good part as you British say, but now they believe it, it is not funny anymore.

"No of course not." Simon spoke in his most sympathetic voice, "I'm sure people don't think things like that about you."

"Yes, or now they say I am Vory, that is Russian mafia gangster, that I am a target because my friend Nicholas Roman is from the Romanov family, though he is very discreet about it. He drives old car like genteel British and does not wear bright clothes."

Simon repressed a gulp of dissent. With his straight back, black curly moustache, plus the jewelled monocle he'd once produced to read the menu at one of the club's invitation lunches, Nicholas Roman looked every millimetre the possible member of a defunct royal family.

Yuri pursed his lips and narrowed his eyes whilst he added in an accusing tone, "It is that beggar. I think he is under-cover policeman."

Simon wanted to laugh, but Yuri's distress was so palpable he controlled himself. "It's not like that here in English golf clubs. There's not exactly much to interest the police here except the odd free game of golf."

"No, they are watching me because they think I have bad plans for the golf club; maybe I will dig it up."

67

Hard to deal with this paranoid assertion. Simon had to restrain himself from remarking *That's probably your wife's fault.*

Ekaterina Sokolov did flaunt her glamorous body in what he understood were designer clothes when she visited the club on social occasions. The Russian's wife was a noted personality, especially as it was rumoured, she had been heard to say more than once *When Yuri owns this club.* Better not admit to her husband that caused great indignation amongst older club members in case the unlikely happened and one future day the big man opposite him did own the club. He waited until Yuri paused in his rant before he said calmly, "I think you are mistaken. People here like you for who you are."

"Not that Madam McTavish," insisted Yuri. "She gave me a bad look. She does not understand I help Elmsleigh. Now I need you to help me."

"Tell you what," replied Simon, glancing at his watch and noticing it was past eleven thirty in the morning. "Let's go into the lounge and have a coffee and I think you'll see our members are just happy friendly people without any particular hang-ups about you."

"I have had coffee already this morning."

"Well, have another one." Somehow he must assuage this emotional man no longer looked droopy but sat up straight, his shoulders stiffened with anger. There should be other people in the lounge who could distract him. Simon rose out of his chair. He went over to his filing cabinet, unlocked it to get out his special packets of sweetener for the coffee. Now he needed it.

Rather to his alarm, as followed by Yuri, he entered the lounge, the first people he saw were not those he would have chosen for Yuri's relief or comfort.

Sitting nearest in the lounge, was a loosely assembled group containing Helen McTavish alongside her boyfriend Greg Burgess. From their body language, bodies almost entwined with one another, Simon assumed it must be him. There he sat in what were probably jeans with a sweatshirt on his vast chest, but no collared shirt underneath it. Simon glanced down at the man's feet to see what he expected; Greg wore trainers, which were in theory not allowed to be worn in the clubhouse.

Simon looked at the other people at the table, noting with relief Vice-Captain Hector Bravo was there. That meant it was not up to Simon to remonstrate with Helen for bringing such an inappropriately dressed visitor into the club, or turn him out. Happily too, unlike Helen, Greg seemed to welcome the sight of Yuri. The massive amount of black hair on the lower half of his face parted as his thick-lipped mouth spread into a smile which looked. He nodded as though he knew him too.

Though Vice-Captain Hector might have sounded off against the club's potentially predatory rich, he was now talking to Ozzie Reynolds in a most amiable manner. The two had started early that morning to finish a match begun yesterday, which Hector won after a tough battle

Simon, followed by an apprehensive Yuri, strode over to join them. Ignoring Yuri's suspicious look at the two men, he deftly pulled a couple of nearby spare chairs to squeeze in alongside Greg. "Mind if we join you. I thought you being in the iron business Greg, might like to meet Yuri here. He's a miner."

Whilst Yuri's face lit up for a moment, Greg smiled awkwardly. "Yes, yes, we do know each other but I'm afraid I've changed my job." His long narrow mouth twisted down on one side, "I'm a gardener now."

"A special kind of gardener," chimed in Helen. "Greg's studying wilding gardens, getting them back to nature. Something we might think of here. That's what I want Hector to consider for next year."

To Simon's relief, Yuri laughed as he eyed Greg. "Yes, we do this in Russia. We get back the woolly mammoth too in Pleistocene, our nature reserve in Siberia."

Simon repressed a smile. Though Yuri's tone was humorous, his intonation suggested a hidden meaning to his words. He glanced round the table to note people's reactions. From their expressions, he guessed only Sir Bill Chambers picked up the woolly mammoth reference as jovial slight about Greg's untidy appearance, but he, a former diplomat was far too discreet to laugh. "I'm getting some coffee," Simon said quickly, "what does anyone want?"

All, except Helen, asked for coffee of various different types.

"You do realise," said Simon with a gesture towards Ozzie, "who we have to thank that we can be so specific with our orders." He repeated their various requests whilst he stood up to go over to the bar.

"Yes," Hector nodded. "Thanks Ozzie. It was very generous of you to present us with the coffee maker.

70

I suppose we'd soon have to have bought one ourselves, but we felt anything we could possibly avoid to add to our debt should be forgone."

"Good coffee with the various varieties is what visitors expect," said Ozzie. "If we want to compete for custom with other clubs in the area, it's what we need."

"Really?" queried Sir Bill Chambers. The polite tone of the tall lanky older man, known as one of the club's great traditionalists, made Simon smile as it belied Bill's acid response to Ozzie's generosity, "I don't think golfers are fussy about frothy coffee, types of beer maybe and certainly wine."

"You'd be surprised these days," said Ozzie as Misty came towards them with a tray of various mugs and cups of coffee plus shortbread biscuits. "You've only got to consider the coffee bars all over the world, the Costas and Starbucks, to see how important the drink is today."

To Simon's relief the good-natured argument about coffee that ensued, whilst the various cups were dispersed to the people who wanted each brew, along with different bowls of brown and white sugar, obliterated any conversation about re-wilding. Even Yuri had an affable expression on his face whilst he drank his latte.

Though Simon feared he would have difficulty not repeating Yuri's joke about Greg being the woolly mammoth, his presence was helpful as he chatted with Ozzie and Yuri about scrap metal. It appeared Yuri actually dealt with the business where Greg had worked.

Maybe he felt more comfortable once Helen was not around since she had departed to play a game with another lady. Then Simon saw the retired diplomat, former

Captain and President, Bill Chambers had also slipped away, leaving possibly a more congenial group for Yuri, which would enable Simon himself to depart.

Even Hector putting forward his views about the necessity of the club's survival owned by the members, not bought out by either a single person or a consortium, did not appear to upset Yuri. Maybe it was the mollifying influence of the congenial Ozzie who suggested they should all stay on and have lunch together.

With a nod to them all, Simon stood up to go back to his office. He assumed and certainly hoped Greg in his jeans style trousers and floppy sweat shirt would forgo going into the dining room. It was surprising he was happy to visit, having been turned down for membership. Would he apply again if heard the club had revised its dress code?

After his own lunch of a sandwich in the spike bar, during which time Misty reassured him Greg had departed without visiting the dining room, he was able to settle down to an afternoon's work with minimal interruptions. His relief, when he was packed up, ready to go home at five twenty and half-way through the office door was interrupted when the telephone rang.

At five twenty-two, a time he would remember as he so often had to repeat it officially, he answered the phone to a furious Ekaterina Leonov. "Yuri is very sick," she cried, "he has to go to bed. He says he has been poisoned at your club.

7. Death discussed by Cabinet

The phone rang at seven o'clock in the morning.

Sam rubbed her sleep sodden eyes. Yes she was awake. No she wasn't dreaming. Yes she'd better take the call. It probably spelt trouble. People didn't usually ring this house number early without bad cause. Yet at the moment all her close friends who came to mind were in a good place so why, unless there was some emergency, should they ring her now?

Blearily she reached for the phone standing on her bedside table and clasped it against her ear to hear Simon's apologetic voice. He wanted to know if she was available for a special committee meeting today, or failing that, tomorrow.

This was odd. The next committee meeting was scheduled for a fortnight's time, hardly a long time to wait. Sam's antennae prickled. "What's happened?"

"Can't discuss it over the 'phone. I'm sorry I've had to ring so early, but please can you tell me which of these times you are available."

Sam rolled out of bed to reach her handbag on the floor with a mobile inside it. Fumbling inside she found her phone, switched this one on, and pressed on her diary. This afternoon today was taken with a meeting with a prominent Australian female golf professional who was entrancing the wider world with her humorous tricks. She could not forgo that commissioned interview for a newspaper which could be syndicated all over the world.

Tomorrow morning, Simon had obviously forgotten, was ladies' morning at the club. She could not,

73

as Lady Captain, miss that, especially not for a meeting at the club where she would be seen, something Simon picked up on before she started to explain.

"Count out Wednesday morning," he said quickly. "This meeting has to be confidential, or as confidential as we can make it. I'm afraid I have to give you the times Roger is free. I know he's meant to be retired but he's still involved in hospital life. Can you do tomorrow evening at about five? Most of the ladies will have gone by then."

So next day Sam, having cancelled a drink with Toby, a former journalistic colleague, always a fun occasion, joined her fellow Cabinet members in a hastily converted large first floor bedroom. They sat around the vast boardroom table which the ground staff had moved upstairs from the former ground floor committee room.

"Surely," said Sam who had arrived first in the room, having stayed on in the club house after her unsatisfactory golf game, "the girls, seeing all this palaver of the groundsmen coming in to move this table and chairs up here, will suspect something fishy is going on."

"There is nothing *fishy* going on," said Sir Hector Bravo, the Vice-Captain, the only other person there at exactly five o'clock. "It's simply that what we have to discuss is confidential and we have found the downstairs room is not soundproof."

Sam wanted to say the committee itself might not be leak proof, but the penetrating stare Hector gave her, plus the aggressive way he spoke, stopped her. She recognised that look as the one he all too often used when she tried to defend some or other subsidy for the Ladies, and he'd retorted, "You must be joking."

It made her wonder why she had accepted the role of Lady Captain. This was meant to be a fun year, squired around by the handsome, but safely married to a non-golfing wife, gallant men's Captain, Roger Turpin. Her year as Vice-Captain had made her realise that with the club's parlous financial situation, there would be much tedious discussion about money, but what on earth could be so urgent that an Extraordinary meeting should be called at such short notice. It was not surprising some other committee members were unable to come.

Roger opened the meeting by thanking all those who were there. It was, he stressed, hugely important they should know what had happened before the club had to make the announcement that Yuri Leonov had died.

"That's so sad," exclaimed Sam.

A hostile silence greeted her lament.

"Well in terms of diversity, he was an asset to the club. He partook in events and brought his wife along. Ekaterina's such a live wire, always helps make the party go." Sam turned to Matthew Borden the event's organiser. "He was going to take part in the True or False evening pretending..." But she did not have time to finish.

"So it's your fault," said Hector, curbing his loud aggressive tone by speaking through almost clenched teeth and lips. "If you suggested he had criminal relatives, that's probably what did it."

Sam tried not to cringe at his aggression. He had been incandescent with irritation when she had suggested he might take part in the True or False entertainment as someone with Charles Bravo, the renowned nineteenth-century murder victim or a potential murderer who accidentally killed himself rather than his wife, on his family tree.

"Did what?" Sam leant backwards away from Hector's large torso stretched across the oval end of the table towards her.

"Got him thinking people were against him, possibly," said Simon.

"I don't think he did, or at least not when I spoke to him."

"Oh come on," said Matthew Borden. The social events manager turned to smile at Sam and gave her a quick wink of a blue eye. "I think Sam's idea is splendid. Anyone with a sense of humour wouldn't be offended. I'm playing. After all Lizzie Borden of the famous rhyme is on my family tree."

Sam gaped at him. In her investigations of famous criminals, she'd forgotten about Lizzie Borden, whom she'd assumed was a fictional character. "What?" She gasped. "The Lizzie Borden who *'Gave her mother forty whacks, Then when she saw, What she had done, Gave her father forty-one.'* You mean you are related to the real Lizzie Borden."

The broad-shouldered man stretched his short body upwards as he looked around the assembled committee members, a wide grin on his face. "That will be for the audience to decide, but put it this way, I do know that the nineteenth century Lizzie Borden was of English extraction and she had two sisters, Emma and Alice, which happen to be the same names as my two sisters, one of whom is, as you will know, a member here."

"Of course," agreed Sam, with relief for his support. "I mean, that's a great help Matthew."

Captain Roger held up his hand. "Thank you, Matt. Actually this is not entirely helping matters in hand at the moment. Sam, you and everyone else here needs to know the reason we've called this meeting is not only that Yuri has died but, more serious for us, is that Ekaterina has accused the club of poisoning him."

Sam found her mouth drop open. *That's ridiculous,* she wanted to say, but to her relief before the words fell out of her mouth, Jason, Crystal's partner, whose job was the house manager responsible for the club's food and drink, spoke worriedly.

"Now the ball's landed in my court has it?"

Captain Roger shook his head. "The point of this meeting is to declare our joint rejection of Mrs Leonov's accusation. We need to act together in our repudiation of Mrs Leonov's assertion this club killed her husband."

"How could we have done? I mean how did he actually die?" Asked Sam, irritated that everyone else in the room seemed to have been given prior information about the details of Yuri's demise.

"We're not privy to the exact diagnosis," Roger said calmly. "All we have been told by Ekaterina in a phone call, is that her husband died of food poisoning a couple of days ago which she puts down to his last visit to the club a couple of days previously. That same afternoon he started to be sick. It is an outrageous accusation, probably instigated by shock and grief, but we have to take seriously." He turned to look at Simon. "Do we know when the post mortem is?"

"I'm not sure, but it might be tomorrow." He fingered a file of file of papers on the table in front of him. "I've done a search on him to see who we can enlist to assist us. Yuri joined in the days when people who wanted to join had to be proposed and seconded by members, and I see his proposer was Sir Bill Chambers, a former captain."

They still play a fair amount together," said someone.

"Yes," Simon agreed, "and he was in the clubhouse a couple of days ago when Yuri came to see me on that last visit to the club. "We had a coffee with him afterwards."

"How was Yuri then?" asked Roger.

"Okay-ish."

"What does that mean?"

"Before we had the coffee, he came into my office in a terrible state," said Simon. "I've never seen him like that before and frankly I didn't know how to handle the situation. He made weird remarks about people not liking him, or rather, saying nasty things about him, calling him a spy or a gangster. It was, as I said, weird."

"Do you think his state of mind might have been disturbed?" Suggested Hector. "In that case he might have made all sorts of peculiar accusations to his wife when he got home."

"Possibly. More than that, he looked so upset, he could have been suicidal. His behaviour was bizarre."

"Do you think his wife might want to find someone to blame for his taking his own life." Pointed out Hector.

"I don't think he would have killed himself," said Sam. "People probably did accuse him of things, maybe in his hearing, but I can't, from my last conversation with him, imagine him killing himself."

"That's your journalist's instinct is it?" sneered Hector.

"Possibly. The thing is that when I talked to him about what famous character could possibly be in his family tree, I didn't mention any Russian criminals, not that I know any. To get him to join in, I suggested Russians we all admire like the writer Leo Tolstoy. He flatly rejected them because they were what he called 'tortured souls'. He didn't identify with men who were sensitive in any way or found life hard. He wasn't crippled with self-doubt."

"I don't see how you can judge on the basis of one conversation," remarked Jason pleasantly. "It ties in with Simon's first hand experience." He turned to face Simon who sat next him and pointed to the file on the table in front of him. "You did say you looked through Yuri's bar account and found no reference he bought food."

"That's right. He had a coffee before the one I bought him later. Then, according to Misty, he did eat a light lunch with the fellows which could have been paid for by someone else. I understand they all had the same pasta and sauce." He glanced apprehensively at Hector.

"Yes," agreed the Vice-Captain in an aimable though officious tone, "My understand is that we all ate the fusilli on offer with a bolognaise sauce. There was actually a lot of moving around with other people coming and going so I don't know who paid for Yuri."

"The thing is," queried Sam, frowning as she spoke, "that you didn't sit at the same table as Yuri?"

"That is indeed not the thing," responded Hector coldly. "Once that ghastly friend of his, Nicholas Roman turned up and started making accusations and winding him up again, I made my excuses and sat further away, especially since Bill Chambers was there to sort things."

"I thought he disappeared earlier," said Simon.

"Only to the cloakroom," said Hector. "He came back into the dining area and joined them. He's an old friend of Roman's too. Don't know what happened then because I had to leave to get to work that afternoon."

"If you, Bill and all the others are okay, it's unlikely he could have had food poisoning from any source here at the club," announced Jason, breathing heavily with relief.

"That appears to be the case," agreed Roger.

"Couldn't you in your professional capacity take a look at his medical records to see if he's on some anti-depressant he might have over-dosed?" Asked Hector.

"The result of the post mortem will be in the public domain," replied Roger coldly.

8. A look at the shed

The following Wednesday, Ladies morning Sam decided she must not let Yuri's death enter her mind again, or it would wreck her game, especially if she was lured into talking about it by her playing companion. Tabby might be a good friend but she always wanted to discuss the latest club drama.

Although Roger as club Captain had impressed upon the committee the need for discretion, Tabby's husband Hector would be bound to have told her about Yuri's death, if not Ekaterina's accusation of poisoning. She might have to talk about it, but that conversation with Tabby could come later. Now she must focus on hitting the ball, she told herself firmly as she changed into her golf shoes in the clubhouse.

Initially her resolve worked well. She did not think she would have a problem with Tabby for whilst they stood by the first tee waiting to start, Tabby herself said she wanted to concentrate on her game because she needed to have a good score today. Sam agreed. Before every shot she took, she lightly slapped the side of her golf bag to try to stop extraneous thoughts and bring her mind back to hitting the ball.

It worked until the ninth hole where she drove wildly into rough grass alongside the fairway. As she was some way from the white post which marked the hundred-yard distance from the fairway to the pin in the middle of the green, she took her golf binoculars into the rough grass to measure the distance she would have to hit. Swivelling them round to decide upon how to hit her next shot, she spied the beggar.

Yes, it must be him. There he stood in the doorway of one of the sheds. That ragged old chap could not be one of the green staff. They were a young team. None of those energetic chaps would loiter in the doorway of a shed. What was he doing there? Guiltily she remembered she was meant to be checking him out, but she had become so caught up with organising the social event. with its dual purpose of discovering more about personnel, that she had forgotten about the beggar.

She must take a photo to ascertain it was him. As quickly as she could she ran back to where she had parked her trolley with her bag strapped to it and selected another golf club from it. At the same time, she deftly whipped her mobile out of the side pocket. Then she raced back to where in her ball lay in the rough grass, and tried to hack it out. Inevitably with her mind on the impending photo, she almost missed the ball and moved it only a few feet. Cursing she gritted her teeth and was about to try again when she decided that it would be better to take the photo first in case the old chap moved whilst her head was down looking at the ball.

With a quick manoeuvre she snatched the phone out of her pocket, held it disguised beneath the binoculars and snapped a couple of times. She hoped Tabby would not realise what she was doing. By the time she managed to catch her up, the couple playing behind them stood with their hands on their hips looking irritated at having to wait whilst Sam moved out of the range of their shots.

Tabby was annoyed by the delay too. "You took your time there, faffing around. I thought you of all people realised we must play at a decent speed these days."

She complained having to hurry now would upset her game and inevitably it did just that. She muffed her next shot. Mentally Sam cursed Laurie for the emotional pressure he'd put on her to take part in this investigation. She must put the silly distraction behind her. Again she slapped her bag before she hit the ball, which worked for a short while until a few holes later, she saw the old chap again on the footpath.

Now she averted her eyes; she must keep going. She did not want Tabby grumbling to Hector; the Vice-Captain was known to be manic about people playing at a good speed. Yet however much she told herself *not* to think about the beggar, she could not stop herself.

Luckily Tabby's game bucked up, so back in the clubhouse over their sandwich lunch Sam did not feel she had to apologise for her own parlous performance in case she had put Tabby off, although Tabby herself did keep saying how she should have done better. It was taking a risk but Sam still thought it worth asking, "Did you see that beggar who hangs about the Visitors carpark wandering about."

Tabby wrinkled her nose. "I haven't seen him around on or near the course, but Hector has and I gather so have some other men. Hector says he's getting bolder, a damn nuisance roaming around; he could get hit."

Sam grimaced. "That would be awful." She stopped herself from adding, especially after Yuri Leonov.

"Yes," agreed Tabby. She lowered her voice. "I gather Simon's such a softie; he says as long as the beggar sticks to the foot paths we can't do anything about him because he's on a public right of way."

"Is that so?"

"Yes, but actually," Tabby looked round conspiratorially before she whispered, "Hector himself is getting something done about him. He's got a detective agency looking into it."

Sam gulped; she hoped she wasn't blushing. "Really?"

"Yes, you obviously know the committee agreed to get the catalyst converter thefts being looked into by a private detective." Tabby lowered her voice as she leant forward, her blonde hair cascading in front of her face, but through the veil of hair, Sam could still hear her say, "Hector's briefed the same chap about the beggar."

Sam wanted to say sarcastically *Well thanks for telling me*, but refrained. She should not be surprised; she could feel Hector's frustration with Roger Turpin's easy-going attitude. Hector wanted all unsatisfactory loose ends cleared up before his innings as Captain.

With this in mind, she excused herself from having coffee with Tabby and said she must hurry home. Time for her, she decided on her way out, to stop and have a word with the beggar.

Before that she would drive over to the half-way parking place near the tenth hole which was a short walk to the green keepers' sheds. Although members were not supposed to enter the sheds, certainly not inspect them, she would poke around to see if there was any reason someone other than the ground staff, might go there.

She was glad to find no-one around when she arrived at the sheds. Half way through the afternoon seemed early for the ground staff to finish work, but then they did start very early in the morning. Anyway, it gave her a chance to look around unchallenged. She did not need to enter some of the sheds because their doors were open revealing lawn mowers, leaf blowers and other obvious machinery for ground clearance. Another couple of sheds had closed doors which opened easily to reveal similar equipment. Although there were sacks of stuff which appeared to be fertiliser and weed killer, nothing looked as if it might be of particular interest to a vagrant.

She tried to envisage which of these sheds she might have spotted from the rough grass by the ninth hole. It must have been round here, she decided, as she walked round one of the end buildings to see another free-standing chalet type wooden building. *This could be it.* She put her hand on to the door knob, but it wouldn't turn. The door was locked.

How irritating. What on earth could they have in there? Poisonous materials of some sort she supposed. Dog walkers used the foot paths all over the course, enjoying the views and scenery that Elmsleigh Park provided. If a dog having managed to enter the shed, got poisoned there could be trouble for the club, she supposed. She turned around to walk back to her car and found herself facing a couple of young men, one of whom she recognised as Kyle. The slim young man with bushy red hair, was a handyman who often helped out as a dog walker, much to her black Labrador Monty's delight.

Though from his services to the dog walking agency, he must have known she played golf, he eyed her with surprise, but to her relief, no suggestion she was somewhere she shouldn't be.

Assert yourself as Lady Captain, she told herself. Whatever the other chap's business is, presumably if Kyle's here, he must be helping out the green staff. Then she remembered she had seen him here at Elmsleigh before, presumably working for some gardening agency taken on by Alan, the head of the green staff. Speaking in an authoritative voice as she could muster, she said, "Why is this shed locked?"

Kyle shrugged. "You tell me," he replied nonchalantly. He shook his head with its bushy mane of red hair, which looked a bit incongruous against the dark stubble protruding from his chin. "Belongs to the club don't it."

No argument there. Best to thank him and move on. She would ask the beggar himself. Without a backward look, she hastened to her car to drive to the Visitors carpark.

The beggar's ragged appearance made it difficult to assess what age the man might be, but his quick glance at her car when she drove into the Visitors carpark made her think he was more alert than he pretended. Yet in a trice his head quickly drooped back into its usual melancholy position as she slowed to decide where amongst the empty spaces she might park.

He sat motionless as she approached him and even when she stood next him, he did not lift his head until Sam said "Hello, how are you today?"

"All right." The beggar stirred and raised his head slightly.

Sam opened her bag and got out three pound coins. "Do you have a bowl for me to put these in?"

The old man took the cap off his head and laid it down on the ancient duvet on which he sat. "This'll do for now." He said.

Sam dropped the coins into the cap as she asked, "But what do you usually use?"

The nostrils on the wide nose of the man's oblong wrinkled face seemed to stretch whilst he spoke. "Anything handy. Sometimes I have a bag. I'm not just a beggar you know."

"Why do you come here then?"

"Family property. I should own the place so I like to look at it."

"That's impossible; I mean you owning the place. It was given legally to the club members in nineteen thirty-two."

"Yes, but it shouldn't have been. My grandfather was off his rocker."

"Doesn't seem like that from the records." Sam spoke as sympathetically as she could. Not that she had studied them, but her understanding was it was a legally binding agreement. The previous owner of the land in the early twentieth century had passed the house and grounds over to the people who played golf on the course they had built on his land, with the provision he would live in the mansion used as a clubhouse until he died. Thereafter the estate would belong to the Elmsleigh Park members.

The expression on the old man's large brown wrinkled face, indeed his whole relaxed posture as he sat on the large faded and crumpled and rumpled dark blue duvet gave credence to his story, as did his clothing; the tattered sports jacket he wore, besides the grey trousers both looked as though they might have once been tailor-made.

"It's very sad," said Sam as sympathetically as she could, "but a lot of people are cut out of their parents' wills for all sorts of reasons. Had your father and presumably his siblings upset the old man in some way?"

"My mother." The old man wrinkled his nose again. "What's that got to do with you?"

"Just interested," persisted Sam. "It doesn't seem to get you anywhere stalking the place out here. I thought you might like to move on."

"Not exactly anywhere else to go."

Good point. "Yes, I suppose we are rather countrified around here." Sam's face puckered as the question occurred to her, "How do you get here anyway?"

"Hitch a lift usually."

"But where from? I mean where do you spend the night?"

"Inside, outside, wherever I can find to lay my head."

"Not outside today though." Sam eyed the possessions he had with him which included a battered rucksack as well as a tattered bag besides the duvet, but he was short of the amount of baggage she associated with the homeless she usually saw sleeping rough.

"I might." He looked up at the sky. "Doesn't look as though it's going to rain. Anyway, what's it to you?"

"I thought I might give you a lift," she lied, half-hoping he would refuse but thinking that at least she would be doing a good turn as well as finding out something to report back to Laurie if she could provide an address for the beggar.

"You can take me to Petersfield if you like," he said nonchalantly.

It was at least ten miles out of her way, but Sam nodded. "Okay, where in Petersfield do you live."

"No fixed address. Just some good hostels there." His tone was even more casual.

No information gained from that, but maybe once he was packed with his belongings into the car, he might be more informative.

9. Inside the shed

In some ways the trip with the beggar was informative, but in other ways Sam felt she had not discovered as much as she might have. At least she had some information for Laurie when she was to meet him tomorrow to pick up his master keys, which should allow her to enter the locked shed in the Elmsleigh Park grounds to inspect the contents inside.

She would have liked to be able to report to Laurie that she knew whereabouts the old chap was based, his home address, but that he was not giving away.

"Drop me in the carpark," he'd said when she asked him where she should deliver him in Petersfield. "I'll find my own way to one of the hostels."

To insist on being given a specific address might she feared make him put up his defences. She needed to establish a positive rapport with him if she was going to discover more about the underside of the golf club. Already she had enough material to earn her keep from the Old Alresford Investigators.

"But why did your grandfather disinherit your mother?" She had asked companionably as she drove the old man slowly along the busy country road as the rush hour with the end of the school day had started.

"He didn't like my father, didn't approve of him," came the sulky reply.

"Why was that?"

"Well he was a Jew wasn't he? And the Elmsleigh Park Golf Club," here he put on a superior posh accent, "didn't accept Jews in those days. Not one of us, they used to say." He finished in a sneering tone.

"I'm sorry to hear that. That's appalling." Sam winced as she gripped the steering wheel. She wanted to deny anyone in her world could ever be tarred with anti-Semitism, but then recalled odd references to the "chosen race" made in a sniffy tone by her late mother-in-law.

"What about your mother's siblings? Weren't there any brothers or sisters who might inherit the house."

"Two brothers but they were killed in the second world war."

"Oh dear." The exclamation seemed painfully weak. "And your father, he survived I suppose. Didn't he go into the army?"

Nah, he was interned as an alien in the Isle of Man. Worked out quite well for him actually; he learnt a skill and made himself useful."

"I see. What was that?"

The old man sighed, "Carpentry, which he turned to making musical instruments after the war; did well out of it."

"If he made a new life for himself and your mother, why do you want to hang around the golf club?"

"I find it fun, like you do." He gave an ironical chuckle. "And it's my birth right."

****

That she explained to Laurie, as she sat in his office the following afternoon giving him an update, was all she could get out of the old man. "Thing is, I think the old boy is genuine. He didn't throw the information at me

91

like liars tend to do. I had to draw it out of him gradually with question after question."

"You didn't get his name I suppose," asked Laurie, drumming a pencil on his desk.

"That wouldn't be relevant since it was his mother who was the original owner's daughter. I'm much more interested in the contents of that shed. I did see someone else though, a man called Kyle. He's not a regular member of the green staff, so I'm not sure why he was lurking in the grounds in the late afternoon."

"You don't know his surname I suppose?"

"For goodness sake no," retorted Sam. "But with his red hair he's very recognisable. Anyway who's paying for me to investigate this beggar? I do wonder what the point of this is when he's not actually on the golf course but roaming in the park. The committee agreed, and it's in the minutes, that we should employ an agency to assist the police in their enquiries about the thefts of catalyst converters, nothing to do with the beggar."

"Maybe they're connected," suggested Laurie. "Like I told you: it was your Vice Captain, Sir Hector Bravo who came to see me personally about that vagrant."

"I'd still like to drop it; I can't see airing long past prejudices against certain people joining the club being helpful to the friendly club it is today."

"I don't know about your club politics," scoffed Laurie, "but it's still agency business. I've had to stall Bravo a couple of times when he's rung up since to ask whether there's been any progress. What you've got is okay but we need more."

"So that ball's still in play," sighed Sam.

"Definitely. You must keep tabs on that beggar."

"Okay, in that case I'll have to look in the shed he was loitering near the other day. Can I borrow your master keys?"

Laurie delved into the drawer of his desk to fiddle around before producing a large bunch of assorted keys. He handed them to her with the suggestion she never knew but she might find a catalyst converter inside, to which she replied she would not know one if she did.

He laughed. "Anything else of interest."

"Yes, it may not be relevant, but we've had a death of a prominent member, Yuri Leonov."

"A Russian? Was it not natural causes then?"

"We don't know. We haven't been told the result of the post mortem yet, only it's another awkward situation for the club because his wife has suggested he was poisoned at the club, got food poisoning that is."

"Yes, I can see that would be a bit disastrous. What sort of age was this man?"

"Early sixties, I'd guess, but he could have been younger. Don't think there's anything for me to investigate, but thought I'd better pass on the info to you."

The next minute Sam wished she hadn't mentioned Yuri, for Laurie told her to "Keep an eye on that situation too. The Russian element's certainly significant for us."

So much work and so little time. Tomorrow she had to go to report on a Seniors golf championship the other side of the county. It should be a pleasant enough day, but it meant spending a lot of time for in terms of work, on what would not be a particularly interesting story, annoying when she wanted to move forward with the problems at Elmsleigh Park so she could enjoy her captaincy without complications.

Although she usually enjoyed a cup of tea or a drink after her meetings with Laurie, this afternoon she refused his hospitality, explaining she must go straight to Elmsleigh Park. She needed to take advantage of arriving during the late summer daylight, but after the green staff had departed. Then she hoped she would be able to enter the locked shed unobserved.

To her chagrin as she reached the Visitors carpark, she noticed the beggar was still there at six o'clock in the evening. More frustrating as she drove into the Members carpark, she saw the Captain's car parked in its allotted space, as was the President's car. Also, there in his reserved slot was Simon's, the Manager's car. She had automatically headed for her own Lady Captain's place beside the other Captain, but with a quick reverse she spun the car round. Silly of her; she should have gone straight to the shabby bit of ground near the tenth hole, used as a parking area. It should be safely anonymous since no one would expect cars to be parked there now.

However, when she parked her Mini, there was one other scruffy little vehicle, an ancient Renault, parked there. It might belong to a member, but there was also the possibility some non-members, trespassers were taking advantage of the good early evening weather to play at Elmsleigh Park without paying a green fee. There would be few players around to report them.

Sam could not worry about that now. She must get to the locked shed to look inside. With her handbag safely over her shoulder and Laurie's bunch of keys rattling in her trouser pocket, she made her way along the path beside some bushes to the small screened dirty wooden building. Now, close to, she reflected on how shabby the larger old dark wood chalet building looked in comparison with the other lighter coloured huts which housed the smart new machinery in which the club had invested to bring the course up to a higher standard.

She hoped one of the ancient master keys which Laurie provided would fit the lock. Only one, the largest black iron one looked possible. She pushed it into the keyhole apprehensively, surprised it entered without a problem. To her relief, with only a slight wobble, she was able to turn it. A couple of seconds later she pushed down the door handle to enter the shed.

It was full of jumble, or what appeared to be useless bits and pieces. Strange bits of machinery with no obvious use were half covered with an aged once yellow blanket. Nearby on a table were a few odd bits of metal and about half a dozen shiny grey stones with gold glints. Alongside that, an ancient check rug covered something else with black iron legs which she supposed might be machinery. On a large wooden shelf, which looked like a table jammed against the side wall were tools, secateurs, shears, trowels and forks. There was also a ring on which stood an ancient looking copper kettle.

How silly I've been. She reflected. *There's obviously nothing here. What a waste of time. No, I had to look, to know what's in here. Still, better take a photo, have something to show Laurie.* She took out her mobile phone for a quick snap of the interior before she turned to go. Then she swivelled round again. *There must be something here.* Her instinct told her that. With a couple of steps forward she reached out to tug the rug off the large object with short black iron legs.

She almost laughed out loud. In front of her stood a foldaway bed. Dusty though it was, at a glance she could see it was a relatively modern design. There was even a cover over the enclosed mattress. As she stared at it, presuming the obvious, that the old man must sometimes sleep here, she noted that the top of the folded-up bed, which would act as the bed's headboard, was not flush against the wall.

The gap between the bed and the wall was disguised by a shelf running along the wall above the end of the bed. Maybe there was something of interest hidden there? Easy to find out since the bed was on castors.

Sam pulled the end of the bed to one side, proving with the ease it moved, that she was right not only about the age of the bed but its purpose to hide stuff. She lifted a cardboard box with some tins of baked beans off a piece leather to discover an ancient dark grey leather jacket with a torn lining lay on another carboard box. *Still wearable,* she decided, lifting it up to examine it. She felt in the pockets. Nothing there. Disappointed she dropped it back, realising as she looked down in the darkness of the unlit shed, that a long black object stood behind the box on which the jacket had laid.

She put her hand down to feel the top of the object. It had a curved shape but she was able to pull it on to one side without difficulty and once she had it on its end, she could see it was the case of a musical instrument, almost certainly a guitar. She lifted it out and placed it on a space she cleared on the large table like shelf.

Excitement mounted in her. Surely this must tell her something. The case was not locked. She was able to twist the silver catch on the case and lift the lid open to reveal the guitar inside. It was, she could tell from the wood, obviously an old instrument, she had expected that from its case, but its presence here still must mean something. Instinctively she plucked a couple of strings. Not only were they taut, but they sounded somehow right, as though they might have been tuned. Sam had never played the guitar but she had once learnt the piano and loved music. Ancient though this instrument was, she felt sure it was still played by someone.

She felt around the inside of the case. On the inside of the lid there was a bit of material, something stuck to the surface. Propping the lid open, she got her mobile out of her bag to use the torch to see if it was a label with a name stuck there. Yes, it was.

"David Barvaz," she read the name in gold letters on a black leather patch stuck to the dark red velvet interior of the lid.

Who on earth is that? She was getting her diary out of her handbag to peruse the list of members on the back pages, to see if there was anyone with that name when she heard, to her horror, voices outside.

"You think there's someone here then?" Said a male voice that sounded like a youngish man.

"Could be, maybe in our shed," said the other.

"Nah, they can't get in," said the other.

Despite her alarm, in a trice Sam had moved as quickly and silently as she could to the door to lock it from the inside, quaking at the slight squeak the key made as it turned. Then she looked for somewhere to hide.

"Better see," said the other. "Don't like the look of that car parked there."

"That's like the Lady Captain's car. Can't see her dossing down here."

He's right there. Sam was stifling cough after cough in her hiding place squashed against the bed under the smelly old tarpaulin.

The sound of their steps came nearer until they were right outside the door. There was a squeak as the handle turned but the door did not open.

"Told you," said the younger man who'd spoken first. "No one there. Car belongs to some old bird out playing."

"Better look inside all the same," said the other voice and there was another scratching sound whilst a key was evidently placed in the lock before it was turned.

Beneath the tarpaulin Sam felt a rush of air as the door opened. She held her breath, grateful for all the years she spent swimming under water, but still feeling she might faint before, after seconds the door closed again.

No more conversation other than a "Told yer".

Gradually the sound of their footsteps lessened whilst Sam tried to remember where she'd heard the younger man's voice before. After a few minutes she concluded the voice sounded like Kyle's, the friendly dog walker she had spoken too only a couple of days before, loitering around these sheds. The other man she presumed must be a ground staffer, although she did not recognise his voice.

Had he checked out her car then so that he knew it belonged to the Lady Captain? More worrying for the moment was whether the men had left the park, or whether she would find them messing about the place when she went back to her car.

Best to wait for a bit.

She got her mobile, then decided it was not sensible to use it as a phone or for the internet. She did not want to give away her location now or in the future.

Bored she stared around the shed again. Other than the guitar and the foldaway bed, there did not seem to be anything of relevance to her investigation here, but she reminded herself, *You never can tell.* She got out her mobile again deciding to while away the time until she was sure those guys had departed, then she would take a load more photos of the shed's contents.

The tools, lumps of metal, the large greyish black stones lying around might mean something or nothing. Still, as far as Sam was concerned, there was one thing of real interest, that guitar in the box with the name on a label stuck on the tattered velvet lining of the lid.

10. News of Yuri

As she edged out of the shed, locking it behind her, she saw quickly, to her relief, that hers was the only car in sight. With a spring in her step, she walked quickly to the Mini. It was after seven in the evening and she was hungry. Time to get home to get something to eat.

She had just started the car when the phone in her handbag rang. Her automatic response kicked in making her switch the engine off. In the mirror she saw herself screw up her retroussé nose as she wondered why she imagined this might be an urgent call worth answering at this time on a Friday night. Nonetheless she delved into her handbag for the mobile which was just turning into answerphone mode as she said "Hello".

"Oh good, you're there," said a relieved sounding voice which she recognised as Roger Turpin's. "I wanted to tell you some good news."

"Oh," Sam repeated, "what's that?"

"The tests confirm post mortem on Yuri Leonov. He died of antimony poisoning."

"Good news?" Sam questioned, hardly believing what she was hearing.

"As far as the club's concerned, yes. Although there might have been a trace of arsenic, that's covered by the antimony because there can be arsenic with antimony, but all his symptoms as well as the autopsy point to antimony poisoning. That clears club as far as the accusation of our food poisoning him is concerned."

"I see," gulped Sam, "but what does that mean about…?

Roger cut in before she could finish her question as to any perpetrator. "Why he died is still not answered. There'll have to be an inquest to decide whether it's natural causes, possibly some sort of accident, or suicide, but that's up to the coroner. We here at Elmsleigh Park know from Simon that Yuri was in a disturbed state of mind the day his illness started."

"This is just awful." The phone in Sam's hand shook as she trembled. "I knew him a bit, was drawn as his partner to play with him a few times. He never gave me the impression he was the suicidal type."

"I don't think type is quite the word and it's not always obvious if someone's depressed," said Roger in an authoritative professional tone. "Anyway, I'm sorry if this comes as a shock to you, but I felt you ought to know how we stand as soon as possible. You'll be relieved the club's in the clear."

"Er yes," Sam managed to agree before the Captain of Elmsleigh Park bade her goodbye.

Definitely not suicide. She kept telling herself as she drove home. A man who, if not scornful, does not want to identify with someone like Solzhenitsyn because he's got a "tortured soul" or more appropriate Tolstoy, is not the suicide type. *There's nothing wrong with a tortured soul. I sometimes feel I've got one myself.* She mused. *To claim you're not like that should mean you're different. It may not be scientific, but it's my instinct.*

What did Roger mean by the alternative of natural causes? How could death by something she understood to be a metal be "natural causes"? It did not make sense to her. Still the post mortem was only a preliminary giving

101

them evidence from the Yuri's body. They would have to wait for the inquest ending with the Coroner's verdict to understand why or how he imbibed antimony.

As she drove along, she realised she was glad Laurie was paying her; she didn't want to wait for the inquest to find out more. She must investigate further.

Once her car was tucked in the garage beside her house, she walked through the adjoining door into the utility room beside her kitchen. She shook herself; she must not take this personally. Her suggestion Yuri took part in the true or false game could not have any bearing on his death. He was pleased at the idea of joining in, playing a part; she had not suggested he should pretend to be descended from criminal or a murderous dictator.

She felt for Ekaterina, even if she did turn up at the club's parties or social lunches looking rather more magnificent than the occasion demanded. She participated as a social member which helped the club's finances. Sam's hand shook a little as she switched on the kettle to make a cup of tea, thinking she would prefer a gin and tonic. She knew what it was like to be suddenly widowed, like half the house falling down in an unexpected tornado.

With her mug of Earl Grey tea in her hand she walked through to her office to browse antimony poisoning. The tea almost dropped out of her mouth as Mozart's name cropped up. There was the suggestion that he died, poisoned by antimony. Shaffer's play about his murder might have been fiction, but here it was mooted as a factual possibility. Still that was hundreds of years ago and in another country. Roger might bask safely in the notion that Elmsleigh Park was in the clear, even if Sam herself was not so sure.

She must go and see Ekaterina; she could go on behalf of the club. Sipping her tea, while Monty, her black Labrador dog, rubbed his muzzle against her legs as she scrolled down more references to poisoning. There was, she decided, no need to mention the visit to the Cabinet or they might tell her not to go, that it was unnecessary or unwise in view of Ekaterina's accusation. Now the club's Lady Captain was equal with the Men's Captain in theory, she need not ask Roger's permission, however courteous it might be to tell him or indeed Simon.

A weekend might not be the best time to visit the bereaved, but sooner rather than later would be good, Sam decided as she walked into the local flower shop next morning. Penny Norton, the President's wife, always ensured she had a splendid selection of flowers in her shop on Saturdays, the day when Hampshire folk would want to pick up a bouquet to take to their evening's dinner party. Besides Sam liked to support the flower shop which was in the centre of the village, not only helping to bring custom to the other couple of shops there, but also promising all the produce it sold was sourced locally.

To her alarm Penny, who normally ran the place from behind the scenes was there, in the shop this morning. The tall voluptuous lady with silver curly hair was actually serving, bending over a flower pot full of roses, for another customer. Although there was a sales girl there to help Sam, Penny excused herself so she could rush to attend to her.

"Who do you want them delivered to?" She asked when Sam chose a beautiful bunch of white lilies whilst she wondered whether Ekaterina, unlike Penny, would appreciate that they were a traditional choice for bereavement.

"No, I'm going to take them with me," replied Sam, "she's a non-golfing friend." She must be careful to avoid mentioning Yuri's death.

As far as Sam was aware, the club's flag outside the clubhouse, did not yet hang at half-mast announcing a member's death, but Penny would surely know about Yuri's demise from her husband. How much detail Dick would have given her, Sam couldn't guess.

Whatever her husband might have told her, Penny would certainly be fascinated with Sam's point of view, especially if she could impart further information about such a well-known club character as "The Russian". To involve her in sending flowers to Ekaterina would cause trouble indeed.

"How would you like them wrapped?" Asked Penny, pulling at a sheet of black tissue paper.

Sam almost groaned. Her choice of Arum lilies had made Penny assume her anonymous friend was bereaved. Bracing herself she shook her head. "No, no, for this occasion I think something else would go better. Don't want to be dramatic. White will be fine."

"If you're sure," insisted Penny. "Anything else I can help you with?"

Sam would have liked to ask if she knew the Leonov's address. Her talk of delivery made Sam realise she had no idea where the Leonovs lived now. The list

Laurie gave her with names, jobs and addresses was years old. She was sure she had heard Yuri moved house recently. Penny might know his current address, since she might well have delivered floral condolences to the Leonov household, but Sam quelled the urge to ask her.

Back at home she searched various telephone directories on the internet. No luck. The only place where she knew she could find the address was at the golf club. It must be somewhere in the office, but she would not be able to access it because the office staff did not work at weekends. In any case she did not wish Simon to know she planned to visit Ekaterina. She eyed her handbag, now sitting on the desk in front of her. In it was Laurie's bunch of master keys. Once again, they could come in useful.

She knew there were likely to be people around in the hall of the clubhouse on a Saturday morning but as it happened the couple of men chatting to each other did not appear to notice her standing there before they departed into the men's changing room. All the same, with her shoulders back and head held high to give the impression she was the Lady Captain on official business, she put one key after another into the lock of the office door, finding thankfully, on her third attempt, one which fitted.

She locked the door from the inside so as to give herself fair warning should anyone else try to enter, although here there was no shabby rug to throw over herself should Captain Roger Turpin, or more alarming, Vice-Captain Hector Bravo charge into the room. Then she stared around at the numerous drawers of the desk and against the side wall wondering where in this densely packed place an address list could possibly be. Presumably a paper file was somewhere. Now it hit her that a better option would have been to get a friendly hacker to break into the club's hidden website for the Leonov address.

As she was here, she pulled at a couple of drawers in the corner of the room where an old-fashioned dark wood filing cabinet stood. This could be where Simon kept files of names and addresses. A couple of these drawers were locked, but again she found a tiny iron key amongst Laurie's master bunch which fitted, but all there was inside were a couple of cash boxes, also locked. They would contain the petty cash the manager might need. There was obviously money inside because they rattled when she picked them up to see if there was possibly a file underneath them, but all she discovered was, rather oddly, a half full packet of sugar stashed behind them. She re-locked the drawers and despondently pulled at the third unlocked drawer underneath which flew open easily.

Oh joy oh rapture! In front of her was a file with ADDRESS LIST on a printed label stuck there. In two minutes, she had noted the Leonov's Alresford address on her mobile. She would go straight there to deliver the flowers with the Ladies of Elmsleigh Park's condolences. She would like to say the club itself, but that would risk Ekaterina writing back to Captain Roger Turpin, or worse still, the President Dick Norton, which she must avoid.

It crossed her mind, as she drove away from the clubhouse that maybe she should wait for the result of the inquest, but dismissed the idea. She needed to find out why Ekaterina blamed the club, before complicated medical information along with various legal ramifications blurred everything else

11. Visiting Ekaterina

The town house in New Alresford was not what Sam had expected the Leonov residence to be. The moment she walked through the door, she guessed she entered a rented property. Although the house itself must be over a hundred years old, the interior had been so reconstructed to need such minimal maintenance that the effect was to take away the house's character.

Ekaterina stared at her. "What do you want?" She asked brusquely, in her deep voice, the perfectly enunciated words still spoken with a faint Russian accent. "I did not ask for you to come here."

"No," admitted Sam, hoping the straight black trousers she wore looked sufficiently respectful without looking too formal. "I'm here to pay our respects to you from the ladies of Elmsleigh Park. We're so sorry to hear that Yuri has been so desperately ill and died."

Ekaterina, who was at least six inches taller than Sam, stared down at her with a frown. "You know I do not trust your club," she said with a slight shake of her head, making her dark-haired chignon bob loose. Putting up her left hand she pushed in a couple of pins to secure it.

"Yes, I'm sorry about that, but I've brought these for you." Sam held out her hand with the bunch of white lilies wrapped in white tissue paper tied by a pink ribbon. Though she knew Ekaterina usually wore yellow or orange Sam had not wished to argue with Penny Norton who had insisted the pink ribbon was the prettiest she had to offer.

"Thank you." Again the brusque tone. "Will you come into my kitchen whilst I put them in water."

Sam nodded. She felt an underlying urge from Ekaterina to be friendly despite her inhospitable tone, but why would she behave any differently following the horror of her husband's harrowing death? As she followed Ekaterina into the small modern kitchen with its white kitchen units one end and pine dining table the other, the thought struck Sam that when he started to be ill, Yuri himself must have blamed the club.

Ekaterina reached for a tall plain jug from a shelf of a large pine dresser behind the table to fill with water for the flowers, off which she deftly hacked the ends of the stems, whilst she offered Sam coffee.

"Thank you. An Americano would be nice." Sam eyed the modern coffee machine wondering whether it belonged to the Leonovs, who were now of course, only Ekaterina, or part of the furnishings of the house.

Sitting beside her at the pine table it seemed more than inappropriate, almost cruel to ask details about Yuri's death, but Sam hardened her heart. To learn the truth must be to everyone's benefit, as well as to reassure Ekaterina club members were not prejudiced against her husband. "I suppose the doctors didn't realise until too late what caused your husband's sickness," she ventured.

Ekaterina shook her head vigorously. "No, he would not let me call a doctor. He say he do not like doctors here. Then when I do call the doctor, he gives Yuri an injection and says he must go to hospital, but it is too late. Yuri dies in the ambulance." A tear rolled down her face as she continued, her strong lower jaw sticking out as she breathed through clenched teeth to say, "They say antimony has poisoned him, but that is impossible."

"Why's that?"

"We have no antimony here. The officials say that in their post more-thing because that suits them. It works for them."

"No, no, that sort of thing doesn't happen here in the UK. Doctors here wouldn't say that if it, I mean if they didn't believe, have some sort evidence it was true."

"Then poisoning must happen at the club. I tell you we have no antimony here."

"But surely, I mean possibly, Yuri had exposure to it, I mean dealing with it?"

"What do you mean dealing with it? Yuri was not a miner. He was a money man; he raises the money so our mine in Russia can produce. It will be amazing, but it is so terrible Yuri will not be here to see it." Ekaterina gave a sob. Another tear rolled down her cheek.

"He must have seen the antimony coming from his mine?" The words fell out of Sam's mouth embarrassing her. Yuri was known as rich, not a gambling speculator.

"Only a little now," reiterated Ekaterina. "We will have fantastic mine one day; it will be our Golden Moon."

"Golden Moon?" queried Sam. What on earth was the woman talking about now? Surely she couldn't mean a honeymoon.

Her puzzlement made Ekaterina give a faint smile. "Golden Moon is what we call our mine because it will take over from Twinkling Star."

"Twinkling Star?" Sam's face puckered in a questioning frown.

"Twinkling Star," explained Ekaterina "is the Chinese antimony mine which has fed the world for years, but is now running out; our Golden Moon can take over."

"I see." Sam nodded thinking it sounded rather pie in the sky. "You mean you really don't have any antimony around here."

Ekaterina shook her head. "That is what I keep telling you. Yuri raises money to pay miners. He is city man. We have no antimony here, except the one piece."

"Where is it?" Asked Sam trying not to sound too eager.

"Behind you on the shelf." Ekaterina sniffed. "I used to think it was lucky."

Sam turned around to look and gasped. On a high shelf of the pine dresser stood a solid silvery grey object with glinting gold, exactly like the lumps she'd thought were stones in the shed she'd searched beside the golf course. "You mean that's antimony?"

"Why yes, but you would not eat it would you?"

"No," agreed Sam. "I don't see how something like that could give anyone food poisoning. Are you sure there's nothing else here in the house, some broken bits of the stone?"

"It is not stone; it is more like rock."

"Yes," agreed Sam, remembering her research into antimony, "but I understand it can be grated, or at least ground into a powder of sorts because in the olden days it was used as a medicine. There's a suggestion that's how the composer Mozart died; he got poisoned by taking too much medicine containing antimony."

"Yuri was not silly man like that. He understood antimony, and how it is used for the good, otherwise he would not want our boys to go into the business."

"Your boys? Of course." Sam tapped the side of her head with her fingers, recalling Yuri referring proudly to his children after golf games they were drawn to play together. "They went to school here didn't they?"

"Yes, my sons." Ekaterina pushed her chair back to enable her to stand up and stride out of the kitchen; she returned a few moments later with a silver photograph frame filled with a picture of two boys in what looked like their late teens. "Vladimir and Alexei." She pointed to each of them proudly.

Sam stifled a gasp. Vladimir looked very like the young man she'd presumed to be a ground staff, whom she saw loitering around the sheds on the golf course with Kyle. Yet wasn't that man too old to be Ekaterina's progeny? Close to, without masses of makeup, her hostess, even in smart tight jeans and loose-fitting tee shirt, did look older than Sam had taken her for previously. She stared at Ekaterina, then back at the photo, hoping Ekaterina assumed she was looking in admiration rather than to spot a likeness. The resemblance was there, confirming she had definitely met that man.

Then it struck her forcibly. There might be a good reason for a Leonov son to skulk around the sheds. Inside the one she broke into were lumps of stuff that looked remarkably like the antimony on the wall behind her.

"Are they living here in England where they can be a help and comfort to you now?" She asked

Ekaterina shook her head. "No they live in Russia where they work."

That did not fit, unless Vladimir had recently made a trip to the UK.

"Don't they want to come here to be with you?"

Ekaterina shook her head. "They work hard and they do young people's things."

"Don't they ever come to the club?" Pulling her tummy muscles since she'd once been told this was a good Pilates exercise if you wanted to ask an awkward question, Sam continued, "I think I've seen Vladimir around the sheds at the club."

Ekaterina nodded before answering angrily, "Maybe when he is here like now. Sometimes he is with me but he has lots of friends in England; he has been to great public school here."

"Oh, which one?" Asked Sam, whose father had been a teacher at one of the top public schools."

Ekaterina mentioned a school Sam thought she had heard her late father refer to as a less academic, but more expensive place than some others. Whilst her father was critical of what he considered exorbitant fees, they appeared to impress Ekaterina for whom money talked.

Reverting to the club, she said angrily, "Yuri pays good money to store some things in a hut. He made agreement with manager Mr Duckworth that it was to be a secret. Mr Duckworth says the club is short of money and this is a good way for Yuri to be helpful because he pays cash or the money on the internet that is not money."

"Bitcoin?" Ventured Sam.

"Whatever it is I do not know, but it is meant to help the club, only Yuri must keep it secret. The manager cannot make the same agreement with everyone."

"I see. That means your family did actually deal with and sell antimony in a way." Suggested Sam in her most placating tone, "Yuri acted as an antimony broker."

"He was getting people interested, making friends with people who would help."

"Who do you mean? Ozzie Reynolds perhaps?"

"Maybe, I do not know them all, but I tell you this. That shed, supposed to be for our stuff, is being used by someone else. My boy says there are clothes there, a sleeping bag there and even bed."

"Really?" Sam tried to look surprised.

"Truly. Someone spies on us. Our true friend Nicholas Roman, a good man, who is Russian royal family tells us."

Sam restrained herself from commenting that anyone purporting to be from the Romanov dynasty was likely to be a fake himself, however charming.

"He came specially to tell Yuri that the last day he was at your club. He warned Yuri that the day his car thing was stolen he saw bad man like vory gangster there."

Probably that wretched beggar. "I don't think so; I haven't heard anyone say they've seen anyone evil like that. There is a sad old man who hangs about, but we think he's a nuisance rather than dangerous."

"Now Yuri is dead who will protect me?" Tears began to flow down Ekaterina's face. "I do not know what I will do."

"Your boys," said Sam in what she hoped was a

comforting tone. "They'll look after you." She pushed her chair back to stand up. By coming here, she had discovered more than she could possibly have hoped. The only trouble was, it did not move her very far forwards in her investigation.

To her amazement, Ekaterina clasped her hand. "Don't go. I feel you are a friend."

"I'm so sorry," said Sam awkwardly, for she hated to be unsympathetic, "but I really do have to leave now."

She must have been here in this house for almost an hour, during which time she had warmed to Ekaterina, but she could not become her friend, however sorry she felt for her. She could not be certain the antimony mine was not a hoax. It certainly sounded almost unreal. She would have to check it out along with other mentions by Ekaterina. Then she would have to ascertain whether Simon really had given permission for lumps of antimony to be stored in one of the golf club's sheds.

To link that antimony with the catalyst converter robberies did not seem any more probable than the notion Yuri consumed his own ground-up antimony. With a sigh of sympathy, Sam reached out to Ekaterina thinking she should shake her hand but Ekaterina's longer arms pulled her into an embrace, kissing her on both cheeks.

Guilt suffused Sam; she was just doing a job whilst the woman she had been talking to was suffering a terrible loss. She pushed down a sigh, knowing she could not admit that she could see no circumstances when she could fight Ekaterina's corner. Nonetheless she could not deny to herself what the lady clearly instinctively felt; her lack of trust in some member of the club was shared.

12. Audience with the Beggar

She must go back to see the beggar, Charlie as she mentally termed him. The old man claimed he was a direct descent of Charles Elmhurst, the owner of the Elmsleigh Park estate who had generously donated it to the golf club he loved, of which he was a founder member.

No wonder the homeless beggar felt deprived, if indeed he was either homeless or descended from Charles Elmhurst. The bed in the chalet type shed she saw the beggar go into, suggested it was indeed the same old itinerant man who owned the bed. But what of the guitar? Did that belong to the beggar? Was his name really David Barvaz? It was, she discovered a Hebrew name which fitted with the beggar saying his father was a Jew.

To ask him straight was not likely to produce the answer. He would, she expected, prevaricate. She must surprise him into admission. With that in mind she drove into the Visitors Carpark, noticed him look up from his newspaper from where he sat in his usual place on the public right of way, and parked as inconspicuously as possible behind some already parked cars.

Quietly she opened the car door to slip out between the parked cars. After shutting her door, she crouched down to move unobtrusively towards the front of the three rows of cars where she hid until she thought the beggar, sitting on his aged rug with a thermos beside him, was engrossed in his tattered copy of the Daily Mail.

Then she sprang forward with the cry, "Morning David Barvaz."

He looked up, his mouth dropping open in surprised confirmation.

So, she continued: "That is your name isn't it?"

"Could be." There was a slight tremor in his voice.

"You play the guitar though, don't you?" Sam ploughed on mercilessly, despite the way she noted the old man's mouth twitch awkwardly at the corner.

"I did." He admitted.

"Well enough not to want to part with your prized possession which is why it is in a shed here."

"Have you've been spying on me? Sent by the powers that be no doubt?"

"Be that as it may, it won't hurt you to tell me your real name, admit that you are David Barvaz. Why not? I read Barvaz is meant to be a strong lucky name."

"Not sure about that." His blue eyes twinkled and he suddenly laughed. "Okay you're right and wrong. It's the name I was christened with, and yes, my mother got me christened but I didn't keep the name Barvaz. Too much anti-Semitism around. Our family changed it when I was a child. That guitar case you obviously found belonged to my father."

"What's your name now?"

His face crinkled into a laugh again. "Elmhurst obviously."

"Not obvious as far as your father was concerned," retorted Sam. There was, she sensed, something false about the old man's claim.

"So what? I'm entitled to take my mother's name."

"Although you were happy to keep your father's name on your guitar case?"

"Why throw away a good case? He was a great musician and pleased I was able to follow in his footsteps and make a living out of music, if only for a while."

"Were you a musician then, a pop star?" That would explain his change in fortunes. Throughout her journalistic career, having worked on pop magazines, Sam had seen fortunes in music made and blown away.

"Yeah I liked his music. People in the sixties and seventies still liked melodious stuff, not like all that awful banging they do today."

Something about this was beginning to ring chords in Sam's mind. "What tunes are you talking about?"

"Oh things like 'I remember you; you're the one who made my dreams come true'. You know the Bing Crosby, Frank Sinatra stuff."

"Heavens, nothing more modern than that?" She didn't add it was no wonder the old man had not been able to make a living from music in the twenty-first century.

"Yeah surely. I went on to some of the rock and roll, skiffle and stuff. Used to like Lonnie Donegan." He pulled a battered looking stop watch out of his tattered jacket pocket. "Time for me to get my dinner," he said. "I'll be off and good-day to you." He rose unsteadily on to his feet and started to walk away.

Sam hesitated. "You mean you can get lunch at the club?" She called after him.

Charlie, or David, whoever he was, turned his head over shrugged shoulders. "I'll eat what they'll throw out.

Eat by dates are great for people like me. Club can't sell left-overs, but I'm happy to eat them."

Sam walked after him. "What does Jason Goodridge say about that?"

"Who's he?"

"The house manager." Sam checked her indignation, surmising that though he might be her chum, in his role as house manager Jason did extremely little. He left the work to Misty, who benefitted from having a cottage on the Elmsleigh Park estate.

"Never heard of him. Not heard anyone round the back door talk about him."

"They should know about him. He's the member on the committee responsible for seeing all is right with the club's catering and any other household matters."

"Look chuck, I'm just a dustbin," laughed David Charlie, as Sam now mentally christened him. "You don't have to worry your pretty head about me or some grand committee member. It's other cheating sods who belong to the club that you should be worrying about."

"Such as?" Sam asked eagerly.

"You're not catching me there chuck, so run along. You must have better things to do than pester me." He pursed his wide lips in a hard line as he turned away from her, walking now more briskly than she would have thought possible for a man of his decadent appearance.

As he moved away his gait suddenly struck her as familiar. Someone she knew walked like that. She pictured the various club members she had seen recently, then the committee members. No, it wasn't any of them. Yet her instinct told her somehow David Charlie had a more modern connection to the club than the one he claimed.

She wished she could mention this to one of her friends in the club, but that would be folly. The thought of confiding in Tabby made her chuckle out loud. Astute though Tabby was, Sam did not want another rocket from her husband Vice-Captain Hector Bravo, who'd briefed Laurie. Bravo and Barvaz; how similar those names were! That made her smile again. Good to laugh at something before she went back to her desk to swot at more research.

Sometimes to recognise someone, a wade through the names in the back pages of the club diary threw up the answer, but not in this case. Sam dropped the diary down beside her office desk, planning for it to fall into her small shoulder bag lying there. It was a near miss, something she felt horribly redolent of everything she had found out.

Despondently she picked up the mouse to attend to other business, look at her bank statement. A click on the screen in front of her produced the last lot of research she had done into the name Barvaz, the indication that it was of Hebrew origin. She stared at it again. Why did it not strike her before? The name Barvaz was derived from the Hebrew word for duck. It was Simon Duckworth, the manager to whom the beggar bore a slight resemblance.

Could David Charlie, born Barvaz, have given her his maternal grandfather's name to disguise how his father, or indeed he himself changed his name? The more she considered it, the more convinced she became.

There was additional evidence in his, David's talking about his particular style of music. That was the music Simon had told her and Crystal that he liked

119

because it was what his father played. If she needed something more conclusive, there it was when she pressed her mouse's button to look up Lonnie Donegan whom David Charlie said he particularly like to play. "My old man's a dustman". That song Simon accorded his father's favourite, was made famous by that pop star.

If David Charlie really was Simon's father it explained why Simon was reluctant to try to push the old man back on the road, but it was still odd. Why, when Simon was so efficient in so many ways, did he not find a better solution to his father's homelessness than allowing him to plague visitors at Elmsleigh Park?

Sam wondered whether she should tell Laurie what she suspected, but decided against it. Laurie would be bound to tell Hector Bravo of her suspicions which could spark off a terrible row, possibly resulting in Hector firing Simon which was not what Sam wanted. Simon was not only efficient, but helpful to her personally. She did not want to wrestle with assisting a new manager get to grips with running ladies' golf here.

She drummed her fingers on her desk. No, she did not have to tell of her suspicions because they might not be true. Everything she had discovered could add up to coincidence. She would report to Laurie her belief the beggar was truly the grandson of the golf club's founder, Charles Elmhurst. She would say she was going to research his descendants to ascertain his male offspring had died in the second world war whilst his daughter had married a man of whom he disapproved. The beggar himself was once a successful then failed musician specialising in dated last century sloppy songs.

120

No need to talk to him; she would fire off an email outlining her progress before returning to the club. David Charlie must be able to help her more. He virtually admitted to Crystal he knew something about the catalyst converter thefts saying "See no evil".

It was nearly five o'clock in the evening by the time she arrived back at the Visitors' carpark. Seeing David Charlie in his usual spot, packing his possessions into his rucksack evidently about to depart, she stopped the car next to him, wound down her window and asked, "Did you get a good lunch?"

His crinkled old face creased into a smile, "Always a good day if a society's been feeding here."

"What made you stay here so long if you've been fed and watered?" Asked Sam.

"You do go on." He laughed. "It's a nice day aint it?" Again he used the mock cockney vowels.

"Don't you feel guilty, sponging off other people's hard-earned money?" The words dropped out of Sam's mouth, making her feel guilty herself at her own lack of compassion for a man on his uppers, but the feeling passed instantly at David Charlie's scornful scoffed response.

"Hard-earned money? There's worse than beggars belong to this club."

"Such as?"

"Bloody Russian."

"He's no longer a member. The poor man's dead."

"Not surprised someone's probably done him in; that guy could be pleasant and generous as can be, but he was a damn spy." With that he stepped away from her car waving her a firm good-bye.

13. Tea after golf

It was going to be easier to validate David Charlie's own pedigree than test his accusation Yuri was a spy. A few routes through ancestry websites proved what the man had said, with a few additional details about his father, David Barvaz having escaped the holocaust by leaving Germany in the 1930s. Most important, Sam managed to trace a registry office marriage certificate for the man's mother as well as a birth certificate for a David Ezekiel Barvaz. A couple of fore-finger touches on the computer's mouse to research names before she discovered Ezekiel was Jewish for Charles.

"The beggar is kosher, as you or rather he might say," she joked to Laurie when she visited him in his office the next day.

"As your man fears," laughed Laurie. "That beggar has morphed from 'a loose impediment' to an 'immovable obstruction'."

Sam winced at the use of golf rules language. "Not 'my man', just the Vice-Captain's, but he's right to fear potential adverse publicity if David Charlie's identity got known. It could damage the club horribly."

Not helpful to add she had also found birth certificates for Simon, David Charlie's only child whom she strongly suspected to be the current Elmsleigh Park secretary. She tried to suggest that was presumably enough investigation as far as the beggar was concerned. All she need concentrate on now were the catalyst converter thefts which had gone quiet for the moment.

Laurie shook his head. "Mr Bravo also said there's also been a death at your club which we might help investigate with our undercover agent." He smirked. "Presumably that's the Russian man you mentioned?"

Sam waved her hands airily, shaking her long fingers as though she were dusting the problem away. "Yes, Yuri Leonov, but we on the committee have been told we don't have to worry because the post mortem proves he died from antimony poisoning when he actually dealt in that substance. His wife insists there's none in their house, other than one block, but there could be some in garden sheds or stashed away in a cupboard somewhere."

Laurie put his elbows down on the other side of his desk and folded his hands together. "Yup, but the state of affairs is not being left there. The suggestion is that the Russian Embassy, no less, has requested an inquest, so the police will be sending a forensic team to examine the club for whatever antimony maybe on your premises. Not sure how it can poison somebody."

Sam suppressed her desire to smile at her thought *I'm ahead of you there.* "Historically it's been used in famous poisoning cases. The solid substance can be ground down to a fine powder that resembles sugar which has been hidden in medicine."

She wrinkled her nose as she wondered whether to mention Hector's fury at her suggestion Charles Bravo, the handsome dark-haired man with the wide-lipped sensual mouth, whom Hector resembled, could possibly be on his family tree. In 1876 the man of the famous Balham poisoning had been killed with antimony. He denied taking himself, but the suggestion had been made that he took it accidentally, having prepared it into a medicine he intended to administer to his rich wife. Alternatively, if Florence, Charles Bravo's wife of four months had deliberately poisoned him, she might have had good reason because he was reputed to be a bully.

Not so different from Hector at times. No, she must not say that, even in jest.

"Penny for your thoughts," said Laurie, reverting to the case in hand. "Yuri may have lived in England for a while, but he remained a Russian citizen, committed to his homeland where his business was as well as his family. They would have told the embassy."

"He's been here five years at least," Sam's nose was still wrinkled as she tried to recall the first time she was aware of Yuri's existence at the club. "Actually, it could be more like seven or eight." She frowned, puzzled. Odd for someone to be selling interest in a non-productive mine for such a long time.

"How old was he? Asked Laurie.

"Sixtyish, I'd guess. He had two grown-up sons who are in the business."

"Interesting. Can you contact them?"

"Not easily. Anyway, I don't think the Cabinet would want me to get involved." She spoke as firmly as she could, but Laurie's disappointed expression made her feel she must feed something to the man who was her boss. "There is one thing though: David Charlie, the beggar knew Yuri, though I don't know how well, and he said Yuri was a spy."

Laurie's blue eyes lit up. "Really?"

Sam nodded. "Yes. David Charlie said it, but obviously I don't know whether it was true. He might have been talking through his hat. It could be a ridiculous exaggeration, or rather a complete fib."

"He wasn't exaggerating or fibbing before, about himself, when no one believed him," said Laurie.

As she expected, had feared, Sam came away with a new investigation, prolonging the four weeks she had agreed to work on the project. She must now find out everything she could about Yuri Leonov, whether or not he was a spy. This investigation seemed absurd, she protested. It was way beyond her realm of experience, or remit when she joined the detective agency five years ago

Laurie was insistent. "You can do it."

With no other obvious source of information other than David Charlie himself, Sam spent a couple of days periodically wondering how she could best approach him to extract positive information. As he was already suspicious when she tried to question him, she decided the best way forward was friendship. If she cultivated the beggar, she might at least win some favour from Simon, himself, should he indeed be the beggar's son.

This could not be done in a rush. She needed to strike up some form of camaraderie to develop into a friendship of sorts. Bribery was a possibility, but Sam found herself shaking her head as she walked around with Monty her dog, whenever she pictured herself overtly tipping money into the old man's cap, jar or whatever he used for collecting, sometimes a disposable paper mug.

Mug? Drink? That's it. She punched the steering wheel as she drove to the club the following Wednesday for the Ladies golf morning. After the game she would take the old boy a cup of tea. If he was going up to the club's kitchen to scavenge food, the chances were that he would inveigle someone to give him a drink. She would ask the bar staff, or rather just Misty who could be relied upon to be discreet, what the old boy liked. Then she would take him a cup.

Inevitably preoccupied with what she was going to do later, Sam messed up her game. If only she had been playing with anyone other than Penny Norton, the glamourous flower-seller wife of President Dick Norton, she would not have been so upset. Penny was such a good player and so gracious, she managed to suggest tacitly that it was an honour to accompany her round the course. This always made it particularly annoying as well as humiliating to play badly with her. Penny compounded this by saying at intervals how golf was "Such a psychological game.". The implication some character foible caused Sam to flunk drives and miss putts invariably made her play even worse.

After the game, when Sam longed to proceed with her plan, Penny insisted on buying her tea in the clubhouse, to comfort her. She then expanded on her theme of psychological forces, only finishing her lecture when through the open floor to ceiling glass door, she spotted a tall muscular young man wearing scruffy jeans. The casual way he lounged in a wooden deck chair on the terrace next the club house, with his long legs crossed, showed the tattered ends of his trousers. A massive amount of facial hair was on his bronzed face besides the long dark hair pinned in a bun on top of his head.

"I don't know what we can do about him." Penny shook her head as she spoke in an undertone, surreptitiously eyeing the man.

"Who?" asked Sam, swallowing a mouthful of chocolate cake. She hadn't intended to eat something fattening but felt she needed comfort food, at the same time wishing she had asked to put it in a doggy bag, since it might have been useful to offer David Charlie. Perhaps she would do that after she had got rid of Penny.

"Greg Burgess," whispered Penny. "Can't think why Hector has to bring him here."

"Doesn't look as though they're getting on very well," commented Sam, making herself look properly outside to turn her mind to Penny's conversation.

Of course. That's the man who was gardening at Ozzie Reynolds' house. He was fun. What was more, she recalled, Ozzie had mentioned he once dealt in scrap metal. David Charlie could wait. She should definitely try to talk to Greg first.

"He looks such a mess," complained Penny, "does it deliberately 'cos years ago when Sir Bill Chambers was captain, and Dick was on the committee, they turned him down because he was so rude about the dress code amongst other conventions the club has." She blew out through her pink rosebud mouth in an irritated fashion. "Greg turned up for the interview looking an awful mess, but Dick tried to be nice to him, told him that the club really would like to admit him, but we did have a dress code which members were expected to adhere to. He was as nice as pie to the wretched man, even telling him where he might shop to get a discount as an Elmsleigh Park member and how he might as a desirable low figure handicapper, get credit at the Pro's shop."

Sam winced. She could guess what was coming next.

"And you know what?" Penny continued, "Greg was incredibly rude back. He made some remark like he wasn't a charity case and he didn't want to look like a toff. Well that was the end as far as Bill was concerned; he dismissed Greg; told him he would hear from the club. We do have standards here."

Sam controlled her impulse to mention the club's one-time anti-Semitism. Instead she said, "He's probably dressed like that because he's been working on the land here." She hesitated before saying in a rush, "Penny, I hope you don't mind but I understand he's a gardener and I'm desperate for some help in my place. Would you mind awfully if I went outside and collared him now. If I could just get an email or better a phone number to ring him, I…" She had not finished speaking though she stood up.

"You'd better know," interrupted Penny in a suspicious tone, "that he's Helen McTavish's boyfriend." She eyed Sam as though she suspected Sam had some other motive than gardening in mind. "I believe it's quite a serious attachment."

Sam laughed. "Thanks for telling me, and for the game," she added as she hurried towards the open French windows.

"Hello there," Hector greeted her without enthusiasm as she reached the wooden table by which he and Greg sat. "I don't think you know my godson Greg, do you?"

"We have met," said Sam with Greg almost in unison. "At Ozzie Reynolds where Greg was doing the garden."

"Really," commented Hector drily.

"Yes," agreed Greg with a chuckle. "Sam wanted me to join her fancy dress party as the spy Guy Burgess."

"Not as Guy," corrected Sam, "just with Guy Burgess on your family tree."

"Most inappropriate," said Hector drily. "Now, if you don't mind Sam, I must go and leave you two party animals to chat about gardening." With a deft movement, he rose up, pushed his chair away and strode off.

"What can I do for you then," asked Greg, his wide mouth creasing across his long face in a friendly grin.

"I desperately need some help in my garden, advice as much as anything, to make something of the patch I've got. It's not very big but I would like to make it more enticing."

"Sounds just the sort of job I'd like," he chuckled. "When did you have in mind to start."

"Give me dates when you're free and I may be able to make myself available, other than Wednesdays which is ladies day here."

They settled on a date in a week's time before Sam, to make herself more convincing asked, "And you'd better tell me what your rates are."

"Oh, you could take me out to tea or dinner as you might call it, included." His dark eyes twinkled flirtatiously at her. "Or maybe we could do that as a prior engagement."

Tempting. No never mix business with pleasure as her father would have said.

"Best stick to business for a start." She stood up.

"Good to see you," he retorted, standing up, holding out his hand to shake hers warmly before she hurried away.

Diverted by his flirtatious manner, she had not, she realised, asked him anything about metals, as she made her way back into the lounge, noting to her relief there was no sign of Penny. Now she could go discreetly to the kitchen to get cup of tea and possibly a piece of cake to take to David Charlie.

She was glad to find Misty in the kitchen, though unfortunately, with only one helper there, she was rushed to cope with all the orders coming through from the numerous ladies who had played that morning.

"Can I help you, Lady Captain?" Asked Misty in a voice which implied Sam had no right to be in the kitchen.

Sam took a step backwards to hover in the kitchen doorway. Obviously not a good moment to mention the beggar. Instead she asked, "Please could I have a mug of tea to take away?"

Misty gave her an odd look, but did not say she knew Sam had already drunk a couple of cups. She simply nodded, asking, "Milk and sugar."

Sam nodded. Surely David Charlie would be likely to take sugar. She smiled to herself. That packet of sugar in Simon's filing cabinet would probably have been for his father, rather than himself, since Simon could help himself to sugar in the clubhouse any time.

With the disposable mug of tea in hand, she made her way out through a back door, noting with relief that Penny's flower van, which had as usual on Wednesdays, been parked in her husband's presidential parking space beside the clubhouse had gone. Now she could safely drive down to Visitor's carpark to find David Charlie.

He should be there; he usually turned up on Wednesdays, probably because lady members were likely to be more generous than the men. Some of them, when she'd mentioned "the beggar", were more charitable in their reactions than the men.

Glad though she was to see him still around at half past four, he did not look welcoming. There he sat, in his usual place, wrapped up in his scruffy duvet, with his head down, looking rather miserable.

She parked alongside him, opened the car door and whistled as she held out the thick paper mug of tea. "This is for you. Thought you might need it."

He looked up at her suspiciously. "Now why would you think that."

"Just thought a cuppa might be welcome. They're very busy up at the clubhouse at the moment so I thought it might be a good idea to bring one here for you."

"Very kind of you." He reached out to take the cup from her outstretched hand, lifted the lid off and took a gulp. His lips spread out in a pout. "It's got sugar in it."

"Yeah, you take sugar don't you."

"No, no, mustn't have sugar. I'm a diabetic." He poured the tea away and handed her back the cup.

131

"I'm so sorry. I assumed you did, seeing that packet of sugar in the filing cabinet." The words slipped out. Sam grimaced as she slapped her long fingers over her mouth.

"What filing cabinet?" asked the old boy, his suspicious tone returning. He eyed her curiously. "Whose filing cabinet would that be?"

"Oh nothing, I must have been dreaming."

"What strange dreams you do have." He grinned.

"Next time," she said, "I'll bring you a cup without sugar, but you do take milk don't you."

He nodded.

She had made progress, she comforted herself as she drove away. Another time she would bring him tea or coffee without sugar. She sighed as she drummed her fingers on the steering wheel, worrying about the downside of their meeting, her admission she knew about the packet of sugar in Simon's locked filing cabinet.

The old man had looked as though it was no surprise to him that Simon had a packet of sugar in his filing cabinet. Or was it sugar? The label clearly said it was but, other than moving the packet which felt like tiny granules of something, she had not looked to see, smelt or tasted them.

Maybe it was lucky she had not. The memory hit her so hard she nearly drove over a red light. She could see the words again on her computer screen telling her about ground antimony. It resembled sugar.

14. Party preparations.

A couple of days later, on Friday evening, before
she managed to tackle David Charlie again, Captain
Doctor Roger Turpin convened another emergency
committee meeting. As it was eight o'clock in the evening
when the clubhouse was officially closed, with no one else
about, other than Misty to provide them with drinks, they
lounged around in the sitting room.

This was, Roger informed the group, an unofficial
gathering, partly due to the lack of attendance by some
members who could not attend at such short notice, but
mainly because he simply wanted to brief the key officials
as to what was happening.

"We want everyone to sing from the same hymn
sheet," explained President Dick Norton.

"Don't you mean play from the same tee?"
Quipped Amy in a light-hearted tone.

Jason eyed Matthew before they both looked at
Sam to see how she, as the only other woman on the
committee, responded to her Vice-Captain's remark.

Knowing Dick Norton was a keen chorister as well
as pillar of a local church, Sam simply gestured as she said
with a smile, "Let's hear what we've got to sing or play."

Roger gripped his glass of non-alcoholic gin he
had instructed the club to start stocking, and tonic. "You
need to know as it will be out on the county website this
Sunday. The inquest into Yuri Leonov's death will take
place in three or possibly even four months' time."

"Four months," exploded Jason. He eyed Roger's
gin, which, as house-manager he had objected to being

stocked, for who else, he had demanded, would want to pay such a ridiculous price for a non-alcoholic drink. Then he turned to look at Dick. "Can't you do something about it? You're a lawyer for Chr… goodness sake."

"No," Dick shook his head calmly, his half-drunk glass of whiskey on the table in front of him. "If I did try, it would only look bad for us. Mrs Leonov has accused us, as you know, of being responsible for her husband's fatal illness and subsequent demise. We have refuted this as a business, an organisation and a club, as, to the best of our knowledge, he was not ill when he left here last Tuesday, or not physically."

"What do you mean by that?" asked Jason.

At a nod from Dick, Simon said, "As some of you know, there's a question over his mental health. We've been through this before, but to refresh: on the day in question, his last visit to the club, he came to see me in a very agitated mood. He said people were against him and that Helen McTavish, who was in the room before him, looked at him in a hostile way. He was in a funny state."

"Would you corroborate that?" Roger turned to Dick.

The President nodded. "He did seem agitated when he and Simon joined a group of us, but bucked up quite quickly so at the time I didn't think anything of it."

"Are you saying he could have gone back down?" Jason looked at Roger as the doctor in the room.

"We have submitted our report to the Coroner stating our experience of his volatility." Said Roger.

"But what about the substance itself?" Asked Sam. "I mean the antimony he must have swallowed."

"That is indeed a problem," said Roger, the brows of his high forehead knitting whilst he shifted awkwardly in his chair. "I now discover Yuri did indeed store antimony here. An informal arrangement with the club, was made some years ago to help us with our finances, that Yuri Leonov could use one of the ground staff's sheds to store antimony from his mine. It is however in block form and could not be used in food or a beverage."

"Do the police know that?" asked Jason.

"Yes," replied Simon, "we have shown the police the shed with the lumps of antimony there on a shelf and they appeared satisfied that the stuff was not involved."

Sam wanted to ask how they had reacted to the fold-up bed and the guitar, but said instead, "What about the kitchens? Have they inspected them?" Now was not the moment to ask Simon about the supposed packet of sugar in his filing cabinet. Her body stiffened as she told herself she might be making a ridiculous assumption that a packet actually labelled sugar could actually be antimony.

"Calm down." Roger gave her a charming bedside manner smile. "This is something you need to know; the kitchens have been thoroughly inspected by a forensic team, as has this sitting room, I mean the dining area, where Yuri ate his food. Everywhere is clear of antimony. It is a natural substance, used to strengthen material in gadgets like mobile phones and of course range finders so inevitably there are odd traces around here, but as for anything out of the ordinary is concerned, the forensic people have found no evidence."

"Shouldn't we send out an email telling our members?" Asked Matthew Borden. "That would save a lot of trouble."

Dick Norton shook his head. "Absolutely not. It would invite questions. We will treat Yuri's death as we would any other member. We've had the flag at half-mast now for a week so that can be re-hoisted. There is no need for any other ceremony."

"More questions are bound to be asked," said Jason gloomily.

"Yes. That's why we are meeting here this evening," responded Roger. "To give you the information so you can answer them. Now, if there's nothing else can I call the meeting … Yes Sam," he noted her raised hand, "you want to ask?"

"About the social event next Saturday night; should we go ahead with it in the circumstances?"

"Good Heavens. Yes," Dick Norton spoke as he stood up. "Of course we must let events proceed. It's always sad when a member dies, but Yuri never held office here, although he was a great participator."

"Just a bit unfortunate," said Matthew Bordon, with a snigger, "that we are all, or a lot of us, talking about criminal forebears on our family trees."

"All the more reason to go ahead," said Dick. "Anyway, some of us, like me are proud of our ancestors, or relatives of them. It'll be fine. Sad though it is in many ways as Yuri was a fun guy, who I gather was actually going to take part, but we must go ahead, be the club we always are. Agreed?" He turned around the group, raising his hand to indicate he wanted a show of hands.

Everyone responded, even Amy, although some were clearly less enthusiastic than others.

"Thanks," said Sam, rising along with the rest of the group. "I needed your approval, that's all."

"Go for it Sam." Jason clapped her on the shoulder. "Crystal and I will be there to cheer you on."

The more she thought about it afterwards, the more inappropriate the occasion seemed to Sam as she prepared her notes for the game she was going to have to compere. She needed another player to take Yuri's place. Sparked off by Simon's remark about Helen McTavish's possible antipathy to Yuri, she decided to approach her. It would be good to get a younger member to take part, especially if, in the asking, they could have a discussion about Yuri.

Accompanied by Monty, Sam made her way into her study to ring Helen.

As Sam feared, Helen did not want to be involved in the game. "Not my sort of thing," was her response. She was particularly annoyed by Sam's tactless suggestion she might claim ancestry from Simon McTavish, founder of the North West Company, the eminent Scottish born trader, whose name had appeared when Sam googled the name McTavish, before she rang Helen.

"Him, the furrier," responded Helen in disgust. "Me, descended from someone in the fur trade. No way. What an outrageous idea."

"It could be false," faltered Sam. "It's a true or false game. You say you're upset to find this man way back on your family tree. That would sound convincing."

"Dealing in animal skins isn't a game. It's cruel, absolutely dreadful." Retorted Helen who continued with a diatribe against the fur trade, finishing with, "You don't wear furs do you?"

"No, no," replied Sam truthfully. "They've never appealed to me. I don't know anyone who does actually." Then she suddenly remembered. Yes, she did. She had seen Ekaterina once in the Ladies Cloakroom at Elmsleigh Park removing a fur. *Go for it.* She told herself. "Actually, I believe I saw Ekaterina Leonov come to the club in one once. Is that why you objected to Yuri?"

"Oh I didn't see that. Anyway, I didn't object, as you say to Yuri. Never say ill of the dead. What I didn't like was his saying he was going to buy the club because he would have destroyed it, dug it up looking for shale gas or something else buried underground. He was chummy with that rich crowd who talk about saving the club when they're bound to mean profiteering for themselves."

"I heard you were one of the people who saw him with some of that crowd on his last visit to the club," said Sam in the least accusing tone she could manage.

"Oh yeah I was in with a group of people, not my usual crowd, who he joined – or rather Simon brought him over to sit with us. He, Yuri that is, has had some dealings with Greg who was there, not that they were that friendly. He was pretty rude to Greg, or tried to be, thought he was being funny, calling him a woolly mammoth."

Sam restrained a laugh, but not sufficiently for Helen to respond, "You may think it's funny but the joke is, Greg took it as a compliment. He says the world has got enormous benefits from those ancient beasts, the way they chewed up ancient fruits and vegetables then spat out the seeds has created melons, courgettes, pumpkins and other vegetables we eat now."

"How knowledgeable."

Sam's surprise must have registered in her voice for it prompted Helen to inform her in an irritated tone how under-rated Greg was at the club. His refusal to ponce around like a posh boy didn't mean he hadn't got a good brain. He went to Cambridge where he got a first.

"Interesting," said Sam. "Did he read Russian? Was that his connection with Yuri? I heard they had a rapport, presumably something to do with metals."

There was a pause before Helen said curtly, "Not to my knowledge. That's not my scene.". Then with a brief thanks to Sam for the call, she rang off.

If Greg had a grudge against the club because he was turned down for membership why did he hang about the place? If he were still such a great golfer, he would be welcomed at some other club which Helen would certainly also be welcome to join.

Sam smiled to as she considered Helen's notion Yuri might have had an ulterior motive for being part of a group who would buy Elmsleigh Park. She could not believe he'd been interested in digging the place up for minerals when he had his own mine in Eastern Russia.

What did make sense was Helen's repetition of Yuri's "Woolly mammoth" joke about Greg. That was the Yuri she remembered, always jovial when they played together in golf competitions. Joking on the day of his last visit to the club was surely not typical of a man about to commit suicide. That might be the inquest verdict Captain,

Dr Roger Turpin wanted to steer his committee towards supporting, but Sam could not accept it.

Everyone else at the meeting had nodded their heads eagerly, except Amy, her Vice-Captain. Maybe Sam should talk to her. They were not buddies, but Amy did have the virtue of speaking her mind, not agreeing for the sake of it. Anyway, Sam had a good reason to ring her. She needed someone else for the entertainment in. Possibly Amy would be happy to find a famous suffragette amongst her forebears. She could even invent one, tying her in with the criminal theme by saying the woman was treated shamefully by being sent to prison.

Sam knew she must be careful.

Like Helen, Amy had strong feelings over women's rights and the way females were treated over the years, especially at golf clubs. She must be approached in the right way, with the fun element down-played. Then Amy might feel she had a platform to express her views.

To Sam's surprise, Amy complied immediately over the telephone. She was more than willing to claim relationship, albeit distant, with the Pankhurst family. The only downside was her question as to how long she would be expected to speak. More than five minutes can seem a long time if you bore the audience and Amy wanted as long as she was allowed, which Sam feared would bore the aged male golfers, if not their wives.

At least Amy seemed aware of this. "I've tried to talk to Simon about the way women are treated at this club," she told Sam. "In fact, I had a go at him that last day Yuri visited the club. I tried to explain how the old men monopolised the course and they should share the grass here, not be left on it to munch away as they please, but Simon was in an odd mood and not at all receptive."

"Do you think Simon himself might not have been in the right frame of mind to judge whether Yuri was suicidal then?" Asked Sam in as neutral a tone as she could muster.

"Certainly, he was negative, sort of aloof. I could have got irritated at his attitude, except I'm used to it and I'm in for the long haul, got to cope with him next year."

"That's right," agreed Sam, "but I'm sure you'll find him helpful, as I have."

"Don't know about that. You're more compliant than me." Amy made it sound more like an insult than a compliment.

Sam gulped back an indignant retort that she was not a push-over to bid Amy good-bye pleasantly. She had got what she needed from their chat, although hearing Amy question Simon's judgement made her uneasy, a feeling she did not have time to dispel before the phone rang.

Sam was tempted not to take the call. She had had enough conversations for today and who could possibly want to speak to her at nearly eleven thirty at night?

She sighed: only someone in her family like her brother or sister with some problem over their aged mother. As she put out her hand to pick up the receiver, interrupting the start of her answerphone message, she heard with surprise who the caller was.

The panic-stricken Russian accent of Ekaterina spoke in a shaky tone, her words breaking up. "I am sorry it is late, but I could not get through because you are always engaged."

Though Sam tried to apologise back for not being available, Ekaterina was too emotional to appreciate her explanation how she had been preoccupied with finding someone to take Yuri's place at the party.

"We were so looking forward to seeing you both," Sam said in what she hoped was a sympathetic not gushing tone. "Such a lovely idea for Yuri to talk about his famous relation who walked in space."

"Yes we do that," cried Ekaterina. "We do that."

"But how?" Queried Sam, wondering what on earth the sad widowed lady could be thinking.

"My son Vladimir. I told you he is here to mourn his father. He will play; he will say a spy here is not his father."

"Yes," Sam demurred awkwardly, "but what the game's about is your family having spaceman Alexie Leonov on your family tree."

"Yes, yes. Vladimir has good British education so he plays games right; he will speak for our family."

"I'm so sorry but we have got someone else for the game now. Please don't worry about letting us down."

"No worries, I can get pair for Vladimir. Nicholas Roman could be my guest. He is great person really from Romanov family, descended from Peter the Great."

Sam hoped she made it clear in a sympathetic way that it would not be appropriate for either Vladimir or Nicholas Roman to perform or come to the party. Nonetheless Ekaterina's words filled her with dread.

15. The Party

Crystal puzzled over what to wear to the golf club.
"Smart Casual" as guidance was no help, even particularly silly in a place where jeans were not allowed. She could not guess how women dressed for social events at Elmsleigh Park, to a party described as a supper with games? Thankfully there would be only one game, organised by Sam. Had her friend not been involved, no way would Crystal be going, whatever Jason wanted. She was not yet a paid up member of the club.

It was no use asking Jason for advice on clothes. Unless he had a particular dislike of an outfit, he would simply say he was not qualified to give an opinion, which was true since in the army he had spent so much time amongst people in uniform, or social places where everyone knew what was expected. Though he kept saying things were different in golf clubs these days, especially at Elmsleigh Park where they wanted to attract younger members, he still wanted Crystal to wear a collared shirt, preferably with a sleeve, when she played golf. He thought Smart Casual an easy instruction but then he didn't know the multitude of clothes Crystal kept in her wardrobe.

After much deliberation Crystal turned to his ten-year-old daughter Maisie for advice. Though Maisie hated the notion this new woman in her life might be more beautiful than her own mother, she was fascinated by Crystal's numerous clothes. Moreover, Maisie knew how her friends' mothers dressed. So, instructed by Maisie, Crystal put on a fitted deep pink lace dress which had hung in her wardrobe for at least ten years. It showed a bit of flesh and cleavage through its lacy bodice but having sleeves to below the elbow should mitigate that. This aged designer dress must be sufficiently vintage to help her mingle, not stand out or be a "spectacle" as Jason would say, among any oldies present.

Ghastly or perhaps dull as this evening might be, Crystal wanted to support Sam, whom she knew dreaded tonight. It was hardly surprising in the wake of a long-term member's death. She was particularly worried about the possible appearance of the man's son, Vladimir, who she had a hunch, might cause a scene.

Jason was less perturbed. As a fellow committee member and a friend of Sam's missing husband, he told Crystal he'd assured her friend that if anything awkward happened, she could rely on him to sort it out. He was chummy with Matthew Borden who looked forward to relating his possible kinship to the famous Lizzie Borden with the axe. Jason was also biased because, in his role as house manager, he had spent so much time with Misty planning the meal which he had discussed endlessly, booking a catering company to provide the food and waitresses.

The moment Crystal arrived at the clubhouse, she felt she had made the wrong choice of outfit. As she entered the Ladies cloakroom to take off her evening cape, she noted the other ladies, all of whom seemed to be at least ten years older than her, wore trousers or long skirts with tops that might glisten but had nothing like the allure of her fitted dress. Their looks at her, Crystal knew from years of showing off clothes, were not of admiration.

She mustn't be daunted. With a shrug she hung up her cape, swayed her bum as she turned for the cloakroom door. Once inside the sitting room there would be men to look at her. To her surprise, when she found Jason there with Sam, he who had told her how everything was going to go so well and easily, looked as perturbed as her friend.

"What's the matter?" She asked.

Jason did not answer but Sam rolled her eyes towards a table near the dining area of the room where a smartly dressed woman in black sat with a couple of young men at the same table as Ozzie Reynolds accompanied by Cynthia his friendly wife.

"Oh lord," whispered Crystal, "you mean he's here." Her mouth dropped open in horror as she spotted Cynthia, Ozzie's wife. "I'm so sorry," she gasped.

Yet Sam seemed oblivious to any sartorial error. She put her mouth up to Crystal's ear, "Not him, her."

"Yes, Cynthia, his wife," whispered Chrystal back. "I'm sorry; I never thought anyone would turn up wearing the same dress as me, let alone Ozzie Reynolds' wife."

"Don't care about her." Sam continued in a low tone. "There's Ekaterina. When she suggested she might turn up, I hoped I'd put her off. The worst of it is, she's determined her son Vladimir must perform." She gestured at the other side of the room. "Apparently the Captain, Roger Turpin, says it's okay; he'll have Vladimir in his team. That means they're the Captain's guests."

"Who's the man with them, who looks like something out of a comic?" Asked Crystal, remembering Ekaterina from her presence at fashion shows. "He's too wide awake to be the normal guy who accompanies her."

145

Sam groaned. "That's the worst of it. Her husband's dead and she wants this man, Nicholas Roman, to take part as a descendant of the Romanovs, the erstwhile Russian royal family."

"Hell no," groaned Crystal, remembering the conversation at the end of her last visit to the club with Sam. He's the man who's a relative and might be a friend of Prince Andrew's."

"Don't worry," said Jason not bothering to subdue his voice. "I'm here to help. We have to go with it. You can't stop him playing if the Captain says it's okay."

"Yes, but I'm meant to compere this game and it means the President's team have to have another one. Oh, there he is, I'll go and mention it to him." She hurried off to consult the suave looking elderly Dick Norton.

After a short exchange, she returned saying with a shrug, "He's such a smoothie; he says not to worry he'll sort something out. He's more worried about Vladimir Leonov."

Jason nodded. "There you are. Go with the flow. Most people here won't understand what he's talking about; they won't know about his father's death."

That made Sam smile. "In a golf club where it's been on the notice board?"

"Come on," urged Jason. "We'll go and join that little group so you can start a charm offensive."

Crystal pulled his arm to try to alert him that it would be tactless for her to go anywhere near Cynthia Reynolds, but to no avail. With no one else around she had to tail behind her husband, hoping his height and broad shoulders would prevent the Reynolds getting too close a view of her wearing the same outfit, but she failed.

She also wished she'd suggested to Jason that he should have advised the catering company he booked not to send waitresses wearing skin tight black leggings uncovered by a skirt. With men like Ozzie and that Romanov character, possible friend of Prince Andrew's, around there could easily be a touchy-feely incident. She was glad to see Sam still near enough to catch her arm and warn her.

"Thanks," said Sam. "I'll sort it."

Crystal stared after her as her friend hurried towards the kitchen door.

"No probs," she said on her return a few minutes later.

"How come?" Whispered Crystal, concerned Sam had not taken her seriously. She tended at times to suggest Crystal exaggerated when she said a man was after her.

"There's a guy called Kyle helping in the kitchen. They've put an apron round him and he's going to serve whatever tables Ozzie's and Nicholas Roman are on."

"How will he know which one that is?" Crystal asked anxiously.

"He will; Kyle's here a lot, helping out as a temp all over the place. He's the red-headed guy."

Crystal felt her tense body begin to relax, helped when they reached the table as Cynthia called: "Snap, I'm glad this old number passes the super-model test."

Not knowing how to react, Crystal blushed. The question whether Cynthia herself recognised her usual job tonight, when she hadn't the last time they met, or whether

147

her husband Ozzie told her, plus indeed, what he might have said, battered her mind. She was glad Sam took over the conversation, telling Vladimir Leonov he was welcome to mention his father and lament his death.

Once it was established Vladimir should not exceed five minutes, because Jason assured him in an authoritative tone, that would be counterproductive, Sam felt relieved, though slightly apprehensive at the young Russian man's response.

"They should be glad to hear more from us," said Vladimir, his perfect intonation in his upper-class voice. "We bring fresh life to this club, from another continent."

"Yes," Jason nodded, speaking with his strong tenor voice full of tenderness. "We all want to remember Yuri's special contribution to Elmsleigh Park. I know what it is like to be bereaved and how it helps to take the person you've loved forward with you."

Crystal eyed Sam, fearing a lament on widowhood might be forthcoming, but Jason moved smoothly forward into his house manager role, beckoning staff to move people into the dining area to sit down. She turned to Cynthia, glad for an excuse to be away from Ozzie, she said, "We'd better not sit together looking like twins."

"On the contrary, you'll complement each other." Ozzie lowered his voice whilst he leant towards them to include Sam as he continued, "We can help you."

Indeed he did. Seated next Ekaterina, he chatted away to her about Yuri, the fun they had playing golf together, even reminiscing about time they had spent on a boys' holiday playing at famous golf courses around the country.

It boded well for the True or False game which started with a flourish. Captain Dr Roger Turpin kicked off with the claim that, to his chagrin, the famous outlaw Dick Turpin was on his family tree. It was, he asserted, particularly embarrassing as Dick Turpin's father had been a butcher, a trade he inherited from his father. As an orthopaedic surgeon, he did not like to think about this connection, but he had been charmed into playing by the redoubtable Lady Captain.

The way he spoke delighted the audience, most of whom voted his claim as true. Also a success as a speaker was the President, Dick Norton who was believed as having the same pedigree as Mad Dick Norton, the man who had founded a Hampshire village. All went well with Ozzie too; he had been savvy enough to bring a photo of a portrait of Joshua Reynolds which did indeed look like him. Even Crystal laughed at the jokes he made.

The good humour of the audience was not dented by Amy with her earnest talk claiming Emily Davison who threw herself in front of the king's horse at the 1913 Derby was on her family tree. When someone said loudly it wouldn't happen on a golf course, Amy disagreed, but nonetheless gained many votes for her spiel being true as she replied that her relative's violent death had made her emotional about petty discriminations women suffered in the past, especially at some prestigious golf courses who used not even to admit women.

Though Sam's apprehension deepened when Vladimir took his stand on the makeshift stage, the staff had erected, she hoped the general mood would infect him. No such luck. The moment he started to speak, his tone of voice made it obvious he was on the attack.

"My great-grandfather Alexei Leonov," he said in a loud voice that, with the aid of the microphone he spoke into, sounded deafening, "would be shocked at the treatment of my father here."

Sam, who stood nearby, theoretically to give any assistance needed to the performers, took his arm. "You're meant to be proving Alexei is related to you."

"Yes, yes." Vladimir continued with a monologue about the importance of antimony for use in space ships being an inspiration to his father. This was why his dad invested in antimony, which had many uses these days in smart phones and other important modern equipment.

Fearing from the expression on his face what he might say next, Sam tried to interrupt the monologue but Vladimir would not be deterred. Antimony, he asserted, was medicinal. No way would it have killed his father. The post mortem must be wrong. "Murder," he began.

Sam was flummoxed. What could she do? To her astonishment, a most unlikely saviour stepped forward.

The large frame of Hector Bravo appeared out of the awed crowd watching.

"Niet, niet," he said loudly, putting a large hand over the microphone which Vladimir held, before adding something else in a whisper in some foreign language, presumably Russian. Loudly he continued: "I have an ancestor Charles Bravo who was poisoned by antimony. It is a very famous case. Because no one knows whether he was villain intending to use the substance to kill someone else, but accidently took it himself, this has been an embarrassment to my family."

As Hector continued to talk, holding his audience in suspense as they listened to the details, Ozzie moved surreptitiously on to the stage behind him. Whatever he whispered to Vladimir was inaudible even to those standing near, but it made no impression on the Russian who, though he stopped talking, clung on to the microphone. The moment Hector hesitated in his speech, Vladimir put the microphone to his mouth, obviously about to speak again, but he did not get the chance.

The microphone disappeared from view as someone behind Vladimir grabbed his arm. There was the beginning of the sound of a shriek, but the person behind Vladimir put a hand over the Russian man's mouth. Somehow he pulled him backwards, made him relinquish the microphone which was then passed to Hector.

Crystal gasped in horror. She recognised her partner's hand. Jason often talked about his skills in close combat but she had never seen him in action during their three-year relationship. She tried to protest he could not behave like this at a party, but he was too engrossed in over-powering Vladimir, to notice Crystal's subtle gestures.

Sam dared not look behind her to see what was happening. She hoped what Hector said, with the help of the microphone, would disguise the kerfuffle going on beside the stage. Unprepared to speak as he was, Hector was doing well to keep his audience's attention, competing as he was with Jason now evicting the Leonov family from the room.

Extraordinary as it seemed to both Sam and Crystal, most of the audience were not aware Jason had Vladimir's arm pushed up behind his back in a half-nelson hold, whilst Ekaterina was trying ineffectually to pull him off her son. The two men were about the same height with Jason close behind the Russian as he pushed him to the clubhouse door then out into the night.

Other than Nicholas Roman, whose long black moustache seemed to twist in fury as his mouth dropped open, the few people who did notice obviously thought it was part of the performance since they laughed.

Moments later Jason, followed by Ekaterina, walked back casually into the lounge as though he had simply made a visit to the cloakroom for a comfort break.

Never in her life, had Sam wanted so much for an evening to end, but there was another speaker. At the prospect of his talking about more brutal murders, an awful foreboding ran through her as she welcomed Matthew Borden on to the stage

To her enormous relief, within seconds, Matt enlisted the sympathy of the audience, by asking them what sort of parents treat their children so badly that they want to kill them. He told of his great sadness that the awful events had happened, but the acquittal of Lizzie Borden happened because she was obviously mistreated. Yes, it was an amusing rhyme saying she "gave her mother forty whacks, then when she saw what she had done, gave her father forty-one", but it was wrong. Lizzie was an abused child who eventually turned on her parents with one stroke of the nearest weapon. Matt sounded so knowledgeable that everyone believed him. He had almost a full house of people holding their hands up to agree he spoke the truth before he disappointed them with his admission that he fabricated his relationship.

Sam did feel able to say, as she concluded the event, that what Matt said could be true. "Food for thought", she said as a prelude to her announcement of the draw between the Captain and the President's teams. In her hostess role, waiting as everyone came up to thank her for a most entertaining evening, she felt at last that the evening had been a success. Even Hector, whom she thanked profusely for his intervention with Vladimir Leonov was charming. He complimented her on managing the event so that it was entertaining rather than gruesome in the current unfortunate circumstances.

Her relief turned to apprehension as she joined Crystal to collect their coats from the Ladies cloakroom. A terrible clanking and churning noise greeted their ears the moment they left the room to enter the hall. The door to the carpark was open. Outside, standing beside the reserved carparking spaces, Roger Turpin with Simon Duckworth amongst others were talking indignantly to each other.

Crystal shuddered. She recognised that excruciating noise; she knew what had happened, even if no one else did. Her only surprise was the bewildered expressions on the faces of people standing around outside the clubhouse. "Your car catalyst converter," she suggested, "has been removed."

Roger waved his large hands angrily in the air. "That's what it must be. Those damn thieves have pinched it from my car, right outside the clubhouse." He turned to

Ekaterina. So sorry I can't take you home. Can you ring Vlad to come back to fetch us?"

Ekaterina, who stood nearby, shook her head. "I am not so sure." In the sudden silence now of the cool night air she sounded much more Russian. "He is very angry. I shall get taxi."

"We will too." As Sally, Roger's wife, fished in her handbag for a phone, Sam stepped forward quickly. She must save her evening. "I can take you all back," she said hurriedly. "It may be a bit of a squash, but it'll be quicker and easier."

Whilst someone else volunteered to take the Captain and his wife home, Sam was left with Ekaterina standing by her. Her alarm at the thought of conversation in the car was momentarily assuaged at the sight of Nicholas Roman in his black velvet evening jacket coming to join then. He could give Ekaterina a lift home.

"Thank you very much for coming," she said in as calm a tone as she could muster, putting out her hand to shake. "We haven't been introduced but I know who you are and your support is much appreciated."

He grasped her hand to shake it with his own smooth one. "And I know who you are, someone too good for this place. You should be careful. Bad things happen here." Brushing aside Sam's apologies, he warned, "Too many bully boys and worse. Look out for yourself.

16. Apology Party

Simon agreed with Vice-Captain Hector Bravo. Something needed to be done about Vladimir Leonov in the wake of Jason's treatment of him at last weekend's party, successful though it was in terms of fund raising. To date they had avoided the hailstorm of bad publicity they feared, but the potential furore arising from Vladimir's social media was alarming.

Sanguine though President Dick Norton and Captain Roger Turpin were over Jason's manhandling of Vladimir, who, they maintained could bring his personal legal action against Jason without involving the club, Simon shuddered at the prospect. He had already stalled the local paper whose reporter had visited Vladimir on account of the exhibition of his bruised arm on his alarmingly international social media pages.

So What, was Dick's reaction. Since none of the booked societies had cancelled coming to Elmsleigh, it was better to ignore the incident. Though Vladimir had been a junior member as a schoolboy, since his return to Russia ten years ago as a young adult, he had dropped his membership. Only this year had he started again periodically visiting the club.

Hector's proposal of an early evening gathering for drinks with a few sympathetic souls to express their condolences to Vladimir over the loss of his father, whilst also showing appreciation for the Russian's contribution to the club, would, Simon reckoned be a good shot. Extraordinarily also, considering his former fierce denunciations of David Charlie as that scruffy old scrounger, Hector suggested the old man could be a useful addition to the party.

Simon was not sure how he divined David Charlie played the guitar. He wondered why it might be in any way appropriate for the old man to be included, but Hector was adamant that, as the supposed grandson of the club's founder, David Charlie would give the evening an authenticity as well as being an example of how someone's actions might be misinterpreted. The guitar, Hector had said with a smirk, was going to be particularly useful because David Charlie could perform, even sing whilst he strummed the tune of "The Volga Boatman".

The notes of the song Yuri himself had sung in his loud bass voice a couple of times at social events sounded in Simon's mind as he sipped his afternoon cup of tea. He would have liked to have got home in good time this Friday night to see his wife and young children, but thought he'd better stay. Someone needed to keep an eye on the proceedings, even if Hector was going to play host. The Vice-Captain was not accident prone or mistaken in his assessment of people but, despite his reference to the folk he'd invited as mostly sane and reasonable, he was grateful when Simon agreed to stay late.

As a fine evening was forecast, Misty arranged for Rollo the bulky dark-haired East European barman to push some of the wooden tables outside to one end of the terrace into a rough circle with assorted wooden chairs and benches arranged around them. Along with various glasses, bottles, jugs of liquid and for some odd reason, bowls, were three pots of flowers spaced out on different tables to give the scene a welcoming, though not, Hector had instructed, an over-festive atmosphere. Where the plants came from was a mystery, since Hector had said in no circumstances was Penny Norton, who normally organised anything floral in the club, to be approached. This event might take place at the club, but it was not a club function.

Evidently not. Simon's face fell at the arrival of the first guest, the non-member Greg Burgess. Presumably he must have been asked to come since he lowered himself nonchalantly onto the bench nearest the open French windows of the clubhouse lounge, not far away from the armchair where Simon sat. In other circumstances Simon might have gone straight outside to challenge him, but today Greg's appearance was not as provocative as usual. His long dark hair was neatly brushed and tied in a plait clipped to the back of his head. Though he did not wear a tie or a jacket, his open-neck maroon shirt did have a small traditional collar whilst his grey trousers were neither gardening apparel nor jeans.

He did not look as confident as usual. Perhaps it was his more formal attire or the imprecise nature of the occasion that made him sit and fidget his long legs, rotating his large feet, shod in trainers. He must have known that footwear was not welcome at Elmsleigh Park or many other golf clubs. No matter. As one of Vladimir's known associates, Greg had a useful role to play this evening since he was the Vice-Captain's godson.

Maybe it was not this event which perturbed him for Greg's head kept turning sideways towards the eighteenth fairway where a mixed foursome match was progressing. Although this was a quarter final match of a popular summer competition, it surprised Simon that Greg should be interested, unless he wanted to watch the players themselves. Yes, that was it: there was Sam.

As they neared the green she looked across at the now nearby terrace. With a slight nod Sam appeared to acknowledge Greg, which he confirmed with a small wave of his hand. Their exchange was surreptitious, possibly because of Hector's arrival outside on the terrace carrying a box of various bottles. Greeting him with another nod of his head, Greg rose to help Hector unload his cargo.

This must be the main drink which Hector was going to provide for this evening's gathering. He'd made a bit of a mystery out of it, but claimed it should definitely help relationships. It must be something other than vodka because Hector would know the club had plenty of that spirit in the cellars; they kept a stash in store because both Yuri and Ekaterina often asked for it and tried to persuade anyone, either a club member or visitor to drink it with them, so a couple of bottles were already in evidence on the table. How that would be charged for was not yet decided. Rather to Simon's surprise, Hector who was notoriously tight-fisted, had not suggested the club should subsidise this occasion.

Maybe that was because Matthew Borden with his wife Emma were invited. In his role as Events manager, Matthew, who had proved skilled at arranging freebie events, would have been strongly averse to the club providing free drinks, even to assuage a member who might have been wronged. Simon had been definitively told by Misty that Hector would provide drinks. She and

Rollo the barman would simply be on hand to pour them out and pass round some fruit canapés prepared elsewhere.

Time to find out exactly what was going on.

Simon made his way outside on to the terrace to find Ozzie and Cynthia Reynolds as particular friends of Yuri were already there. They both grinned at him as though he must be party to some joke they were about to play. He hoped they did not associate him with David Charlie's presence. He sat at the end of the longest table looking less dishevelled than usual, but rather embarrassed with his guitar in its case beside him.

Luckily Sam had now turned up with her dog Monty, though, as the organiser of what Hector termed that ghastly party, she was not invited. Still, she sat alongside David Charlie, making conversation to him in an undertone whilst he caressed the black Labrador who almost seemed to smile at the old man.

It was at least another half hour before Vladimir himself arrived with his tearful mother. Wearing a long black skirt topped with a peasant style beige coloured lacy smock she looked less flamboyant than usual. To the raised eyebrows of Sam and some other guests, they were accompanied by the unmistakeable upright figure of Nicholas Roman, appearing oddly to be in attendance as he carried a large bag. He was obviously invited because Hector waved his arms to welcome the three of them to join him, indicating to Greg he should move along to let the Russian trio sit alongside him.

With a gracious smile around at the seated guests, Hector stood up. "As most of you know," he began, "we're all gathered here to pay tribute to our late

159

wonderful member Yuri Leonov. Though some of you, especially the younger ones may not recall the name Leonov in any other context than our late member," he hesitated as he looked directly at Matthew and Emma Borden before switching his eyes towards the other side of the table where Dick Norton, Dr Roger Turpin, Sir Bill Chambers and a couple of other ex captains sat.

"This is sad. With regard to our party, I know Yuri valued his connection with the amazing Alexei Leonov of that family who was the first man to walk in space in 1975, before some of you here were born. He was only hours ahead of the American Apollo team, although that team had already orbited the moon. Being a great sportsman, a quality we here at Elmsleigh Park hugely respect. Alexei Leonov was part of the wonderful American and Russian "Handshake in space." This was agreed by President Nixon and Alexei Kosygin in May 1972, a wonderful mission which shows how much good can come with the co-operation of two great countries."

Amongst the smiles and nods which Hector turned around graciously to accept, Nicholas rose to his feet. Standing upright he was marginally taller than Hector and in his black velvet jacket which matched his moustache if not his greying hair, he now looked more regal than the Vice-Captain as he spoke. "You're forgetting what happened in the nineteen eighties."

An eerie silence ensued whilst people stopped eating the canapés and drinking at the authoritative tone of Nicholas's voice which sounded more redolent of an old Etonian than a Russian.

"Alexei Leonov was hauled before the Communist Party's Central Committee. They didn't like his association with the novelist Arthur Clarke or Andrei Sakharov the Nobel prize-winning physicist."

Hector's shoulders shook a little as he appeared to try to smile. "Just a little hiccup. These things happen."

"Hardly a hiccup when Sakharov wins the Nobel Prize and is punished so he can't accept it."

Hector pushed back his chair to step across and behind Nicholas to tap him on the shoulder, a gesture which he accepted with a dignified inclination of his head as he sat down saying, "Yuri was under no illusions about the way his cousin and indeed his cousin's father were treated at times in their homeland."

As he finished speaking, before Hector could reply, the crackling sound of someone singing in Russian with a background of a piano came from a mobile in Nicholas's hand. Captivated by the nostalgia in the woman's voice everyone strained to listen.

"Yuri sent this to me after we last met," said Nicholas. The words are, "Give me your hand for luck, my dear friend."

Ekaterina's eyes filled with tears as she choked back sobs to say, "That was our song, Yuri's and mine."

"We valued Yuri's friendship here," insisted Hector. "He was a good honest club member."

"Here, here," concurred Ozzie, his words echoed by Sir Bill Chambers whilst others nodded.

"He valued his kinship with Alexei Leonov and remember that famous handshake in space went. He replied to the American man Stafford's greeting of

161

'Tovarich' saying 'Very very glad to see you. How are things?' And believe it or not, the pair had a bear hug before they went on to toast each other."

Clearly prepared for a sceptical audience, Hector delved down into the box he had brought. Out of it he produced a yellowy newspaper Obituaries page which he handed to Ekaterina who sat beside him.

"I have read this wonderful piece," she said as she passed the paper to Matthew Borden. "You must see this." She pointed to the attractive smiling face of Alexei Leonov inside a space helmet, at the top of the page.

Emma stared at the page in front of her husband, taking in the laughter line at the edge of the warm brown eyes and the upturned mouth in a cheerful open smile as she commented, "He was very attractive."

"Just like my Yuri," said Ekaterina staunchly.

"He was our good friend," said Hector. "Let's drink to that, have a toast." He started pouring vodka into some glasses. Then opening a large bottle labelled "Blackcurrant", he added fruit juice to some of the glasses.

"Can we now go for the real thing?" Asked Ekaterina. She put out his hand for Vladimir to pass her his bag.

Pulling out a thermos, Vladimir held it up for all to see as he said, "This is it."

"What is that?" asked ex-Captain Bill Chambers, suppressing a laugh.

"The borscht," announced Vladimir. "And Nicholas has provided some extra blackcurrants from his garden to flavour it." He pointed to a bowl on the table.

162

"We've provided some too, with black currants from our garden." Cynthia Reynolds waved a flask in the air before placing it on the table alongside the bowl

"Soup?" Queried Bill.

"Yes, that's it." Tabby read a short passage from the obituary where it related how Alexei Leonov offered a toast, handing out tubes labelled "vodka" which turned out to be borscht."

Greg muttered something about duplicity, whereupon Hector rounded on him sternly, pointing out the Apollo-Soyuz project was a great success. "If only," he said, "there could be more such projects."

Godfather and godson eyed each other coolly but their lack of rapport did not dispel the good humour of the occasion. Whilst all the guests had sipped the vodka and blackcurrant, raising their eyebrows as though in surprise at how enjoyable such a cocktail could be, most of them looked in askance at the offer to try the borscht.

"I'd like some." Sam raised her hand. "I didn't have any lunch." With a smile she accepted a helping which Vladimir poured into one of the bowls Misty had thoughtfully provided and handed it to her.

Whist she was watched with some scepticism, especially by Greg, she tentatively tasted the mixture before giving it her accolade. "Actually, it's really nice." She turned to Greg, "Why don't you try some?"

"On your recommendation," he said, the corner of his mouth turning down at the side, "I certainly will." And he accepted a much larger bowl full from Vladimir before agreeing that it was tasty, particularly as he too had not eaten yet that day. He shook his head when offered more, but when the couple of other takers refused extra helpings, he happily accepted a second flask to take home for later.

Such was the convivial atmosphere in the group that Emma turned to her husband Matthew to suggest maybe he should organise an international drinks evening with different speciality drinks from various countries.

"Music is better," said Vladimir. "My father was a man of many talents. As you've already heard he had a song for every occasion. Music runs in our blood as well as vodka." He gave a deep throaty laugh making those who remembered Yuri's bass voice smile with nostalgia.

"Yes." Hector beckoned to David Charlie. "I understand you can accompany Vladimir to sing us, a communal song."

Whilst David Charlie stood up awkwardly, Vladimir made his way over to him. "I will sing my father's song," he said. "My father understood all men are in the same boat as the English say and that was celebrated by the men of space because we are all mankind. So now I'll sing The Volga Boatman to you."

"In Russian or English?" Asked Greg.

"I do both," replied Vladimir coolly, "first in Russian and then in English for you to understand."

He proceeded to sing with the slightly less than perfect accompaniment of David Charlie on the guitar, but the performance worked, mainly because Vladimir had inherited his late father's deep powerful voice that resonated with the frequent "Heave hoes". By the end many of the guests joined in the chorus which, when it was finished, even provoked requests for an encore.

No. Vladimir refused. He had done enough. His tearful mother needed to go home, but they would come back. Elmsleigh Park had proved they were not hostile to his family or indeed his nation and he thanked Hector profusely for his hospitality.

As the other guests departed, the only one who looked less than happy was Greg. Possibly Simon thought because he should not have been there as he was neither attached to the Leonovs nor a club member, like all the other participants. Indeed, both the President and the current Captain were averse to his joining. Why Hector included him was puzzling, especially as Greg himself did not seem to be too happy to participate this evening.

"Are you okay?" Simon asked him as people were saying good-byes to one another as they began to leave.

"Yeah well," Greg replied.

"Not too good?" Suggested Simon.

"Yes, I do feel a bit ropey," agreed Greg, "but don't let it worry you."

"Okay. Do you want me to call a taxi or organise a lift home for you?"

Greg shook his head. "I'm okay. I've got my bike."

"Are you sure?" Asked Sam who was still hanging around. "I've got my car here; I haven't got anything organised for now so I could easily give you a lift home."

"Really? That would be great actually." Greg's wide mouth twisted into a watery smile.

At that moment Hector bustled up, almost shovelling Sam away with enough force to make Monty give a little growl. "Thanks, Sam, for your concern," he said officiously, "Don't worry; I'll look after him." He took Greg's arm. "Come on young man." He pulled Greg to his feet, but even in his weakened state, Greg summoned up the strength to push him off aggressively.

"No need, thanks. I'm fine," Greg insisted, despite his shaky voice. Throwing his shoulders back he staggered away from the lights on the terrace, but was just visible collecting his bicycle from some railings before he disappeared into the dusk.

"That seemed very successful." Sam congratulated Simon as she left.

"Hm. Not so sure about Greg," said Simon in a low voice as Hector was only a few paces away back towards the clubhouse.

"I think he was probably all right if he could cycle," said Sam adding casually, "It was a nice idea to involve your father." With any luck, she hoped, taking Simon off his guard, he might now admit the connection.

"Don't know what you mean by that, but thanks for coming yourself," he said as he stepped away, departing before she could elaborate.

Since David Charlie had already disappeared, Simon would not, Sam supposed be giving him a lift anywhere. *Time to put them both out of my mind*, she decided until she got ready for bed later that night when she was disturbed by a phone call. "Something is wrong in our shed," Ekaterina cried hysterically. "Vladimir is worried. He cannot get into the shed but he has looked through the window and he says there is a body, someone dead on a bed in there. Can you do something?"

David Charlie must be dossing down there, thought Sam. *I can't deal with that now.*

17. Finding a body

Ekaterina wanted Sam to go straight out to the golf course to inspect the shed, telling her that she could take a torch when Sam protested it would be dark.

Sam refused; she could not face it. If somebody were sleeping there, or even lying injured, it was not, Sam explained, her job as Lady Captain to deal with it. That responsibility belonged to someone else, possibly the course manager who had jurisdiction over the Elmsleigh Park grounds or the general manager if he were available.

By midnight Sam managed to persuade Ekaterina it would not be in her boys' interest if she went out in the middle of the night, at their instigation, to find someone, presumably David Charlie Elmhurst, Barvaz or Duckworth, whatever his name might be now, dossing down in that hut. Better to let others discover him there.

To assuage Ekaterina, Sam did agree to take her dog Monty out for an early morning walk on the golf course. Should they find anything untoward, she would alert the green-staff responsible for the grounds, there because they started work early in the morning.

Inevitably with the prospect of rising at dawn, Sam spent the night drifting in and out of sleep deciding one moment to abandon the visit to the sheds whilst another time scolding herself for not being more sympathetic to Ekaterina. By five o'clock in the morning she could bear worrying no longer, with the result that, bleary eyed she rose at a quarter to six, dressed and made herself a cup of tea in a portable mug to take with her to drink as she drove herself with Monty to Elmsleigh Park.

To her alarm when she reached the carpark area near the tenth hole, she saw a red Mazda car already parked there, one she recognised although she could not place the owner. It must have been frequently parked in the golf club car park so presumably belonged to a member. Was it Yuri's car, now being used by his son? She wondered as she strode with Monty at her heels, round the shrubs towards the sheds.

Would the body be David Charlie's? She imagined it must be. Who else would want or need to sleep there? Yet he did not possess a car. The sudden fear he might be dead made her shiver. Ekaterina had called the person a body, but that did not mean her sons had proof the person was dead. Since Ekaterina did not seem absolutely certain whether the person was a man or a woman, maybe her sons simply panicked when they saw someone lying asleep in the shed.

Obviously a man. Sam realised as the shed came into view. For lying against its wooden wall was a large old-fashioned man's black bicycle with a crowbar from saddle to steering wheel, which looked remarkably similar to the one Greg had shuffled away on the previous night. *Not necessarily*, she surmised as Monty dashed up to it sniffing. She scolded herself for being sexist; a woman could easily ride that old-fashioned bike. Hector said he was going to see Greg was all right. He would not have wanted his godson sleeping in a shed if he were unwell.

Monty's excitement at the bicycle made her snap the lead onto his collar. If it was evidence of anything, she did not want Monty's paw prints all over it. Nor did she want to touch it herself, although it would have been

168

useful to climb on it to look through the shed's high window. Better not, she decided. Nor should she take her dog into the shed in case he sniffed into something he should not. Thankfully he was a good-natured dog, although he did whine as she tied him to a nearby sapling beech tree.

Now for it. She pulled Laurie's bunch of master keys out of her pocket, taking hold of the one she thought she remembered as fitting the lock, but when she rounded the corner of the shed, her mouth dropped open in alarm. The door was obviously not locked. Instead of fitting tightly, it was not flat against the shed's wall; it was marginally open. How could this be possible if Vladimir could not enter the previous night?

Alarm rose inside her. Surely if David Charlie were asleep in here, he would have shut the door properly, even locked it from inside? As she pulled the door open, horror overtook her as she looked around. Not only was there a stench of vomit but she could indeed see a shape which looked like a long body lying beneath a rug on a bed in the middle of the room.

The face of the person lying there was obscured by a mass of long dark hair. No wonder Vladimir did not know for certain the person was male. Her heart pumped as she realised the shape of the long body beneath the blankets looked remarkably like Greg's but surely it couldn't be. Even if he were ill last night, he was able to get on a bicycle. Yet the silent stillness of the shape confirmed what she had then thought an exaggerated fear of Ekaterina's but now she shared.

What was she to do now? Sam pulled her mobile out of her pocket to ring Ekaterina. Her finger was poised to press the key before she pulled it back upwards. No. She would have told Sam if her boys had been back here to unlock the door. Whatever happened last night did not mean her family was now friendly towards the club.

The memory of David Charlie's remark about Yuri being spy came back to her. Whatever was going on here, or had happened needed to be shared with other club members. Involving Ekaterina further could not, Sam's instinct told her, lead to any good, or be helpful to herself. Now was the time for proper authorities to be informed.

Simon was the first person she would call. She must do it fast. On a Saturday, his day off, he would probably be playing golf anywhere other than Elmsleigh Park, but she might be able to reach him. No, she did not have his home number or a mobile for him. She gritted her teeth. She would have to try Roger Turpin; he was a doctor so he should know the best procedure.

Sally Turpin, Roger's wife, answered the phone. In a weary tone she told Sam that Roger was on his way to the magnificent course at Royal St Georges in Kent for a special game. She doubted he would want to turn back for anything except a truly dire emergency, which would be awkward anyway as he was being given a lift by a golfing chum who did not belong to Elmsleigh Park.

After a quick apology for bothering her, Sam dialled 999 for an ambulance. Though she could not bear to look closely she guessed the person might be dead. A glance at her watch told her she had been in this shed seven minutes, during which time she had not seen a stir in the rug covering the body. If there were any breath left there, she should have seen a twitch.

"Yes, I am sure the person is unconscious, if not dead," she told the operator as she gave her reason for wanting the ambulance. "No, I don't know who it is." She stared at the head as she spoke, relief suffusing her that she did not recognise David Charlie lying there. Yet there was something frighteningly familiar to Greg about the shape, its length as well as the long body, too long for all but the tallest of woman, she thought.

Hairy mammoth. No, Woolly mammoth. The nickname struck her. That was what she'd heard Greg was called, although the last few times she'd seen him, his hair was in a bun. Grief as well as remorse that she had not insisted on helping him yesterday hit her. She crept up to the bed head. Though there was a sickly pallor on the long usually bronzed face, despite its strange rigidity, the head strongly resembled Greg's.

Should she ring Helen? No, because it would be awful if she were wrong. Tragically there must be many homeless men who looked similar because they had untidy long hair. She tapped her head. Wrong. With the wondrous play of professional Tommy Fleetwood, there would be plenty of other good-looking male golfers who, like some of the top professional golfers, also had long dark hair on their faces as well as the back of their heads.

Suddenly she thought she saw the body twitch. Maybe the man was alive. Good thing she called the ambulance, not the police. She turned away; she could not bear to stare at the inert body any longer, but when she looked around her, she noticed something odd about the

171

shelves. There were still tools around, but those grey stones which she had decided must be antimony now looked different. Three of them were on the table whilst another couple were on the shelves. To check if her memory was right, she got out her mobile to look at the photo she took when she first visited the shed.

Her recollection was correct. There had been seven pieces of antimony placed at random on the shelves. Now there were five in different places. What did it mean? Something or nothing.

David Charlie's guitar was not obvious either. Maybe that was hidden behind the bed or camouflaged by a couple of boxes on the floor? She was debating whether to search the place when Monty's frenzied barking alerted her to the ambulance men arriving with a stretcher.

Once inside the shed, one of the paramedics had only to pull back the rug covering the body for Sam to see from the rigidity of the body, the man there, was indeed dead. She had never seen a corpse, prior to being treated and dressed by an undertaker, so the tautness of the expression on the man's face indicating pain, chilled her, especially the unfocussed open eyes. To her horror, she now recognised the man was Greg.

With a shaky hand she started to dial on the phone she still held in her hand, as she guessed right what the ambulance men would say next: the police must be called.

To her relief the police were sympathetic to her plight when she told them she had come out early here to walk her dog because the previous night she had taken a phone call suggesting someone was sleeping in the shed. She had momentarily debated telling them it had been

172

anonymous, but knowing how easy it would be for them to trace the call from Ekaterina to her, decided that would be pointless. More sensible now to admit the truth. At least she did not have to break into the shed, which was, after all, part of Elmsleigh Park property, even if rented to the Leonov family who had asked her to investigate it.

Inevitably she had to go to the police station to make a statement. She explained she was merely an acquaintance of the man she had found. As far as she knew, she told man and woman interviewing her, whom she guessed were about her age in their late thirties, he was not a member of the golf club.

Even so, the female police officer asked suspiciously, how did she not recognise immediately, someone with this man's distinctive features?

"Yes." Sam agreed with them. "I thought I did recognise him; I have seen him around on the club's premises."

"His name's Guy Burgess," supplied Police Officer Collins, the man, adding as he noted the surprise on Sam's face, "we found a bank card and a bus pass in one of his pockets."

"Really?" Queried Sam. "I thought his name was Greg. Are you sure?"

"He's Guy Burgess all right," said the female police officer. "His photo's on the bus pass."

Sam winced, feeling rather stupid. "Well you've obviously found out more than I can tell you."

Doubtless Laurie would disagree, but there were times like now when it was a relief to be ignorant. She was glad she had had the foresight not to touch the body or indeed, look in his pockets.

Guy Burgess though. Somewhere she'd heard that name before? Yes. Guy Burgess was the name of a notorious spy who defected to Russia – except he hadn't ended up there. She was sure she had heard someone say something about his coming back to Hampshire to be buried; she seemed to remember it arose from a mention of the Burgesses as a well-known respected local family.

She gulped. She must not let her mind go there. *Stick to what's relevant.* There was little more she needed to say now, other than mention the Leonov family because they rented the shed. She readily volunteered she had known Yuri. That would have been hard to deny since their names were printed linked together on an honours board in the clubhouse where they were listed as the winning pair of an annual competition. She guessed she looked adequately appalled at the snide suggested insinuation she might have had an affair with him, for that nonsense to be shelved. Otherwise she agreed she had met his wife Ekaterina on various occasions, but denied any knowledge of the Leonov boys, other than their existence. With that she was allowed to depart for home.

It was a relief to be within her own four walls, to open her mail, none of which concerned Elmsleigh Park, then boil an egg for lunch since she had left home without having breakfast. With the rest of the day to spend on her own, she thought she might go to one of her favourite relaxing places, Westbury Manor Museum for something completely different. As she sipped her coffee with one hand, she manipulated her i-pad with the other to find out

174

what the current exhibition was. Staring up at her was "Surviving the Stone Age" in which bones of the woolly mammoths, that apparently existed in Hampshire were on show. What an unhappy coincidence.

She thumped the kitchen table with her fist. Yes, she would go. It was something utterly different from golf club politics. The ancient woolly mammoths were nothing to do with today's events, or so she thought; she should enable her to enjoy, as usual, the culture on offer.

Her worries about Greg did not disturb her again until Dr Roger Turpin rang that night at quarter past eight to ask why she had rung him so urgently that morning.

He was very sympathetic over her ordeal and so sorry he had not been able to help her, despite his most enjoyable day playing golf in great weather which would have been wrecked had he known about her ghastly experience. Anyway, now he was home, he could take responsibility for any further investigation into the matter, such as liaison with the Coroner.

Thankful when she put the phone down, Sam decided it was time for a relaxing bath, but she was barely in it before her phone rang insistently again. *Let whoever it is leave a message if it's urgent.* She forced herself to ignore the rings, but once out of the bath, wrapped in a towel, she moved quickly into her living room to play back the message from Roger.

"Sorry to disturb you again, but thought I'd better confirm that the man you found, Guy Burgess, is known to the club, but by the name Greg, the guy," he then corrected himself, "the man who was at our little gathering last night. I've been in touch with Hector, who says you gate crashed the party. You weren't invited because he knows Helen McTavish is Greg's girlfriend, and his family thinks she was a good influence on him, getting him involved in gardening. He knows that because he's Greg's godfather, and he is needless to say, extremely upset but also very angry. That's why I thought I ought to warn you ASAP. He will almost certainly contact you PDQ as he understands you arranged to meet Greg."

Roger's tone of voice made the implication clear; she was chasing another woman's boyfriend.

Hells Bells. If only she had not got involved in this wretched catalyst converter robbery business.

18. Gossip in the clubhouse

The club was awash with gossip. The success of the party evening, as far as Simon was concerned, meant that a week later club members were busy discussing whether the Captain's relationship with the famous highway robber, Dick Turpin, had any bearing on the robbery of his catalyst converter from his car, rather than yesterday's discovery of a body in the green-keepers shed. Whenever he went to the cloakroom or into the bar for a drink, someone would waylay him to mention it. He tried not to start in alarm whenever anyone waylaid him.

"A coincidence", he told them with a vein of humour in his voice, without adding there had been other similar robberies. The question that vexed him was how the robber knew cars would be parked at the club that Saturday night. It suggested an insider, a member or someone on the staff, knew cars would be parked there. With such a racket going on inside the clubhouse, a car could be robbed without people in the building noticing.

More difficult to handle were the members who continued to complain about Jason Goodridge. "He's not in the Parachute Regiment now." Mark Dinwiddie, a former Captain complained. "Members of Elmsleigh Park do not frogmarch guests out of social occasions. "Can't think why Dick didn't put a stop to it."

Simon shuddered at his mental picture of Dick Norton, the President, making his way through the seated audience to argue with Jason's impetuous shovelling of Vladimir plus Ekaterina out of the clubhouse. Her return to the clubhouse had diffused that incident, especially as some of the audience had assumed Jason's manoeuvring of Vladimir was part of the act, something Hector had tacitly suggested when he took over the performance.

Simon certainly did not want repeat discussions about the accusations of Yuri Leonov's poisoning with any of the regular members. He tried to discourage ponderings about whether Yuri might have been a spy, or worse, about to finger a member as a Russian spy. The presence of Nicholas Roman, reputedly a Romanov, did not help, particularly with Mark, another local solicitor and respected pillar of society, tipped as a potential future President. "The Vice-Captain has soothed things over. He with other friends of the Leonov family have had a most convivial meeting." Simon reassured him.

"Huh. Lucky he didn't break Vlad's arm," continued Mark. "I understand Ekaterina took him to hospital to have it treated, but fortunately it is only badly bruised."

Simon said he was sorry to hear that as he slipped away behind Sam, who might have been coming to talk to him, but Simon pretended he thought she was heading for Mark. He was cornered by her later in his office doorway as he was about to leave for home.

"We need to speak," she said, "about Greg or Guy or whatever his name is, who died on our property yesterday."

Simon sighed. He knew this approach was likely. "Yes," he nodded, the mouth on his round face spreading into a half smile which he hoped looked sympathetic. "A terrible experience for you. It's most unlucky Ekaterina chose to involve you."

Worse than that. Sam's eyes rounded as she put out her hand instinctively to catch Simon's arm as he tried to dodge past her, but thinking better of the gesture, let her hand drop before she touched him. "What are you going to do about it?"

"It's not really our problem," replied Simon, with a slight shake of his head to emphasise his point.

"You must be joking. A young man's death on our property is not our problem?"

Simon sighed. "I don't mean to be unsympathetic but he was trespassing and I understand his death was not violent. We've yet to have it confirmed by a post mortem, but Roger, our Captain, who as you know still practices as a doctor, suggests the likely outcome will be that he took a drug overdose."

Sam frowned. To her chagrin now she realised she had looked away after the ambulance men uncovered Greg's body, but as far as she could see when she turned around, he was fully dressed. From what she saw of his face not hidden by his hair, there did not appear to be any blood or bruises, but she had not looked closely. To enable the men to have enough room to bring their stretcher into the shed to carry him out, she had moved out of the shed.

"How strange," said Sam. "I didn't know him well, but I'd be surprised if Helen McTavish would have anything to do with someone druggy. Wouldn't have thought that was her scene."

Simon shrugged as he walked towards the clubhouse door with Sam keeping pace alongside him. "You could be right. Someday the truth will out."

179

I'll damn well see it does, resolved Sam as Simon's tubby frame somehow slipped through the door leaving her to have to pull it open and run after him if she wanted to question him further. He had, she noted whilst she stared after him through the glass door, forgotten to lock his office as he left. *Great.* This unexpected consequence of their meeting meant it would be much easier for her to return to his office later to search the place. For some reason she could not fathom, her instinct told her the last two pieces of antimony, no longer in the shed, might be in there."

Now was not the time with so many golfers coming into the clubhouse having finished their game for the day. Many were heading for a drink in the lounge where others were still eating scones or pieces of cake with their cups of tea. They might know Simon had left the building since his car would not be in the space immediately outside the club house which was reserved for the club's Manager.

Undecided what to do next, Sam was still loitering in the front hall ten minutes later when Simon returned. He did not seem unduly perturbed to see her still there, presumably not realising she had skulked there waiting for a quiet moment to enter his study unobserved, so he smiled at her, making an ironic joke about being glad she was there to guard his office which he forgot to lock.

Hard to know how to reply to that, so Sam merely smiled back, making some remark which implied she had a good reason to be there because she was waiting for someone. Then, as he turned his back on her to click his key in the lock of his office door, she thought perhaps she might get more out of him if she startled him with a question about the missing pieces of antimony. When he turned around, she stood in his way to the door.

"Something I've been meaning to ask you, on Ekaterina's behalf. - As you know she propelled my going into the shed where I found Greg. Apparently a couple of those funny looking rock things they keep there, antimony, I believe it is, have disappeared. I don't suppose you know where they might be?"

His mouth turned down at the corners in a doubtful expression, that suggested he was not fooled at all by the innocence she had injected into her voice.

Later Sam wondered how she had the nerve to speak as she did, but the only other folk in the foyer were a couple of elderly men quite a few yards away from her who were engrossed in discussing something on the noticeboard. She hoped they wouldn't hear what she said as she leant forward to Simon to speak in a loud whisper.

"Did those lumps of antimony disguise something else? Your Papa said Yuri was a Russian spy. So was that bit of rock actually a router or something like that?" She spoke in a jokey voice.

"My father?" Simon's forehead wrinkled in a frown. Through clenched lips he added. "I don't know who you mean."

No point in arguing with him. She might, Sam knew, have made a colossal error in jumping to the wrong conclusion, so continued in a jovial tone, "David Charlie the old guy from the carpark who came along to play the other night. I've become quite chummy with him actually."

181

Simon could not stop himself wincing. "Oh, you have, have you?"

"Yes and he said Yuri was a spy; that's why I wondered whether in this day and age he would have had some Wi-Fi equipment in his shed, disguised of course."

"Very imaginative." Simon took a couple of long strides around her, whilst he spoke, but he looked startled. "Now if you don't mind, I really must be going, get home to my wife and children."

The moment he was out through the door, the two elderly men rushed over to Sam. Not only did they move remarkably quickly, to her alarm, they had obviously listened to her entire conversation with Simon. Close to she saw one of the old chaps, a club regular whom she knew by sight, had an unobtrusive hearing aid tucked into his ear, whilst the other, seeing his face, she recognised as the ubiquitous former president, Sir Bill Chambers.

"Is that old beggar really Simon's father?" They both asked almost in unison.

"Explains a lot," said Bill.

"Not sure," replied Sam. "I can't prove it and it might be a wild guess, but one or two things made me think it's a possibility."

"Hmm, very interesting," said Bill, the larger of the two men.

Despite his weather-beaten wrinkled face suggesting he was long past retiring age, his interest in golf club matters had not dimmed. He was someone who regularly stood up at the club annual general meetings to criticise the report and accounts. After a nod to his companion, who also wore a shirt and blazer with an emblem teamed with cavalry twill trousers, for support, Bill said, "All the same, Lady Captain, you should be careful about throwing those sorts of accusations around. Don't you think Arnold?"

Sam gave an involuntary shudder. She remembered one of the ladies once warning her that Arnold, prior to being a high court judge, had been a high-flying barrister, quick on the sue for libel, something she, as a journalist, needed to note. "It was a jokey suggestion."

"Yes," Arnold, who had the hearing aid, whose thick white thatch of hair was cut in an old-fashioned short back and sides, nodded, "Interesting Simon did not deny it. He didn't react as it if was slanderous."

"No, he didn't make a very convincing denial," agreed Bill. "And what was that business about a router in one of the groundsmen's sheds? How did that come about? A lease on the groundsmen's sheds has never been mentioned in the accounts."

"No I don't think it has been," agreed Sam. "I suppose it was covered in some sort of general income thing, but Ekaterina told me they leased it to store their antimony."

"A bizarre arrangement," growled Bill. "You should definitely try to put a stop to that sort of business, Lady Captain, especially if now you're telling us our secretary…"

"We call him the General manager these days," corrected Arnold with an ironic chuckle.

"Okay, well are you suggesting whoever he is might be storing this antimony stuff in his office?"

"Not exactly." Sam shifted awkwardly from one foot to the other as she recounted her concern about the missing pieces of antimony possibly not being antimony, but have some ulterior purpose which she wanted to discover. She did not mention finding Greg's body, although she felt shaky at the mere mention of the shed.

"That's the problem," nodded Bill, "if we don't know the purpose the shed is really being used for. There are all sorts of rumours doing the rounds about Yuri Leonov wanting to buy the club and naturally we Venerables are all very worried about getting into a Dangerfield situation."

Both men agreed that it would be disastrous for a club like Elmsleigh Park, approaching its centenary year, to be bought by someone possibly in trouble with the National Crime Agency, like the foreign lady who now owned the club they nick-named Dangerfield. What if Ekaterina, Yuri's widow were to follow suit?

To her own surprise Sam found herself protesting that Ludmilla Gorski, who bought the plush Dangerfield golf course in the middle of the home counties, was not Russian like Ekaterina, but Ukrainian. Ludmilla wouldn't or couldn't say where her funds came from, whereas Yuri, or presumably now Ekaterina, owned an antimony mine plus other mining assets in Russia.

As she finished speaking, Sam's lips turned down at the corners in doubt. A memory surfaced in her brain of Ekaterina once boasting she'd met Ludmilla in Harrods when she was shopping there. Sam winced as she recalled Ekaterina, a renowned shopaholic, if not on the same scale as Ludmilla, reputed to have spent millions at the

Knightsbridge store, being impressed by the scale of Ludmilla's possessions. Ekaterina talked as though Ludmilla was a friend of hers, a "lovely person

"But you're now saying," said the lanky Bill, in a slightly argumentative tone, "that actually you suspect the stuff Yuri kept in our shed was not antimony at all?"

To Sam's relief his attention was distracted by the energetic Misty bustling up to them to warn them she was about to lock the clubhouse for the night as it was nearly six o'clock. "We're just about to go," she said.

"Yes, but we'd really like to look into this shed on our way," said Bill. "What do you think Arnold? Let's inspect the sheds now."

Sam groaned inwardly. "It may be locked."

"Well you got into it," said Arnold. "How did you get in?"

"It was open then."

"It might still be open now. We'll go and have a look. Why don't you come with us? It's obviously of great interest to you Sam."

"Shouldn't we have permission from the Leonov family?" asked Sam.

Both Bill and Arnold shrugged off that suggestion with the retort that the shed was golf club premises. It was owned by the members, with no official lease drawn up giving the Leonov family any legal right to use it for any purpose, private or business.

Sam agreed to accompany the two men there. They were, she felt, correct that there should not be arrangements kept secret from the members who owned the club. Both Arnold and Bill were much more long-standing members than herself. Even if Arnold, unlike Bill had not held office in the club hierarchy, he had, through his yearly subscriptions, supported the club by helping fund the means to survive.

Walking at the octogenarian Arnold's pace, it took them ten minutes to reach the groundsmen's sheds which, despite the fading light, all looked remarkably innocuous. Nonetheless, Sam hoped the specific one, set slightly apart from the others, might be locked again; somehow the prospect of seeing inside, even with the knowledge Greg Burgess's body had been removed daunted her.

Once she had pointed it out, Bill's long legs paced ahead. His large hand on the metal door handle threw the shed door open wide with an easy thrust that suggested there could be nothing sinister inside. Moments later when she and Arnold followed, her first impression was initially confirmed. The bed was neatly stacked up against the wall as it had been the first time she had entered the shed whilst various gardening type tools lay on the adjacent table.

"So those funny looking rocks are antimony, are they?" asked Bill, with a flourish of his large hand towards the shelves.

Sam nodded.

"They don't look very suspicious," said Bill. "Don't know why he couldn't keep them in his own home."

Sam swallowed. Being here again made her feel slightly hysterical. "Maybe I just got the wrong impression." She stared around. "There's just one thing."

"What?" Arnold asked gently. He inclined his head towards Bill, giving it a slight shake as if to suggest Bill should not speak.

"There are seven pieces of antimony here now. What worried me before was that a couple of the pieces had disappeared. There were five instead of seven."

"So," said Bill, "someone, maybe Simon, put them back."

"They're not the same. They're bigger."

"But how can you tell?" asked Arnold in the same gentle tone. "To me those pieces of rock look much of a muchness."

Sam fished in her handbag for her mobile, got up the gallery of photographs to point out the differences between the rows of stones, which she had taken twice.

"And what's that?" asked Bill, instantly picking up the end of the bed in which Greg had lain.

"Oh just that bed was out once," explained Sam.

"With someone in it?" Bill continued mercilessly.

Before Sam could admit or deny it, the answer came through on her phone. A voice message from Captain Roger Turpin blazoned out in the confined space. "Sorry to bother you Sam, but we will have to discuss that death on our property."

As she instantly switched off the phone she realised her action spoke louder than any admission that the part of the club's property mentioned was where the three of them stood.

"In here," confirmed Bill with a grimace. "There's been a death in here in that bed."

"Unfortunately, yes," admitted Sam, "but we don't think it was violent."

"Can't always tell," said Arnold grimly. "Plenty initial impressions are wrong."

"But you'll know tomorrow, or have some idea," said Bill eagerly. "Gosh, it's like something out of Cluedo."

Large though he was, for a moment he dwindled in Sam's eyes to seeming like an eager child. "It's awful, a young man's death."

"Yes, terrible for you being involved," agreed Bill in a much more sober, sympathetic tone. "But don't forget we're here if you need some help from old stagers not in the Cabinet."

Sam looked from one man to the other. "Thankyou."

"Count on us, Lady Captain," said Arnold.

"Thanks," said Sam again, wondering how much more tangled things at the club could become if she enlisted them to help her.

Evidently sensing her thoughts, Bill gave a slight shake of his head as he recited, "Oh what a tangled web we weave, when first we venture to deceive."

"I suppose so," said Sam trying to laugh and change the subject as she continued, "but that saying's nothing to do with golf."

"Wouldn't be sure about that," said Arnold with a knowledgeable smile. "Comes from a romantic poem by Sir Walter Scott and there are golfers in his books. You need to watch out for yourself and remember who your friends are."

19. An Emergency committee meeting

Amy's shift work at a local hospital meant she was unable to come to the emergency committee meeting next day, leaving Sam the only woman present. *A pity,* reflected Sam since Amy's medical knowledge would be useful. Amy would have had no compunction in questioning facts about Greg's, or rather Guy Burgess's death, put forward by Doctor Roger Turpin, despite his being a renowned orthopaedic consultant whilst she was a physiotherapist.

Though scheduled for seven o'clock in the evening, the day after Sam had visited the shed with Arnold and Bill, Sam arrived at six forty-five to find Misty hovering around the newly appointed upstairs committee room. She held out a plate with shortbread biscuits and a selection of cakes to Sam.

"Just in case you missed tea," said Misty brightly.

"Thanks." Sam, who had not eaten since her cereal breakfast took a shortbread biscuit. She bit into it hungrily only to find it was dried up and stale. To wash it down she asked, "Any possibility of a cup of tea? No don't worry, I'll come downstairs and get something from the machine."

To ask Misty to bring something up here was beyond the call of duty since it must be after Misty's working hours. Nonetheless she was glad when Misty insisted it would be no trouble to bring a pot of tea up here since others who would soon arrive might also like a cup.

"We really ought to get a hot drinks machine for this room," said Sam, "for after hours meetings."

"Don't suggest it," shuddered Misty, as she placed the plate of biscuits on a side table in the corner of the room where cups and saucers stood ready for service. In a warning tone she added, "There's enough trouble with that Mr Reynolds giving us the other coffee machine, especially as he's now offering to set up those warning cameras outside the club house."

"CCTV cameras?"

"Yes, those things that tell us about everyone who's coming and going, proper spy equipment."

"Thanks for telling me," said Sam, thinking how well-informed Misty was and probably she would make a better sleuth as far as the club was concerned than herself.

Reminded of her work, the moment Misty left the room, Sam took a searching look round the chest of drawers and shelves that lined the walls of the room. To her surprise, when she bent down to pull open the large bottom drawer of the chest of drawers, she spotted there in a back corner, scarcely visible, a greyish black lump which might be antimony.

Sam knelt down to reach forward into the back of the drawer. She was just pulling the rock towards her when she heard heavy steps in the room behind her which did not sound like Misty's light tread. Still holding the antimony, Sam jumped up to see Hector Bravo standing alongside her.

He eyed her, clearly waiting for her to speak, as though she should explain herself.

She gritted her teeth. No, she must not feel guilty. He might not, at her request, be aware that she, at his employment of the Old Alresford Detective Agency, was

engaged to find out any skulduggery at the Elmsleigh Golf
Club. Since she knew she was acting in the club's best
interests, she would brazen out her actions. "I've just
found this piece of rock in these drawers. I wondered
what it's used for and whether the club needs it."

"Yes, well Sam, that would be for the Powers that
Be to decide wouldn't it?"

"We are the Powers that Be," laughed Sam, "in
case you've forgotten Hector. We've got to work out how
to improve matters here." She glanced down at the piece
of antimony she held, suddenly realising that it was far too
light to be solid rock. "This stuff is very odd. Look, it's
not rock, it opens." She pulled it apart to find it was a
hard rocky case with a square object inside resembling a
small radio. "What's this? Looks like a router. Why
should we have one here when there's a perfectly good
one in the office?"

"Give it to me," ordered Hector in an authoritative
voice. "I'll look into it."

Sam was tempted to refuse on the grounds that she,
as the current Lady Captain, these days theoretically on
equal terms with the Men's Captain, currently out-flanked
the Men's Vice-Captain. The days when the old
committee room was the men's Spike Bar, where men
were allowed in wearing their golf shoes, a chaps' place
where the men's dogs were allowed to enter, but not their
women, were gone forty-seven years ago. She might have
reminded Sir Hector of this, but at that moment, the arrival
of the other committee members, who, without Amy, were
all men, was too strong a deterrent. Handing the object to
Hector, she managed, nonetheless, whilst he fiddled with

it, before he said it would have to go back into the drawer for the moment, to take a quick picture of it with her mobile without his noticing.

She sat down next to Jason who had pulled out a chair for her. As she thanked him, she noticed he was looking strained, which was unusual for someone generally so confident.

After thanking those able to attend at such short notice, Captain Roger quickly got on to the reason for summoning them. For those who had not already heard, he announced the death of Guy Burgess, whom he described as a "pleasant young man", known to many members of the club. However, he continued, this did not mean the club had to take any responsibility for the man's death although he was found deceased in property belonging to the club in the club's grounds. As far as the club was concerned, the man was a trespasser.

Some of the men sitting around the table nodded, but Matthew Borden frowned as he said, "Provided he wasn't with a member when he went into the shed. How do we know one of the ground staff or a club member didn't accompany him into the shed, then left him there?"

"We don't," began Roger, but stopped speaking as there was a knock on the door. "Come in." He waited to continue until Misty, with her usual deft movements, had threaded her slim body between chairs and chests to put down the tray she carried with the extra cups and saucers needed, taken the crockery, a large teapot, a pot of hot water, a jug of milk and a bowl of sugar off it, then picked the tray back up and left the room.

"We don't," repeated Roger, "know that and we have to admit that the shed is not far away from a public footpath through our grounds. However, if someone else is involved in the young man's death, that is for the police to ascertain. I have to tell you that fortunately it is unlikely any of our members are involved because Guy Burgess died of Atropine poisoning."

The rest of those present all turned to each other with puzzled frowns.

"What on earth does that mean?" Asked Matthew.

"Hard to explain," admitted Roger. "What I can tell you is that atropine is on the World Health Organisation's listed medicines, although it's used with extreme caution these days. However, Guy Burgess was not taking any prescribed medications so he should not have had a dangerous drug like atropine in his possession. We therefore have to assume that he took the drug for recreational purposes. As he was a wildlife gardener, we must assume that he knew what he was imbibing."

Jason leant forward. "What's significant about his being a wildlife gardener?"

"He would know how to get hold of atropine from a flower I suppose," said Hector, with a shrug of his shoulders. "That's possibly why he took up wildlife gardening."

"You're his godfather, aren't you?" Said Matthew. "Did you know he was taking drugs."

"No." Hector shrugged. "At his age, with his outlook, Greg as we know him, hasn't been very interested in an old stager like me. I introduced him to golf as a child, and he got very good at it, but then he was turned down for membership here which put a bit of a strain on our relationship."

"What did Guy's parents do?" Asked Sam, wondering how Hector Bravo could have maintained a close if strained godfatherly relationship with Guy and be happy to call him Greg.

The look on Hector's face suggested this was none of Sam's business, but he was saved from saying so by the President, Dick Norton who said authoritatively, "I don't think that's relevant anyway, or something we want to discuss. I hope everyone here agrees it is in the club's best interest to hand any investigation into Guy's sad death over to the police who are the appropriate authorities." He looked to Roger for support. "Don't you think so?"

Roger nodded. "The result of the post mortem suggests accidental death resulting from poisoning. Off the record I can tell you there is evidence in his medical records of an addictive personality so the net result of that and the post mortem means there is no suggestion of unnatural causes."

"Surely a drug overdose is unnatural?" Queried Sam. "I suppose it's not so bizarre that he changed his name to Greg rather than suffer being called after a notorious spy." Raising her eyebrows, she turned to face Hector who, as the man's godfather should know why his parents chose the name.

Hector scowled back at her. "He was not called after the spy Guy Burgess, although some people might regard that man as an unfortunate tragic person, gay at a time when it was a criminal offence. To the best of my knowledge his parents simply liked the name, although when they arrived here, because his father became a vicar locally, Guy became embarrassed by the proximity of his late notorious namesake having lived here."

So shut up about it. He might have added, judging by the expression on his strong rectangular face as he turned, his beaky nose pointing to address Roger again. "Sad though it is, don't lots of young people take recreational drugs these days?"

The doctor nodded. "I'm afraid so. Now to move on to some other problems. Although our relationship with the Leonov family has improved since the gathering we had the other night, we have had a claim from Vladimir Leonov for a private ultrasound examination and physiotherapy treatment." He continued to explain that Vladimir claimed how in hustling him out of the clubhouse, Jason had damaged soft tissue in his arm as well as bruising a rib.

"Bugger that," exploded Jason. "I stopped him from making outrageous allegations against our club members."

"I think I'd already stopped him," interrupted Hector, "and saved that ridiculously stupid game."

"It was a bloody good game." Jason's voice rose. "And I can tell you the only problem with getting him out of the clubhouse was that we couldn't keep an eye on him in the carpark where he wrecked your car Roger."

"What, you think he took my catalyst converter?" asked Roger, evidently too surprised to protest against Jason's use of swear words.

"Bloody sure of it," said Jason.

President Dick Norton raised his hand. "Please would you desist from swearing Jason. I know the rules of golf have been relaxed, but courtesy is still an important part of the game and swearing is still outlawed at all respectable clubs, especially here at Elmsleigh Park."

"Sorry," Jason apologised in a softer tone, "but Vladimir swore worse at me when I let him go and said he'd get our damn club back; and his arm couldn't have been that bad or he wouldn't have been able to drive himself off to the hospital. Probably injured it when he crawled under your car to take out the catalyst converter."

"You've got no proof of..." began Hector hotly, but stopped mid-sentence, letting his breath blow out of his large mouth as he saw Dick Norton raise his large gnarled hand like a policeman to halt traffic.

"That point's been made." Said the President. "Now we must move on. Roger has an important announcement to make which in present circumstances needs the support of all the club's directors."

"This really follows on from that unfortunate event," said Roger in a soft mellifluous tone, clearly meant to mollify any possible disagreement. "We've had an extremely generous offer from a prominent member of the club, to provide CCTV cameras outside the clubhouse, covering the professional's shop as well as the entire Members' carpark."

"That would be Ozzie Reynolds," remarked Sam before she could stop herself. "Not quite sure why he's prominent." She forebode to mention he was not one of the club's best players. "Why don't we ask him to pay for Vladimir's treatment? He was friends with his father."

196

Hector shuddered. "We certainly don't want to involve him with that, or anything else as far as I'm concerned."

"Yes," Roger nodded. "He's been a generous benefactor to the club already. However, I do feel our acceptance or refusal of his offer should be a communal decision. There's more than the cost of the lights and the installation to be considered. Someone will have to monitor the thing." He turned to Simon, sitting at the end of the long oak table. "Either you Simon, or the professional, would have to take the responsibility."

"I'd have to do it," said Simon. "Far too many people help out in the Pro's shop. Very good of them of course, but we'd need the observation to be done in my office by myself or my assistant, when I get one."

The tone of his words made the committee members grimace at one another. Simon had been promised a full time assistant three months previously, but Jason, as house manager, had yet to find someone suitable, with the result various temporaries, sometimes female members, had been helping out in the office.

Matthew Borden wrinkled his nose. "This all sounds horribly commercial, not at all in the spirit of our club. We're a club; that's a group of friends for heaven's sake, not a department store."

Jason nodded vigorously. "And do we want to give power to this or that rich guy? Sooner or later it'll mean they can call the shots which we won't want. We've already got too much input from some members."

"What do you mean?" Sam asked.

"In the kitchen stores," replied Jason. "I know it's generous and may have been started with the best motives, but as house-manager, I don't like this custom that's grown up of members supplementing our club store-cupboard."

One or two others on the committee stared at him, wondering what he meant.

"It's getting like some fff...., Jason hesitated drawing back from the f-word as he went on to say "foodbank. I've only been house-manager for three months, but I understand it started a while ago with members donating bottles of wine they'd been given and that led on to other products, even breakfast cereals because oats, I'm told can be made into flapjacks which the bar staff can then sell back to members or society visitors at a good profit."

Sam wanted to groan. The older ladies in the club had been magnificent in their generosity, supporting the club through needy times by making cakes for match teas. They had formed an unofficial group to make sure there was always a good supply of sandwiches if ever any of the kitchen staff were off so that the club might be spared the expense of going to an expensive agency. This was the spirit of the golf club. As gently as she could she said, "I think the girls like to support the club."

"Yes," agreed Matthew, "I know my wife Emma and Tabby Bravo have done their bit. What's the problem with that Jason?"

"Health and safety issues," said Jason. "It makes us vulnerable to accusations. I don't think we should accept gifts as we can't analyse everything to see it's okay."

Remembering the packet labelled sugar which she had seen in Simon's drawer, Sam watched his face as she asked, "What about sugar?"

Simon did not comment, but she thought she saw a muscle twitch in his face as he glanced round the other committee members.

"I don't have a problem with that," said Matthew. "Frankly, if I'm organising an event and some farmer offers me a dead pig for a hog roast, I'd go for it just as I'll accept fallen apples to make apple pies. It's a far cry from having aggressive lights around the place. Not sure that doesn't suggest there's something worth stealing."

"Hardly the case with our food," laughed Jason, reaching a long arm back to pick up a biscuit from the plate on the side table. "Anyone for a stale biscuit, presumably donated because the packet is past its sell-by date? Were you worried about stale sugar too Sam?"

"Not really. Only wondered how far the donations went. Did anyone give these biscuits?" She asked quickly, suddenly fearful she might give away her knowledge of the sugar in Simon's filing cabinet.

"I believe they're the remains of a bundle of shortbread made by Mrs Reynolds to go with the coffee machine her husband donated," said Captain Roger.

"Really? That was kind," said Sam wondering why her instinct told it was ominous.

"Yes and no," said Jason. "Any gift is a problem with Vladimir going around accusing us publicly of poisoning his father. As house manager I find that absolutely unacceptable."

"Okay, okay," said Roger. "You've made your point." *Rather too aggressively* added the expression on the Captain's face.

With that he rounded off the meeting, telling Simon there was no need to minute all the proceedings, other than the reference to Guy Burgess's death. There was he concluded, no other business to discuss.

With relief the committee members trooped out of the room leaving Simon behind to lock up. Would he, Sam wondered, take the fake piece of antimony out of the chest of drawers? She could not wait around to see; she wanted to catch Jason to ask him if he had any further reason to suspect Vladimir Leonov was the catalyst converter thief.

No, but yes, was the answer when she cornered him in the carpark. It was not only his gut feeling and Vladimir's threats, but something Crystal had said after that party. She had thought she recognised Vladimir from the day her catalyst converter was stolen. The man looked familiar she'd said.

That did not help prove anything, Sam reflected as she drove home. Nor could she accept that Guy, or rather Greg as she knew him, had taken a drug overdose. Messy though the man might look, what she could see of his face did not suggest the unhealthy pallor of a drug addict.

One person could confirm this, tell her whether she was right. Much as her instinct told her not to get involved, Sam felt she must get in touch with Helen McTavish. It was her duty to comfort a lady member of the club who had lost her boyfriend. The moment she opened her front door at home, she was given such an ecstatic welcome by Monty jumping up at her to lick her face that she nearly missed the voice mail on her house phone, but she heard enough to realise a distraught Helen would welcome a visit from her.

Maybe not tonight. It was nearly eight o'clock. Then she remembered; Helen was a working girl. Tomorrow might not be possible. With a sigh Sam dialled the most recent number on her list of calls. Helen had obviously tried to get in contact with her already.

20. Consoling Helen

"I'm okay." Helen's Scots accent disguised the tremor in her voice. "But I would like to see you. It's all such a shock and it doesn't make sense."

"What doesn't make sense?" Asked Sam.

"Oh everything. Listen, I can't explain over the phone. Would you like to come over here? Or is it too late for you?"

Sam looked at her watch. It was now nearly nine o'clock. "Where do you live?"

"West Meon."

Her irritated puff of air at the phone made her agreement so inaudible Sam had to repeat it in the least reluctant tone she could muster. The village of West Meon was not much more than five miles from where she lived and at this time of night there was unlikely to be much traffic on the rural route she would take to get there.

The small terraced house where Helen lived was easy to find. She opened the door before Sam knocked, explaining she had been watching the road from the sitting room window, waiting for Sam's car, which being the Lady Captain's car regularly parked in the Lady Captain's space in the club carpark, she would recognise.

With a shock, Sam herself recognised Julia, the girl, or rather older woman, with whom Helen shared her house. Although it was a long while since the powerful lady golfer had played at Elmsleigh Park, the former Lady Bravo, was unmistakable. Presumably since Sir Hector's ex-wife had evidently not married again, she might, unlike Tabby, Hector's current wife, who never used the title, still call herself Lady Bravo. With her long floral skirt and tasselled patent leather brogue shoes, besides the way she sat upright in her chair, turning her head to see who Helen's guest was, she exuded the complete air of the posh Hampshire lady.

After the necessary re-introductions were made, with Julia saying in a charming way that she felt after she'd parted from Hector, it would be more comfortable for them both if she played golf elsewhere, she asked if Sam would mind talking to Helen somewhere outside the living room, which she called the "drawing room", because there was a television programme she particularly wanted to watch.

Sam said she did not mind at all. She could have added she would actually prefer to speak to Helen elsewhere, since she might be more relaxed without Julia present. So with alacrity she accepted Helen's offer of coffee in the kitchen "or something stronger if you like".

Mindful of her drive back home as well as the uncertainty about what "something stronger" might mean, Sam settled for coffee. No, she did not mind if it was instant. She might have said she would prefer it, seeing the beverage come out of a recognisable branded glass jar rather than some unknown packet. As they sat down Sam said, "I'm terribly sorry about your loss."

Startled, Helen replied with a sniff, "Thank you, although he wasn't exactly mine."

Noting the height of the cottage doors as well as the neatness of the modern kitchen with its smart wooden built-in cupboards, Sam could not imagine how someone as large as Greg could possibly have felt at home here. "I understand Greg was your partner, but did he actually live with you?"

"What do you think?" Asked Helen aggressively. "No, he wasn't my partner either. We are, were merely good friends." Her voice went down a notch as she suppressed a sob. "He didn't live here. Julia wouldn't allow that, and this is her house. I'm her tenant." She switched on a tall grey modern design electric kettle standing on what looked like a marble worksurface before walking over to a large pine dresser to pick two mugs off brass hooks.

"Oh I see," said Sam, thinking perhaps she didn't. "Erm, do you mind if I use your loo? I rushed out in rather a hurry."

"Not at all. It's by the front door."

Deciding she could say she thought it was occupied, Sam hurried upstairs to take a look at the bedrooms. The first one she poked her nose round the door into was evidently the master bedroom with its large window looking out on to the gardens of the terraced houses. It had a pretty dressing and makeup table built into the oak bedroom cupboards which lined the room. In the middle was a small double bed. Presumably this was Julia's room, since she appeared to be calling the shots with regard to watching television in the sitting room.

Sam closed the door quickly. Alongside it was the door leading into what Sam supposed must be the bathroom by the size of the space between it and the next door. That opened into another bedroom inside which was a single bed, probably three foot wide but single nonetheless. However, standing near it, covered with a rug was an object similar to the covered fold-up bed in the shed in the Elmsleigh Park grounds. With a few quick strides, Sam reached the object to pull back the rug where she found what she expected, a fold-up single bed, which she guessed, rolled out would turn the single bed into a double.

Round the walls were the same styled oak fitted wardrobe furnishings with plenty of drawers, but without a fitted dressing table. Instead there was an inset which resembled a desk, giving the room a unisex look. This was modified by numerous attractive plants in pots on the desk as well as covering the long windowsill. Sam wondered how rare they were since she did not recognise most of them as the usual sorts sold in supermarkets.

Talk about bringing work home. She thought. *But did Helen ever bring Greg here?*

There was no sign he might have stayed in the house until Sam pulled open a large long drawer at the bottom of the oak wardrobe unit. It was stuffed with men's clothes, tee-shirts, long ragged trousers, collarless shirts and even a couple of windcheaters, one of which looked familiar. Had she seen Greg wearing it or was it someone else, possibly Hector Bravo? The garment had the club's familiar elm tree logo.

With a quick dip into her handbag, Sam flipped out her mobile to take a couple of photos, putting it away speedily as she heard a step on the stairs below. She ran to the door and was just out in time to dash into the lavatory.

To her initial relief when she came out Julia, rather than Helen stood on the tiny landing, although she was rather daunted when Julia asked accusingly why she was in the bedroom, almost as though she thought Sam might have stolen something.

"I had to sneak in and see her flowers," lied Sam, she hoped convincingly. "There's such a wonderful aroma coming from that room don't you think?"

"Can't say I've ever noticed it." Julia frowned as she sniffed.

"So good for one, I gather," Sam gushed, "to have foliage in your room at night, counteracts gas that might be expelled from other people's chimneys coming through an open window and contaminating your bedroom."

"Plants are good for you," agreed Julia, her large blue eyes widening, but her tone of voice sceptical. "I'm glad you appreciate them."

"Yes, yes," agreed Sam as she ran downstairs, apologising to Helen as she entered the kitchen for the length of time she'd taken and explaining that Julia had waylaid her, before she said in as innocent a tone as she could muster, "So Greg didn't live with you?"

"No, I told you that." Helen shook her head as she put the two mugs of coffee down on the pine table beside which Sam sat. "I liked Greg; I liked him a lot but he always said he didn't want to tie me down, not in his present," a small groan escaped her lips, "his past circumstances."

"A man without a proper job or a home? But he had become a wildlife gardener." Sam raised her eyebrows questioningly at Helen.

"Gardening is a proper job," retorted Helen, "but he'd only just started on wilding and it could have worked out well for him. He was very interested in it, but it was all new to him. I got him going on that because it's what I do, or rather want to do."

"I see," said Sam picturing in her mind's eye Helen's recent application form to join Elmsleigh Park on which was written for her profession, "Gardener". "I thought you worked at a garden centre."

"I do, but I'm starting my own business. That's why it was going to be so great having Greg and I'm so lost without him. He was awfully strong you know, besides having other sorts of knowledge; he'd been involved in scrap metal as you know. Anyway, he got fed up with that which is why he wanted to turn his hand to re-wilding with me. It's terribly useful to have someone who can lift things and move anything about. They really could use him at the club."

"Yes," said Sam, wondering briefly if Helen's real motive for involving Greg was to do with her own business, then dismissing it. "I'm not sure whether his role at the club might not have conflicted with the works the course manager's planned."

"That's why they bumped him off is it?" Sobbed Helen. She took a large man's checked blue and white handkerchief out of the pocket of her jeans to wipe away the tears that were falling down her cheeks.

Startled, though she knew she should not be, Sam replied, "We were told tonight by Roger, properly informed, Greg died of a drug overdose, not murdered."

"Greg didn't take drugs. He couldn't afford to."

"That doesn't seem to stop some people, but I take your point. It does seem out of character, from the little I saw of him and thankfully drug takings not a problem we've had at Elmsleigh Park, or as far as I know around here."

"What's he supposed to have taken?" Helen wiped her eyes again, picked up her mug from the pine table and took a gulp of coffee.

"Atropine. Seems a bit odd. I've never heard of an addiction to it before." Sam grasped her coffee mug with both hands to calm herself as the memory of Greg lying in the pulled-out bed under the aged motheaten blankets assailed her. "I gather it's a recognised pharmaceutical, but how he would get it heaven knows."

"Belladonna," exclaimed Helen straightening up in her chair as she lifted her head up in indignation. "That's ridiculous. Don't think it's been used medicinally since the ancient Mesopotamians used it. It's poisonous. Surely you've heard of deadly nightshade, the plant."

"Er yes," agreed Sam feeling ignorant of the connection, "but do people drug themselves with it? I mean take it for pleasure."

"Has been known, but not Greg." Helen thumped the table with her fist. "And he certainly wouldn't take so much it killed him."

"Why would he take it in that particular shed anyway?" asked Sam. Seemed unlikely but possible the Leonov family had a side line in drugs.

Helen stared at her momentarily. "Because he used to bed down in that shed." She noted Sam's surprise and continued, "Didn't you know? Obviously he came here sometimes," she lowered her voice, "when Julia wasn't around, or sometimes stayed in one or other of the hostels, but it was useful for him, as a homeless person to be able to doss down at Elmsleigh Park."

"Homeless? I didn't realise he was homeless." Sam stared at Helen. "You mean that bed in the shed was his?"

Helen nodded.

"How did he get the key to the shed anyway?"

"I don't know. Presumably through his godfather Hector." Helen sniffed.

"Bit odd Hector didn't offer him a bed in his own house," said Sam shocked.

"No, no. It suited Greg to be homeless for what he wanted to do." At Sam's puzzled expression, Helen continued, "He wanted to be a spy. I mean he wanted to work for M15 but they wouldn't have him, so he decided to prove to them that he could unearth a real spy and then they would have to employ him"

Sam made a throwaway remark about supposing having the name "Guy Burgess" didn't help with an M15 interview, then cursed herself for tactlessness in the circumstances. To her relief, Helen agreed.

"Too right. His interview with M15 was years ago, straight after university. That's why he changed his name to Greg when he tried again later. Ridiculous really, he should have to do that when there's a film actor called Guy Burgess who's much more famous now, but Greg had a thing about being as different from the other Guy Burgess as possible. He couldn't bear the idea anyone might identify him as a posh boy Etonian, like the other Guy Burgess when they're not even related."

"Did he go to Eton?"

"Yes and then Cambridge which he thought was a bit of a No No. One of the things he liked about me was my Scots voice, said it made me sound like a rrrreal person." She rolled the r of real. "He hated the fact that though he was born here, he couldn't speak like a real Hampshire lad."

"But was he really a Hampshire lad? What did his father do?"

"That's it. God knows where his father came from; he was a clergyman based in a parish somewhere near here for a while when Greg was a child, which is why he always wanted to come back to what he said he felt were his roots."

"But what about his mother?"

"Goodness knows but I gather she was a very efficient vicar's wife, made a bit of a career of being a fifties type woman." Helen pulled a disapproving face.

"Did he want you to help him in his project?"

Helen shook her head. "Far from it, he didn't want me the slightest bit involved in what he was trying to do."

"I suppose his mission was to prove Yuri Leonov was a spy," said Sam.

Helen nodded. "I guess so. The strange thing is, and that's why I wanted to see you, instead of being pleased he was getting near the truth of the thing, he got upset. It started the day he was with a group in the clubhouse and Yuri publicly called him the 'Woolly Mammoth' which was his spy nickname. I knew him well enough to realise something big bothered him. He kept saying it was nothing and that it was better I didn't know."

She sighed. "Obviously I went along with that; then Yuri died which stressed him even more and now this."

Tears flowed again down her face as she spoke. Her lower lip trembled as she continued, "He didn't talk about himself being in danger, but said he was in an awkward situation and it was better if I wasn't dragged into it. I went along with it." She cried out loud now. "Now I wish I hadn't. I should have insisted he stayed here instead of going to that silly party for Vladimir. He could have done. I was so silly." She looked at the kitchen door as she lowered her voice. "God I hate her. Bloody snob. I should have left this house when she said that awful word 'inappropriate', that having Greg here would be 'inappropriate'."

She had not noticed the kitchen door had opened whilst she spoke.

Julia stood in the doorway. "If you feel like that, you'd better go now." She said through clenched teeth. "I always told you that boy – well man if you can call someone so immature a man – was bad news. Posh boy indeed. He'd sponge off anyone: he was a class act at that."

Sam flinched. A glance at her watch told her it was past ten o'clock. Easily late enough to make her excuses and go home. She didn't like to leave Helen in this state, especially since she seemed to have caused this row. *No you haven't.* She told herself sternly. *This was coming. That's why Helen wanted to see you.* "I'm afraid I must go now. Work to do tomorrow. Will you be all right Helen, or would you like to come back to my place for the night? I've got a spare room."

211

It was an offer she did not expect to get taken but to her surprise and slight alarm, Helen accepted with alacrity. "Yes please," she gasped.

"Give her another opportunity to rifle through your drawers." Julia gave a cynical chuckle.

"What? Was that why you took so long upstairs in the loo?" Helen sniffed as she gaped at her.

Sam did not reply. With her bag slung over her shoulder, she made her way to the kitchen door. Hesitating in the open doorway, she turned to say, "The offer's still open, but hurry."

Helen stood up shakily. Then she sat down again, her shoulders slumped in a despair whilst she threw the back of her hand out towards the door to dismiss Sam.

"Better the devil you know that the one you don't," chaffed Julia. "Except maybe the devil is in the detail. You may not have told your golfing chum, exactly where you've told me that deadly nightshade grows."

Now halfway out through the doorway, Sam could not restrain herself from turning back again to ask where exactly.

"Your ruddy Elmsleigh Park. Never saw it when I belonged there, but Penny Norton also tells me it's all over the place there now."

21. A change of role

Sam had hardly time to gather her thoughts after last night's episode with Helen following the stormy Cabinet meeting when she was woken up by her beside phone ringing. Once she heard Laurie on the other end, she wished she had let it ring, but supposed automatic pilot made her hand reach out to pick up the receiver to hear him tell her he needed to see her, but he would not say why at this juncture.

Sam sighed as leaning on her elbow she managed to speak. It was all too complicated. She was tempted to resign from the job this moment, nine fifteen on a Friday morning, but decided she should deliberate over the weekend. With Laurie reporting back to Simon Duckworth, then the Elmsleigh Park Cabinet, she felt more and more she wanted to be let off this hook.

Staring at the time on her phone she wondered why Monty did not wake her. Usually by this time he was desperate to go out, especially when, as last night, he was left alone in the house by himself with nothing to do but prowl around. Then when she saw the reproachful look on his face where he lay the other side of her bedroom, she realised he must have barked and pawed her bedside as usual, but she was too fast asleep to notice. He must have more attention today which fitted in with last night's resolution that today she would walk him over the Elmsleigh grounds to look for deadly nightshade.

"Can I see you on Monday?" She asked.

"Better come today," he said, "if you can make it."

Wearily Sam agreed she would be with him in Alresford at eleven o'clock.

To her alarm, the moment she opened his office door she spied the upright figure of Nicholas Roman in his shirt, tie and blazer, sitting in Laurie's best visitor's chair beside his desk. She almost stumbled as she stepped into the room, biting back the question, *What the hell's he doing here?* Seeing the usual coffee pot with three mugs on a tray on the table, she was tempted to add that she didn't think she was coming to a coffee party.

"Welcome Sam." Laurie greeted her in a tone of voice suggesting he noticed her unease. "I don't know if you know Nicholas Roman."

"We've never been introduced," replied Sam coolly, "but I am aware of who he is."

"No need for anything like that," said Nicholas, holding out his hand for her to shake. "We were actually at a small party together recently."

"Yes," Sam nodded as she put out her hand to receive his firm grasp. "I'm afraid I wasn't certain what side of the fence you were on."

"Maybe different from yours." Nicholas's ironic tone belying the smile which twitched at the corner of his mouth beneath the black moustache as he turned sideways to look at Laurie, as though inviting him to take over.

"I'll come straight to the point." Laurie, sounded apologetic rather than accusatory as he handed Sam a mug of coffee he had poured out for her "We haven't got very far with finding out about the converter robberies which was the main thrust of our contract with Elmsleigh Park."

214

"That's putting it mildly," agreed Sam. "I told you at the start it was not really my thing, but in any case, surely we shouldn't discuss it in Nicholas's presence."

Nicholas's mouth remained firmly clamped shut whilst Laurie continued, "Well as you know Nicholas's car was robbed at your golf club. At the time he wanted me to investigate it, but I told him there was no need because we were already on the job."

"So why now?" Asked Sam in as soft a tone as she could muster.

"Because the club are taking the converter thefts out of our hands. Simon Duckworth, rang me late yesterday to say the club has passed on their suspicions about the son of a late member to the police. It appears this young man all but confessed to a member of your club's ruling committee, whom I understand you call the Cabinet, that he took the catalyst converters."

"It was not exactly like that," protested Sam. "I was at the meeting yesterday when Jason said he thought Vladimir Leonov, the son of the Russian guy who died, was responsible for taking our Captain's catalyst converter after a club party was going on, but there's no proof."

"Yes, that's the point. The police are looking into it more seriously now, concentrating better resources on it, I should say; they've got forensic people involved who have skills and equipment beyond our reach."

"So I'm dropped." Sam cradled her coffee cup.

"Not as far as I'm concerned," said Nicholas. "There's no way Vladimir needs to filch bits of cars."

Not even for the antimony in the converters?

Sam wanted to suggest but said instead, "I'm afraid I'm obviously not suited for this job."

With a look of something like remorse in his large brown eyes, Laurie lent back defensively in his chair as he spoke, "Yes and no. It was always going to be a tough call but you are involved: you need to go on investigating what's going on at your club to protect yourself."

"What on earth do you mean?" Sam asked indignantly.

"Bob, you know my friend in the police, says you found a body on the club's premises, which I might add you never told me about, and there's a theory doing the rounds you might be involved in that man's death."

"But I hardly knew the guy. I mean Greg." Sam objected. She frowned and almost gave an involuntary laugh at her misuse of his name. "I didn't even know his real name was actually Guy."

"Doesn't matter what you called him. Apparently he was also known to some as 'Woolly Mammoth', but the fact that's getting them is your presence at his bedside when he died, which ties up with a tip off they've had."

"They've what?"

"I haven't been told the details, but someone, presumably from your club, has fingered you, suggested you had, or might have had a relationship with him."

"I can't believe anyone would finger me in that way," protested Sam, feeling to her irritation heat rising in her cheeks to make her blush. "Elmsleigh members aren't like that. I was voted into my position as Lady Captain. People at the club are my friends." She looked again at Nicholas. "And I'm sorry, but I can't think it's

216

appropriate to talk about this in front of someone who doesn't belong to Elmsleigh Park."

"I appreciate the way you feel," said Nicholas, "but I think this young man's death may be linked with the death of my friend Yuri Leonov."

"But they're both rated as accidental deaths," protested Sam, feeling rather hypocritical since she did not believe that verdict either.

At the other side of his desk, Laurie raised his hands in a surrender motion. "I'm telling you this for your own good as they say. Obviously I want to update you as well as make sure you're all right."

"Laurie, I had nothing to do with Greg's death." Sam banged her coffee mug so hard down on his desk that some liquid spilt out of it.

"Absolutely. I believe you of course, but others evidently do not. We need to make sure it's not laid at your door. You're an easy target. He was reputed to be quite a lady's man and you are single woman."

Sam stood up. "You're not serious. I don't like…" she was about to say 'hairy men', even if it shortened a girl's choices these days, but bit it back at the sight of Laurie's facial hair which had grown since their last meeting. Instead she finished, "Doesn't matter what I like. More important is whether I'm being paid."

"Certainly; I want to keep you on my payroll. This is also where Nicholas here comes in." Laurie's voice took on a reverential tone as he explained Nicholas would fund this investigation.

Nicholas was his first and a permanent client of the Agency. He often wanted to check the credentials of the

217

people he met. There were a great many factions in modern Russia, people who might wish to use his royal ancestry for some dubious purpose, financial or political. On Laurie's advice he changed his name to Roman to deter anyone googling the Romanov name

"I didn't think…" began Sam.

"No," interrupted Nicholas. "Most people think royal families other than here in Britain are defunct, but it doesn't mean we're extinct, or other people might not want to use us for their own nefarious purposes."

Sam wanted to groan. She loathed the idea of being bank-rolled by Nicholas Roman. Some county ladies might enjoy being in the presence of a Romanov, descended from ancient Russian Czars, but not her; she'd rather not work for someone so conflicted about his heritage he kept a bit of his name and a moustache like Peter the Great's. She'd prefer to suss out whether he was a pretender. He might be handsome with aristocratic features, but no man over fifty could have so much black hair on his head. And where did his money come from? She would like to ask.

"Why would anyone belonging to Elmsleigh Park want to harm Yuri when he'd put money into the club?" She asked instead.

"Precisely for that reason," replied Nicholas quickly before Laurie mouthing *No* at him could stop him. "Since it was in lieu of membership fees you wouldn't have to pay him back."

Sam wanted to shout that was an outrageous accusation but controlled the impulse. A better response would be to prove him wrong.

22. Searching for Deadly Nightshade

It was, Sam reflected later, as she parked in a general carpark on the edge of the Elmsleigh Park grounds, good to be rid of worrying about catalyst converters, although she wished she had pointed out to Laurie, that it was her task in investigating those thefts which led her into the unfortunate involvement with the Leonov family, where one death it seemed led to another.

She struck her forehead with her fist as she let Monty out of the back of the car. She had forgotten to ask Laurie about the beggar whom she believed was Simon's father. Presumably he told not Hector Bravo about that aspect of investigations, but Laurie had not mentioned whether Hector was satisfied with her other findings or wanted them followed up further. He had not revealed the knowledge to other Cabinet members as far as she knew.

Yet since she herself had told Simon her suspicions of his father within the hearing of Bill Chambers and Arnold Sidley, it was unlikely Hector would not have heard of them by now, especially since both Bill and Arnold seemed to find that relationship feasible.

It does not matter, she told herself whilst she strode along the footpath into the Elmsleigh Park grounds with Monty trotting companionably at her side. Now her job was to look for the deadly nightshade plant. Her research on the net, plus in a book of wild flowers inherited from her grandmother, who had always wanted her to take an interest in plants for rather a different reason from Sam's current preoccupation, led her to believe

Julia's assertion the plant grew here. Both her references said it was found in chalk land, like the ground of Elmsleigh Park. One of her sources even suggested deadly nightshade would be likely to inhabit ground which had been not left to nature, but dug up, which made a place turned into a park with a golf course seem the right environment.

She headed for the pretty stream which she understood was a tributary of the River Meon. Even if she found nothing, walking in the summer sunshine along the path beside the clear gently running water was a joy. Around her in the grassland were a few wild flowers, but although, amongst the daisies and buttercups, there were wild flowers she did not recognise, nothing she saw matched the picture of the poisonous plant she had in her head. To make sure she was right, she periodically fished her phone out of her pocket to look again at the photo she had downloaded.

Nothing like it here. Perhaps she should head towards more woody wild ground on the outskirts of the golf course, land which many of the older, long-standing members had fought to save from development because it provided a screen for the course.

There it was. Amongst other plants they stood out, loads of deadly nightshade. Suddenly she thought she would recognise the flowers anywhere, the conical purple petals surrounding the contrasting yellow centres and those deep purple berries which looked so innocent. They looked so edible too.

Could it be that a homeless man looking for cheap easy nourishing food mistook these poisonous berries for blueberries? It seemed a horrible possibility. It might not help her position with the police, but she would point out the possibility to Laurie. On the other hand, surely Greg if he knew about gardening would not eat them.

Nonetheless the berries did look appetising enough for Monty to put his head forward and seem about to quaff a few himself. He opened his mouth, drawing Sam instantly out of her reverie as she leant forward and clutched his collar. "No, Monty no," she cried, although she recalled at the same moment that for some reason some animals, she had read, did not succumb to the poison in these berries with the same fatal results as people.

Realising she must make sure these plants were definitely deadly nightshade, she unhooked her backpack from her shoulder, placed it on the ground and undid the buckles to draw out her phone. She took a few pictures of the plants from different angles. That should be enough. *Better be certain.* Maybe it would be a good idea to pick some plants as well. She dropped her phone on her backpack whilst she plucked three plants, handling them gingerly as she placed them inside her backpack.

Just as she hoisted the pack on to her shoulders her phone rang. Initial relief the call alerted her to her precious mobile, having dropped off her backpack, whilst she put the plants in it, now lay potentially lost in the grass near it, was replaced by irritation when she answered. Tabby was on the other end. Good friend though she was, Tabby somehow always chose the wrong moment, to pick her brains about the rules of golf. Why on earth didn't she ask Hector, her husband?

This time she had a real poser. An adder was curled round her golf ball.

Tabby wanted to do the right thing. It was an important county competition match against an extremely competitive opponent from a rival club who would take advantage of the situation. As adders were a protected species, she could not bash it on the head, even if she only wanted to knock it out, rather than kill it.

"Can't you move the ball?"

"Daren't. The snake lifted its head and I could swear it hissed at me."

"You'll just have to drop another ball at the nearest point of relief and play that."

Though Sam had a copy of the rules on her phone there was no time to trawl through it for an authoritative answer before Tabby came back with, "My opponent says it can't be a free drop because I won't be dropping the ball in play. Anyway, heaven knows where I can drop it since there's a bunker one side and the green the other. My opponent wants me to go back and take three off the tee."

Realising they must be at the par three seventeenth, Sam said, "Drop the ball as best you can avoiding the hazard or the green. If it goes in the rough it goes in the rough. Finish the hole, keep the score but don't count it either way yet until you finish the match. Then when you get to the clubhouse I'll be there and we'll take up the issue with the R and A. Oh and photo the adder."

Poor Simon, she thought as she made her way across the park, skirting the course, to get to the clubhouse. He'll have to deal with this. Then she corrected herself. Why should she feel sorry for him with the problems he'd caused, having his father lurking about, plus the unexplained packet of sugar in his filing cabinet? That could have been ground up antimony, but until she could get hold of it, she could not accuse him of anything. The presence of the stuff in his office did not mean he had administered it to Yuri.

Besides, he might be the one who had suggested she was sufficiently infatuated with Greg to poison him.

Thoughts whirled round in her head as she trudged towards the clubhouse, cursing herself also for coming out dressed in jeans. Although the club had not officially relaxed its dress code, most of the older members, whose numbers at Elmsleigh Park predominated, suggested they were not worried by members wearing the forbidden jeans, Sam did not want to be seen to flout club rules. She especially did not wish to provoke any of the longstanding members, especially if one of their number had been beastly enough to make unwarranted suggestions about her relationship with Greg Burgess to the police.

When Sam reached the clubhouse, she saw Tabby followed by a reluctant opponent heading for the first hole. Sam clenched her fist in the air, forgetting for the moment that she had Monty on the lead and jerking him back. "Oh sorry," she apologised to the dog. "The thing is that means the match's still on. Tabby could still win her match if they didn't finish at the eighteenth."

Monty looked up at her mournfully, as though he wanted to say sometimes her enthusiasm for the game was a bit much. He knew he wasn't allowed in the clubhouse so was bewildered as to why they were there when clearly

Sam, without her golf clubs, was not going to take him out with her whilst she played. He gave a short bark.

Sam bent down to pat him. She would have to tie him up somewhere so she could go into the ladies' cloakroom in the clubhouse. Someone might have left a pair of indoor shoes there, which she could borrow whilst they went out to play. To go into the office to talk to Simon about golf rules, it would be politic not to tramp mud from the stream path into his office.

Alas, luck was not with her over the shoes. There were none left in the Lost Property box or anything her size lying around, so she took off her muddy trainers and walked into Simon's office in her socks. Since he, sitting behind his desk, probably would not notice, why should she care? Her mood lifted further as she saw out of the window behind him, Tabby walking with her opponent, back up the first hole. From their body language the result was obvious: Tabby won. Yet the way her opponent moved suggested she was not happy.

Once Sam had explained what had happened with the adder on the seventeenth, Simon put his elbows on the table and dropped his head into cupped hands. "Ladies golf," he muttered.

"Excuse me," laughed Sam. "Did I hear you right? Are you suggesting an adder would avoid wriggling round a ball if a man had hit that ball at the seventeenth?"

Simon grinned back at her. "If it had any sense it would."

Sam coughed. "Hm. I'll let that pass. Just had to apprise you of the situation in case we have to take this rules issue further."

She spoke hurriedly as through the window she saw Tabby pull the door open for her opponent to enter the clubhouse. Screwing up her eyes in an effort to recognise the other player, who seemed horribly familiar, she added, "I'd better go now and see what's what."

As soon as she stepped out of the office into the large hall, she had to force a smile: there stood the unmistakable tall figure of Veronica Eustace, with her neat cropped hairstyle, known as Ronnie, whatever her surname might be now. Once a member of Elmsleigh Park, she had left supposedly to join a grander, as far as golf was concerned, golf club, although rumours had circulated about an affair with the then much sought after newly widowed Bill Chambers.

That must have been over ten years ago, before Sam joined the club. She knew Ronnie from her role as a senior referee. Renowned for her tough personality, she was not someone Sam wished to battle with over rules. Reluctantly she agreed to join the match pair for a drink in the spike bar where Sam's trousers and lack of shoes, which had already made Ronnie's eyebrows raise, would not arouse comment.

Evidently not realising Sam was already aware of the adder problem, once Tabby had brought the Gunners, ginger beer laced with Angostura bitters, over to the three of them, Ronnie gave her interpretation of the event at the seventeenth hole, beginning, "There I was one up."

Sam listened patiently whilst Ronnie continued to insist Tabby should have suffered a penalty stroke for her unplayable ball which would have altered the result of the match. The major problem was that Tabby in her knee length shorts, leaving vulnerable bare legs, had not dared pick up the ball surrounded by the adder, even to prove it was definitely her ball.

"Problems of an 'outside agency'," joked Sam, trying to lighten the atmosphere by using the golf rules' term often featured humorously in P G Wodehouse's golf stories. This should appeal to Ronnie, even if her grey hair was simply due to the current fashion for being natural, she must be well over sixty. Alas not a bit of it.

"No such thing in the current rules," admonished Ronnie. Clearly pleased to catch out the younger woman, a slight smile played at the end of her wide mouth. "Now the term is an 'Outside Influence' and the adder did not influence the ball, if indeed it was an adder."

"We don't know that," said Tabby indignantly. "It happened before we got up the hill. Anyway it would have been dangerous for me to play it."

The thought of rule 16's "dangerous animal situation" reminded Sam of poor Monty tied up outside, though she guessed the dog-loving club members, most of whom knew Monty, would be making a fuss of him. Still she could not bring the conversation to an end, satisfactory or not. After quarter of an hour, she said how nice it was to catch up with Ronnie and they must have a game together.

"On neutral ground?" Chuckled Ronnie. "Not sure Elmsleigh Park's a safe place these days with all the other perils going on here as well as snakes."

Sam's mouth dropped open. What did she know about the two deaths? The way she eyed Sam suggested Ronnie might even know of Sam's involvement. Was she still in touch with Bill Chambers and if so, had Bill passed on information? "What do you mean?"

"Greg Burgess. I heard he'd died, happening I gather rather quickly after Yuri Leonov. I mean it's unusual isn't it? Two unexpected deaths happening so quickly one after the other."

Sam wondered how to respond. She did not want to be rude whilst Ronnie was a guest at Elmsleigh Park; nor did she want to encourage any further speculation. Yet, was it possible that Ronnie knew something useful? Guessing it would not take much to prod the outspoken guest into revealing anything, Sam sighed. "Two accidental deaths are a terribly sad coincidence."

"Accidental?" Queried Ronnie. "From what I knew of Greg, or Guy as he was once called, he was not the type to let accidents befall him."

"You knew him?" Sam suppressed a gape of surprise. How could this woman in her smart navy-blue cut-off trousers with the white shirt emblazoned with the smart emblem of the club to which she now belonged be acquainted with the scruffy man, attractive though he might have been to Sam. Then she realised before Ronnie admitted she had not known Greg well, that Ronnie, being the age she was and having lived in the area for decades, might have known the Reverend Burgess, Greg's father.

So it turned out. Moreover, though Ronnie did not admit it was through her former relationship with Bill Chambers, she let drop that she knew Greg had been turned down for membership at Elmsleigh Park because he had been so cocky about the bye laws. Without providing any clue how she knew about his death, she did mention she supposed his death might be connected with his being in what she called the "Secret Service" because that was what he said he wanted to do as a child.

With this and David Charlie's belief Yuri had been a spy ringing in her ears, Sam felt she could move on from Ronnie, the Elmsleigh Park opponent who might query the result of her match with Tabby, to the assertion Greg might have suffered for being a spy catcher, when she tackled Simon. He had to help her over this terrible accusation that she herself was involved in Greg's death.

Back she went into his office, having eventually escaped from Tabby and Ronnie, sighing at the thought of Monty waiting longer, but she needed Simon's help.

"Sorry to trouble you again," she said noticing him roll his brown eyes as he peered round his computer screen at her.

"Not at all," he said, "but could you put the rules issue to me in an email."

Sam nodded, "Yes, and I have to tell you that Tabby's opponent, Veronica Eustace, as she used to be, was once a member here, so she's known to some of our long-standing members, as well as being a referee."

The slight smirk on Simon's face suggesting the words *no worries* hovered on his lips, made Sam wonder whether he preferred to deal with older members than possibly tough younger ones. Before he could dismiss her concerns, she added, "And I must take you up on the views you expressed about women earlier. You are absolutely right: we are more vulnerable than men in many ways, one of which is gossip."

Obviously unaware of what she meant, he stared at her.

The problem was, she explained, that it was not simply that rumours were apparently going around the club that she was involved in Greg's death. Someone, reputedly a club member had informed the police she was in a relationship with the man, or wanted to have a love affair with him. She must emphasise this was completely false. No, she recoiled in horror at his instant suggestion; she did not want Simon to send out a communal email to all the club members making this denial, but he should know that there was no truth in it.

Simon agreed that he understood this. He believed Greg had been in a relationship with Helen McTavish.

Sam nodded, then went on to ask whether he also believed what his father, David Charlie, had said about Yuri being a spy whom Greg might possibly be watching.

"David's got a powerful imagination," said Simon, this time not denying the paternity reference, but adding in a detached ironic tone, "he's a great guy in many ways but frankly you're better off asking Helen McTavish anything you want to know about Greg."

Sam smiled in agreement. "Yes, but I've been to see her once already for condolence and I don't want to pester her. I suppose you couldn't help." She did not wish to spell it out but there was a competition coming up next week where playing partners were to be drawn. This list of which ladies were to play with each other in this competition had yet to be circulated. Presumably the draw for the teams of three had yet to be done.

Simon picked up her disguised request. Though secretary Heather should do the draw tomorrow, but he said, he would take the task off her hands to expedite matters.

She thanked him, worried, as she walked out of his office, whether she had been a fool to confide anything to him. Once outside the clubhouse door her concern left her. There was Monty ready to greet her, jumping up and licking her, not reproachful as he might have been left for so long, but growling with love.

He should protect her from Simon, or anyone else if need be, she comforted herself as she walked back across the park to reach her car. Sensing she was upset, she knew he would try to get on to the front seat next her so she strapped him on the back seat, telling herself she must not worry about gossip as she drove home. It could not damage her.

Nonetheless she could not get it out of her head so as soon as she was back in her little cottage, she went straight into the ground floor room she used for an office. She had barely sat down at the computer wondering what to research when it struck her she could find out the club where Ronnie belonged. Automatically her hand went to her computer mouse and within a trice she was on to the appropriate website where the competition was listed. There was the draw with the players named beside their clubs. Instantly Sam knew how Ronnie had acquired any current gossip about Greg Burgess. Her golf club had another ex-Elmsleigh Park member, the redoubtable Lady Julia Bravo, Helen McTavish's landlady.

Sam did not know any details of the divorce between Julia and Hector, but guessed it would not have been amicable. Her mouth twisted into a sardonic grin as she stared at the computer screen. Even if that parting were friendly Julia would be bound to enjoy dissing the dirt on the club she had left, especially as Hector would never have agreed to leave Elmsleigh. With his strong views over family privacy which he'd expressed about her family tree game, she could envisage his making Julia leave Elmsleigh as part of any divorce settlement.

No wonder Helen McTavish had been reluctant to discuss Greg in Julia's presence. Lucky Simon had clearly taken the hint about the draw for the next competition, so they would soon be playing together. It was amazing what could be drawn out of someone on the golf course.

23. An informative game

Helen eyed Sam suspiciously in the Ladies cloakroom whilst they changed their shoes on Wednesday morning. She was sitting on a bench only a few feet away from Sam, but apart from a terse morning greeting, it was obvious Helen was not happy about being awarded the privilege of playing with this year's Lady Captain.

As with any member who was bereaved, Helen should be treated gently with respect so normally the lady golfers would try to be of comfort. Unfortunately today their sympathy was in short supply because few ladies knew of her relationship with Greg. Some had known him only as a large scruffy interloper on the course.

There in the cloakroom on that bright sunny morning, it was clear most ladies were unaware Helen McTavish, their star young golfer, might be suffering emotionally. When they mentioned her name, or greeted her, the tendency was invariably to say what a great team Simon had drawn for the Lady Captain, who was not only playing with Helen, but whose third member was Crystal, thankfully as far as Sam was concerned, now an agreeable probationary member. Her promising play had already favourably impressed the older ladies, briefed by Sam not to look askance at anything she wore.

Crystal's presence meant Sam could speak about Greg more freely than she might in front of someone she did not know. Nonetheless, it would be best, she resolved, not to mention him until they were over half way round the course, which should take at least one and a half hours. She hoped that should allow time to get Helen into a relaxed mood, but it did not happen. Helen seemed impervious to the beauty of their surroundings, the views over the hills and the rolling farmland in the distance.

After the team of three had all struck their balls off the first tee, from which they played as privilege of being the Lady Captain's team, whilst everyone else had to walk to other starting points, Helen strode ahead. Though she helped look for Crystal's ball which was buried in some rough, she kept her head firmly down in front of her, conversing only about where the ball might have landed.

Sam wanted to tell her to lighten up which Helen obviously expected as she made clear after about half an hour's play. She apologised for her shots which flew all over the place, giving Sam and Crystal a lot of exercise walking around the grass and trees helping her look for the balls she hit.

"I just can't put Greg out of my mind," she said tersely to Sam as they walked along a path from the fifth to the sixth hole. "It's so horrible. I came out here deliberately to forget the wretched man, but I can't hit it away from myself."

"Perhaps it would help to talk," ventured Sam, who at that moment had stopped walking to write down her team's unsatisfactory single point scored by Crystal. She too was finding it difficult to concentrate on hitting the ball. "I can empathise with that. Think of the ball as someone's head you'd like to bash when you drive."

Helen strode on to the next teeing ground with a small wooden headed club in her hand. With a firm thrust she pushed a small white tee into the turf, took a couple of steps back and stuck out her bottom ferociously. Back

233

turned her body with her arms swinging with such fervour it looked as though she was throwing the club at the ball.

There was a resounding crack as the sweet spot on the club head's face smashed into the ball. Off it soared into the air. Over the green it went towards the bunker on the far side whilst the three players held their breaths expecting it to fly into the rough grass behind. Sad gasps followed when it touched the raised edge of the bunker knocking it back into the sand.

Helen dropped her club on the ground in disgust. "Ugh: that's an omen. I'll never get the better of them."

"Who's them?" asked Sam in a whisper as Crystal prepared to take her shot.

"You know, the gang," answered Helen out loud after Crystal had nervously driven her ball into another bunker alongside the green.

Sam could guess who she meant, but now it was her turn to drive and her responsibility not to let outside interests obstruct her game. She forbade herself to ask Helen to elaborate; instead she stepped briskly forward to hit her own ball. To her chagrin it dropped into the third bunker beside the green. Forcing a smile to hide her dismay, she made a crack about keeping team spirit which made Crystal chortle but Helen simply sighed.

Nonetheless with a powerful thrust of her iron club down into the bunker, Helen scooped her ball up in a cloud of sand to make it fall a couple of foot from the flag. After Sam and Crystal had both managed to extract their balls less successfully resulting in four shots each, Helen knocked hers nonchalantly into the hole for a three.

"There you are," laughed Crystal. "You can get the better of the gang, but let me know who they are so I can avoid them."

Sam winced. She did not want a conversation to proceed that way in Crystal's presence, knowing her view on certain club members. All local clubs wanted to recruit good young golfers with attractive personalities. They certainly did not want new younger lady members chatting to potential recruits about a nasty gang playing at Elmsleigh. She tried to suggest Helen was "Just joshing."

"Och no I wasn't." The fervour in Helen's voice accentuated her Scottish accent as she bent down to pick her ball out of the hole. Bending over to replace the flag pole with a firm shove, she added as she stood back up, "I'll be keeping out of the way of Hector Bravo and chums."

Sam looked at her in surprise. Whatever her own feelings about the Vice-Captain might be, she understood Hector was popular with the younger better players, male or female, whom he was anxious to promote in the interests of the club.

Yet she still found it bizarre Hector, who had been so suspicious of David Charlie that he'd asked The Old Alresford Agency to investigate him, should have wanted him included in the recent, though possibly fatal informal get-together for Vladimir Leonov. Sam supposed she should take it as a compliment her research's results assuaged Hector's suspicion.

The strange side of this was David Charlie's suspicions of Yuri's activities, saying he was a spy. Was he right? Sam wondered as she pictured the fake lumps of antimony disguising recording equipment and even possibly cameras. Presumably Yuri was one of the chums Helen referred to as associated with Hector?

Tossing the images around in her mind she did not recall seeing them playing together or sitting around drinking together, but her impression was that Hector was not involved with any specific group at the club. "What's the problem with him?"

"Need you ask?" Helen tossed her red curls as she heaved her bag of golf clubs on to her back.

Sam shook her head as she walked along beside her, remembering that Helen was the tenant of Hector's ex-wife. She would be bound to be the recipient of all sorts of undesirable information about the in-coming Captain, some of which was probably exaggerated. Better not to mention Julia after that row when she visited. Instead she tried to alleviate the situation by saying, "I gather he was very attached to his godson."

"Not much God about it."

"What do you mean?"

"Julia always talks of Greg as Hector's nephew. She can't understand why he didn't make more effort to give him a home." She glanced into the distance in the direction of the groundsmen's huts as she plonked her bag down beside the next tee before she took out her driver to hit her ball.

"You mean Greg was actually lived in that shed, not only staying there occasionally?" Sam spoke the moment Helen had smashed her ball straight down the fairway."

"That's right. Some of the time he was with me of course, but Julia wasn't going to have him at her home when she reckoned her ex should be making more effort to house his own flesh and blood. I couldn't explain to her Greg wanted to watch that shed. He made a terrific effort to get friendly with Yuri because he wanted to prove he was a spy. I told him it was rubbish, but he wouldn't believe me until Yuri died. Then he got frightfully upset thinking he'd made a terrible mistake." Helen bit her lip as though to prevent herself from saying anything more.

Despite this information whizzing round her mind, Sam managed to restrain herself from questioning Helen further whilst she concentrated on her own game as well as being encouraging to Crystal, whose alert expression suggested she took in more of their conversation than Sam would have liked. Hence it was Crystal who observed that he must have been Hector's sister's child.

Helen said Julia only mentioned a brother, but she wouldn't ask her anything more about Greg ever again   It was too upsetting, so much so that she was going to move away from West Meon as well as out of Julia's house.

Sam said that would be a pity. Living near the lovely old village of West Meon, she started to defend the area. It was so peaceful and rural with wonderful historic connections.

That made Helen snort so much in indignation that she tossed her next shot into some nearby bushes. "That's it; they're not connections I want. Can't look at the church, but I have to hear it when the bells ring."

Her playing partners looked after her in surprise as she dropped another ball to hit, saying she was not even going to look for the missing one. After she slaughtered it away into the distance, she said through the pursed lips of her usually prettily shaped mouth that it was the church which was too reminiscent of the Burgess family.

"What on earth do you mean?" Crystal's forehead knotted in puzzlement as she watched Helen toss her club back into her bag. "How is the church involved with the Burgess family."

"Don't ask," muttered Helen crossly. Heaving her bag of clubs on to her back, she walked briskly forward.

"What does she mean?" Crystal asked Sam in a whisper as she joined her to walk into the long rough grass to look for her own ball.

Sam shrugged as she said she didn't know, but clearly now was not the time to question Helen further. She resolved herself though to go straight after the game, to West Meon church on her way back home to find out what the connection was.

Though her own home in Steep was a few miles from West Meon, she had never visited the famous old church there, despite her late husband having talked about it. As far as he had been concerned, the most interesting fact about it was the presence of Thomas Lord, the founder of Lords cricket ground who was buried there. A lump in her throat rose as she drove towards the village. Together they had never made the pilgrimage to the church that he wanted to do. She had then thought it would be rather boring, an activity which should be reserved for old age, a destination her soldier husband, lost or dying in foreign fields, never reached.

Now as she drove through the pretty rural village of West Meon, past the turning to the Thomas Lord pub, named after the great man, to go up a narrow hill road towards the church, she mentally said sorry With cars parked along the hillside, the road was narrow and she nearly missed the entrance to the church. With a quick lurch of the steering wheel, she turned into a short gravel drive leading to a parking area alongside the church.

Having parked and alighted from her car she stared open-mouthed around the three sides of the building. The church was almost encircled by a magnificent grave yard, although yard was the wrong word for this beautifully kept grassy garden.

What on earth was Helen's objection to this beautiful church?

This must be it, a grave, some sort of presence here. Sam shivered as she walked tentatively into the grounds feeling a chill as she looked at all the different grey gravestones. If only she had gone home first, she could have put on some comfortable warm trousers.

It would have been comforting to collect Monty too. Strolling through the cemetery, were a couple of dog walkers who looked much less unnerved than she felt. Presumably, unlike Helen, they did not have a deathly connection with the church.

It must be a grave. Again it hit her as she wended her way slowly amongst the large grey stones. Many were so ancient the inscriptions carved on them were barely readable. Others more recently erected had such poignant laments for the departed on them that Sam had to steel herself against emoting herself. She was thankful to see others with pretty flowers decorating the stone markers.

As she looked at the various graves, she tried to work out a pattern as to why they were in one place or another, but found it hard to establish in terms of dates. The most recent graves were not necessarily the nearest or furthest from the church. Her brows knitted as she stood moving from one foot to another trying to work out how to proceed with her search for a Burgess grave.

Possibly sensing she needed help or simply scenting Monty's residue on the flesh of her legs beneath her knee length trousers, a brown and white spaniel ran over to Sam followed by an apologetic owner. "So sorry," she said, "but Coco's a rescue dog. I'm not sure whether she's worked out she's ours now, or just wants to help people in trouble." She hesitated. "Are you okay?"

Sam made herself laugh rather than cry before halting herself as she realised the elderly lady in her long floral skirt and billowy white top might think she was bereaved. "Sorry. How kind of you to be concerned. I'm afraid I'm just puzzling over where I can find a particular grave. I gather the Burgess family are here somewhere."

The old lady nodded, the white curls on her head waving in the wind as she turned to point to a grave a couple of rows away. "There."

Heavens. I must have walked right past it. Sam gaped as her eyes followed the wrinkled forefinger. "Thank you so much. I'll take a look."

The old lady led the way in between the various graves until they reached a long wide oblong shaped grave with a large stone cross on three plinths at one end. There

Sam read the names of the Burgess parents, wondering where their renegade son, the spy Guy could be before she spotted a small stone urn standing at the other end of the grave.

"That's Guy Burgess's ashes in there," said the old lady. "Initially people didn't want his remains back and I think refused to have him, but minds got changed and so there he is now."

A strange emotion swept over Sam. "That's good," she found herself saying with fervour. "He must have wanted to be rehabilitated for people to make the effort to get him back."

"I suppose so," the old lady pursed her lips. "If you're a Christian, you believe in forgiveness."

Hard to know how to reply to that. It was a long time since Sam had been to church.

"His family lived here," continued the old lady. Tall and thin she stood up very straight with her arm in the air to raise again her gnarled forefinger to point down the hill. "There's a large white house they used to live in down there. You'll see it if you go out of the village that way."

"Yes, yes thanks," said Sam, thinking as she stroked the bouncy Coco, that she herself must get back to Monty whom she'd left alone for far too long today.

With a brief further thanks to the old lady she started to walk back to her parked car. Her legs felt shaky, but it wasn't from her round of golf. She had learnt so much in the last few minutes. Greg, the other Guy Burgess, might not be related to his namesake, the notorious spy, other than sharing his name. Yet somehow, even without a definitive connection, Sam now understood what Helen felt.

Here was a world she was not part of. Whether or not the router and cable equipment in the shed belonged to Greg to reconnoitre a spy or for some innocent hobby, Sam could not judge, but she understood why Helen would not wish to be involved with it. The Scottish lass clearly did not believe Greg was a drug addict responsible for his own death, suicide or otherwise. Helen did not want her unfortunate involvement with him to bring her any more grief, or worse danger to herself.

Getting into her car to drive away from the majestic church Sam wished she could do likewise. Her non golfing friends would say she was mad not to walk away. She knew that but she could not. Ridiculous though others might consider her loyalty, she felt she owed it to her fellow club members to fathom what was going wrong. Never mind Nicholas Roman. It was her role to make sure the club was properly run and members were safe.

She must find out what really happened to Greg and Yuri, two men she suspected who know too much about something. Both were unfinished business, especially Greg with whom, she could hardly believe Laurie had suggested it, she herself was in the frame for his unexpected death, possibly murder.

24. A meeting with Julia

Back at home Sam got out a packet of plain cards. She had so many random bits of information, she felt she needed to write them all down on different pieces of paper before she arranged them in front of her on her kitchen table. Then as she sipped a cup of coffee, she could move the pieces around to see if she could see anything tangential.

She did not finish writing the cards before she decided she needed to see Julia Bravo again. From what Helen had said that afternoon, Julia evidently had known Greg far longer than Helen. She also understood the Elmsleigh Park scene, even if her knowledge was limited because she left the club before Simon became secretary or the arrival of David Charlie skulking around the Visitors carpark. Nonetheless it was possible she'd known Yuri who had been a club member for many years.

How to contact her was the problem. Sam did not have a phone number for Helen's lodgings since Helen only used her mobile phone for her friends. Then it hit her. Ronnie or rather Veronica Eustace, the lady who had played that match against Tabby should know Julia Bravo's number, or how to contact her by email, since they belonged to the same club. She could simply ask Tabby how she arranged her match with Ronnie, but with Tabby being Hector's second wife, she would rather not ask her directly about Julia. Since, by a bizarre coincidence, she had just picked up her mouse to start a search when Tabby herself rang to arrange a game, Sam was able to ask her immediately how to contact Ronnie.

Prising Julia's number out of Ronnie was more of a problem, but turned out not to be insuperable, once Sam assured Ronnie she was not acting as any sort of agent for Julia's ex-husband Hector. Remembering how Julia had told her about the belladonna growing at Elmsleigh and understanding Helen, her lodger's passion for wild flowers, Sam managed to assure Ronnie she wanted to tap Julia's brain about horticulture.

"You'll have to come and see me at the garden centre," Julia told her. "It's easier to be there if you want to talk about plants."

Much easier, agreed Sam, especially as Julia said she could bring Monty.

She told herself she was not actually being dishonest, since she did want to talk about a plant, although deadly nightshade, even calling it belladonna, was not one she thought would be likely to be on sale at a garden centre. Turning in from the country lane outside the town of Petersfield Sam's first thought was that she must have come to the wrong place for Peggy's Shack.

The name seemed so inappropriate considering the size and smart style of the place. Even the couple of additional one storey structures alongside the main garden centre did not look like shacks, although one, which had something like Iron Merchant labelled on its door, was much more utilitarian looking. Alongside this was a scruffy area where half a dozen skips stood, a couple of which were over-loaded with ironmongery. There were also two smashed up cars.

Sam parked her small red car, one of the few Minis amongst a bevy of mainly dark-coloured or silver four by fours in the spacious well laid-out carpark. Whatever one kept hearing about the demise of shopping in the High Street, this place was obviously doing well, she reflected as she let Monty leap joyfully off the back seat to trot alongside her until they arrived at the main vast wooden building when he tried to drag her off to the scrap metal shack. There must have been some enticing scent next door, for Monty, now attached to his lead still tried to pull her sideways, even while Sam pushed open the main entrance door.

Inside a bewildering variety of products was on sale. In one corner there were even casual clothes, whilst in another, crockery. This smart respectable shop did not seem quite the right place to discuss a poisonous weed. To Sam's relief, she did not have to raise the subject; the words belladonna or atropa did not have to drop from her lips because Julia said them first.

She invited Sam to join her for a coffee, leading the way to the far end of the large wooden building where the different sections were all to do with various aspects of gardening. As they passed pots of vegetables, herbs and a vast array of colourful bedding plants standing on tables and benches, Julia remarked in her sardonic upper-class tone, "I don't suppose any of this is of great interest to you."

"No, no, I mean yes, yes," said Sam. "It helps me with the big picture."

"I understand," Julia nodded as she ushered Sam into the café where they made their way to a counter at one end of the room to order coffee and some homemade shortbread biscuits. "These are perfectly safe."

"I would hope so," joked Sam back, biting into one, once they had sat down at a small table in the most secluded corner of the room.

"And so is atropine taken in very small doses when it is needed."

Sam nodded. She had investigated it on the web. "Yes, I understand it's present in various vegetables like aubergines too. What I don't understand is how anyone would take it recreationally. I mean, do you sell it here?"

"As seeds yes. We can't be responsible for what people do with what they buy here. Anyway, belladonna, that's the deadly nightshade plant, grows wild in certain places, even at Elmsleigh Park."

"But how would someone take it as a drug? Would you smoke the seeds or what?"

Julia frowned as she sipped her coffee. She put down her cup and waved her large hands, which though brown speckled, looked well-manicured for a gardener, as she spoke. "I don't know." She shrugged her shoulders. "I assume it would be used like alcohol rather than nicotine. People used to use it as a medicine so I suppose a user would make the berries into a drink."

Sam had to stop herself burping in astonishment that she had not thought of that herself. She swallowed mouthful of coffee quickly. Of course, that would be the way Greg consumed the deadly nightshade, but what on earth made an intelligent man who presumably understood plants, since he now worked with them, drink enough to kill himself?

"Apparently the belladonna berries taste like blackcurrant," Julia informed her.

246

"Blackcurrant!" Sam exclaimed aghast. A picture formed in her mind of the party for Vladimir Leonov that Hector had arranged for them all to toast friendship with the Russian by drinking Vodka and Blackcurrant juice. "I might have drunk it."

Julia gazed at her, pulling her lower lip across her white even teeth in an exaggerated expression of disbelief, "You, surely not?"

"Well your ex was offering it at a party he gave the other day."

"Ho ho," Julia chortled, blowing down her nose. "He knows what he's doing when it comes to wine. He's a grown man for goodness sake; he would be hardly likely to offer any guests Ribena."

"No it wasn't Ribena. It was actually blackcurrant juice we were drinking the day before Greg died of Atropine poisoning. Hector made a cocktail of it with Vodka because that was the tipple, or meant to be, that Alexei Leonov celebrated after his first walk in space, with Tom Stafford, the American astronaut."

"Bit inappropriate now Yuri Leonov's dead to be celebrating something," commented Julia sardonically.

Sam sighed as she launched into an explanation of how Hector felt fences needed to be mended with Vladimir after the way he had been treated at the "On my Family Tree" party.

"Yes, he would," nodded Julia, "he's so couth like that."

Presuming she must mean the opposite of uncouth, Sam raised her eyebrows in mock surprise, biting back the retort that Hector could turn on the charm when he liked, but it didn't alter the strange coincidence that most of them drank blackcurrant juice, so similar looking to the juice of the deadly nightshade, the day before Greg died.

"So where were you drinking this blackcurrant juice and vodka?" Asked Julia.

"At Elmsleigh Park, on the terrace. It was just an informal gathering."

Julia shrugged. "Weren't the drinks laid on by the bar staff?"

"No, I don't think so, although they were serving." Sam's face wrinkled as a picture came into her mind of seeing Greg on the terrace waving to her on the eighteenth hole, then suddenly turning away to talk to someone arriving at the table. She thought she remembered that was Hector, who carried a box or something with him. Hard to remember now so much had happened since then. By the time she arrived at the party Simon was helping to pour drinks, assisted by Misty or Rollo, the duty bar man who periodically turned up to help.

Then there was the offering of borscht, that Russian soup, which Ekaterina said was the real thing we should all be drinking because at the occasion itself there hadn't been any vodka to drink in space."

"Space," chortled Julia. Her wide mouth, lips covered with bright pink lipstick, dropping open to reveal perfect white teeth.

Sam nodded then recounted the story of the incident Hector had related about when Alexie Leonov, the Russian astronaut, supposedly related to Yuri, had met British astronauts in space and entertained then with borscht.

"Does borscht usually contain blackcurrant?" Sam asked to Julia's mirth.

Julia shook her head. "Not that I know. You'll have to ask Ekaterina. I thought it was mainly beetroot and potato, although I suppose some cooks would add herbs and other stuff to it."

Surprised at the mention of Ekaterina, Sam drained the last drops of coffee in her cup, "Do you know the Leonovs then?"

Again Julia threw open her brown speckled hands as she spoke, "Of course I do; she's a co-owner of this place; in actual fact she owns next door."

"What? How did that happen?"

Now Julia stared back at Sam in disbelief. "You mean you didn't know the Leonovs ran a business here?"

"No. What is it?"

"Scrap metal of course. They use one of the other buildings."

"I see," Sam joked. "I wondered why this place wasn't called Peggy's Shacks rather than Shack." Noting the lack of humour in Julia's reaction, she added, "Who is Peggy anyway?"

"Was," corrected Julia puffing some air out of the side of her mouth. "My mother-in-law died over ten years ago."

"Before Ekaterina, or I suppose Yuri, got involved here?"

"About the same time. We had started expanding then. More garden centres were getting started around here and we needed to develop our business." She looked at the flower decorated pottery coffee cups on the table as she added, "We wanted get a good refreshment place going and add more luxury products."

"How did Peggy feel about this?"

"Not very happy. She didn't like change." Julia's lips went down at the corners as she said, "Older people tend not to. Peggy was sentimental about the family business staying the family business. That's why she put up with me being involved, because I am the mother of her grandchild who she hoped would keep the Shack going."

"You didn't get on with her?"

"I tried but she never liked me; she thought I was a baby snatcher, stealing her son."

"But," Sam wondered how to continue. As she stared at the woman the other side of the table, she realised she was looking at someone who might be up to ten years or more, older than Hector Bravo. With her finely coloured wavy dark blonde hair framing her oval unwrinkled face, Julia could be any age from late fifties to seventy whereas Hector, judging from his appearance, fitness and strength, was probably mid-fifties, sixty at the oldest. She did know he was much older than her friend Tabby, his second wife, who was only in her early forties.

"But she still wanted you to work here?"

"I told you, she put up with it."

"What about your father-in-law? Was he interested in gardening too?"

Julia suddenly pursed her lips as she reached for the tray on which she had carried their drinks and biscuits. "Why do you want to know about him?" She asked suspiciously. "As it happened, he wasn't remotely interested in gardening, not that he had much chance since he was abroad most of his working life."

Sam wanted to ask what he did, but felt she was unlikely to get an answer. It looked as though Julia felt she'd told her everything necessary and would not give away anything more now she was packing up the cups and saucers. With Monty stirring restlessly under the table, now Sam reckoned clearly the time had come to move on, she asked, "Would you mind if I took Monty to look inside that metal place next door? There's obviously something inside that's intriguing him and I've never been inside somewhere like that."

"Don't ask me," said Julia, standing up with the tray, filled with their empty crockery. "I don't have anything to do with running it." She took a step towards the serving bar, then looked back over her shoulder. "I hope you've got what you wanted. They don't have any plants next door or anything to sell. It's not a retail outlet."

Sam stood up, pulling a relieved Monty out from half under the table where he had been lying, obviously uncomfortably cramped. "Was that why your late mother-in-law objected to it."

"No, she wasn't keen on the Leonovs. She didn't like the fact they were Russian, or Hector's friendship with them."

"Why was that?"

Julia hesitated, frowning, obviously wondering whether she wanted to tell more about her family. Then she shrugged, nearly letting the cups and saucers fall off the tray as she moved, but somehow managed to hold on to the lot as she started singing in a lilting voice:

"How many kinds of sweet flowers grow
 In an English country garden
We'll tell you now of some that we know
Those we miss you'll surely pardon."

As she paused, whether for breath, or because she didn't know the next verse, Sam said, "I get the picture. Peggy didn't like her son's international outlook."

Julia nodded her head in agreement before shaking it as she twisted her lips to speak. "No, Peggy said it was what made her ill, that and the thought of old cars being left to be dismantled next door. Anyway, I must get on, but you go over there and see what you think."

As though he had understood the conversation, the moment they were through the door, Monty pulled Sam towards the scrap metal shed. He even pawed the right door for Sam to push open.

Scrap metal? Presumably that's where people take stolen catalyst converters. And this place is now owned by Vladimir Leonov who's often around Elmsleigh Park where he used to be a member. No wonder the police think he could be involved. But are they right?

25. Lunch with Julia

At first glance it was hard to see what attracted Monty here. Inside was a medley of tables with different odd-looking machinery parts, some simply lying on top and others on stands. There were also boxes of crushed cans and others full of heavier items some of which looked like bathroom taps. Then she spotted the reason. Kyle, the handyman who helped the dog sitting agency she used, as well at the golf club, always made a fuss of Monty when they met him on the course, was there, at a counter in a back corner. He was talking to a man in a uniform overall with Alex Iron written on it.

Sam pulled Monty close to her as she crept up near the counter to hear what Kyle was saying.

The words of the counter assistant shook her. He was shaking his head as he spoke. "No we definitely can't do any more cats."

Could he possibly mean the animals? No, of course not here. It must be a nickname for another sort of cat. Sam's mouth dropped open as the thought of a catalyst converter struck her.

"What's the problem?" Asked Kyle.

"Your boss has told us absolutely not."

"My boss?" Queried Kyle in a tone of disbelief. "Don't have one. Who d'you mean?"

"Mr Roman; he's told us we're not to touch those converters. There's too many disappeared from a local golf club and caused upset. he wants us to help put a stop to it."

"Mr Roman is not my boss. I don't have one but Mr Reynolds, he told me he'd be taking over here or helping out as he put it. That Mr Norman's throwing his weight about 'cos people say he's friends of the Duke of York or that he's royalty, but I say he's conning you."

"That's as maybe, but he's got some clout here, knowing my boss, the one we've got now and we don't want to upset him. Vladimir's temperamental enough over his father's death."

Sam put her hand down on to Monty's jaw to stop him barking at Kyle or rushing forward to greet him as he turned around to walk out of the shed. Under his arm was a dirty black cylindrical metal object which looked oily.

Presumably that was a catalyst converter.

She knew one way to discover. Bending down to place Monty's lead quietly on the floor where she could step on it, with her usual deft action, she whipped her mobile out of her pocket to photograph Kyle with the black object he carried, praying he would not turn around and see her. From the sound of his conversation with the shop assistant, Kyle would surely be suspicious of Sam's motives for being here if he saw her.

Was this where the stolen converters came to be stripped down? It seemed likely, especially as the current owner, the cashier, shop assistant or whoever it was behind the counter mentioned Vladimir Leonov. As Yuri's son here in the UK, he would presumably inherit this business, if he was not a part owner already. He must be the man whom Laurie had been indiscreet enough to hint the police suspected of the catalyst converter thefts.

254

Had they tracked down a stolen converter to this scrap iron business? Could they identify a particular car's *converter?* Surely not. No, any conclusion drawn by the police must be the result of that incident at the unfortunate social occasion she had organised. She drew a sharp intake of breath between her teeth. It would have arisen because Vladimir left the club before everyone else, making a threat, after which the President's converter disappeared.

Sam shook herself. *Better not go there.* Converters were not her business now. Or were they? Nicholas Roman who was unfortunately now involved her employment still wanted them investigated. Was that why he'd involved himself in this place? Seemed unlikely he'd get involved in a racket like converter theft.

A more likely candidate was surely Ozzie Reynolds. He was in the jewellery business, sponsoring designers so it might pay him to be able to point to a source of platinum, gold and whatever other precious metals could be extracted from converters. He had also been a friend, plus a former business associate of Yuri Leonov.

Distracted by her thoughts, she did not notice Monty pull the notch out of his lead's extension to bound up to Kyle who had turned his back on the trade counter to walk back through the store past her.

He stopped to pat Monty, then lifted his head up to give her a friendly smile, "Hiya."

"Kyle," she greeted him back as she wound Monty's lead back, and asked before she could stop herself, "What are you doing here?"

He laughed. "I might ask you the same question." His smile widened as he indicated the black cylindrical object under his arm. "Friend of mine wrote his car off in a smash, but before it was towed away to the knackers, he had the nous to get this out."

"I see," Sam smiled back in embarrassment, yet thinking at the same time here was an opportunity to chat to Kyle who would have known Greg. "Actually I came here to visit next door to talk about Greg Burgess. I expect you know they say he killed himself with an overdose of atropine, from deadly nightshade berries. The plants grow at Elmsleigh, and I wanted to get some expert advice about it from someone who knew about plants."

"Yes of course," agreed Kyle amiably, nodding his ginger head. "Greg used to work here before he got involved in plants."

"Really?" *Of course. I should have guessed that.* "You mean when he was a scrap metal dealer."

Kyle shrugged. "That's right. Not that he knew much about metal, any more than he knew about plants. Sad really. Can't think why, but he was always trying to get away from being a posh boy."

"Presumably he came here because his uncle owned the place next door, Peggy's Shack?"

Again Kyle's shoulders lifted. "I doubt that; he didn't get on with his uncle." He swung round to point to an old man working a machine in the corner of the barn. "Ask Sid. He's been here off and on for ever and a day; he can tell you." He waved as he turned back to walk away.

Sam made her way over to a small bald elderly man who, despite looking as though he might be in his eighties, was handling a large iron object which looked like a giant pair of scissors on a stand. He appeared to be cutting through a vast lumpy sheet of metal. "Hello there. Can I have a word with you?" She asked.

With his gnarled hands still pushing a lever down to push the big blades of the scissors together, he glanced up at her, "What do you want?"

"I just wondered if you could spare a minute to tell me about Greg Burgess."

"What about him?" The old man's hands now hesitated on the handle of the cutters.

"Unfortunately," she swallowed a gulp that rose in her throat, "he's died on the grounds of our golf club at Elmsleigh Park and as I'm Captain there," she stressed the word, "I've been asked to find out a bit about him so we can understand how it happened." She left out the Lady. The age of this guy meant he would be far more likely to reveal something if he thought she ran the whole show.

The old man snorted as he took both hands off the lever he was operating. "Well you'd better ask his uncle then. He belongs to that there club."

"Do you mean Hector Bravo?"

"Robert or Hector or whatever he calls himself now."

"What do you mean? What else would he be called?"

"Bobby like he used to be when he came to his mum's shed as a nipper."

"But what was his other name, his surname?"

"I dunno. Peg liked being called English like her mum, Bobby's grandma, who gave her the dosh to start this place."

"Surely all that was long before this side of the business existed."

"Yes." Sid nodded. "That's right; I worked for Peg as a gardener here when Bobby was a nipper, then they went away for a long while whist Peg's husband worked abroad, and there was a manager looking after the place. Peg always came back regular to see how things were going, only we didn't see the rest of the family, not 'til they growed up."

"So Hector didn't grow up here?"

"Bobby, nah and when he did come back, he was different, gone all posh, especially after he married that there Julia, coming down from London with her fancy ideas. She sacked me the moment Peg died, when she took over the garden centre."

"How did you manage to get back working here?"

Sid tapped his forehead with fingers. "Not what you know, it's who you know and when that there Russian took on people who knew I could make myself useful and keep mum if necessary, they got hold of me."

"Did Hector, I mean Robert, introduce Greg?"

"Don't think so. I heard he just turned up one day." The old chap laughed. "Said he thought he might be useful because he could speak Russian to the boss."

Picking up on what Kyle suggested, Sam asked, "Wasn't he any good?"

The old man shrugged his shoulders, "He picked things up after a while but he was too educated," he blew down his small wide nose, "if you know what I mean. He didn't have a clue about using his hands. All he wanted to do was to talk Russian to Mr Leonov when he turned up."

"Wasn't that useful?"

"No. Mr Leonov, Yuri as he wanted us to call him, spoke better English than Greg did Russian and there's not much use for poetry in a place like this." Sid's wide thin lips spread into a grin. "But Greg's a nice enough bloke and he got the hang of it in the end and then he buggered off next door. Now if you don't mind, I'd better get on." His hands went back on the large lever of the giant scissors to thrust down onto the metal he was cutting.

"Not at all. Thanks anyway." Sam walked back through the barn to the exit.

Could Hector have started life as Robert Burgess? She mused. *That explains why he was* so *unhappy about the "On my family tree" game. He did not want to admit anyone called Bravo was nothing to do with him.* But why did he change his name? Presumably for the same reason as his nephew: he did not want people asking if he were any relation of the former spy Guy Burgess. *Yet that seems a bit neurotic.* Plenty of respectable people are called Burgess – respectable burger's what the name means.

Sam wrinkled her nose as she hurried towards her car since it had started to rain. Unless Hector, whose profession was listed on the sheet Laurie had given her as "Civil Servant", with "Home Office" scrawled by the side, *actually works for MI5?*

One person here should know the answer; that was Julia Bravo.

Sam stopped in her tracks. She looked over her shoulder back at the main garden centre barn where they had coffee, then down at the small gold watch her missing husband had given her. It was only half past twelve so Julia should still be there working. It would be awkward to disturb her again, but maybe something else would work. She could ask her if she would like to pop out for a bite of lunch. Rather to Sam's surprise, when she unearthed her in a small office at the back of the barn, Julia agreed she would like to have a short break outside the business.

At Julia's suggestion they went to café attached to the nineteenth century naturalist Gilbert White's house. To Sam's joy, Julia said she was pretty sure they would admit Monty in the eating area because it was separate from the kitchen where the food was prepared.

Sam's only regret about the café as opposed to a pub was that Julia would be less easily tempted to drink a glass of wine which could help loosen her tongue to release any inhibitions she might have about betraying her ex-husband.

With the excuse of the dog being with them, who might disturb other customers, Sam chose a table in a corner, which meant their conversation should not be overheard. As they munched the quiche and salad which Julia had recommended as being a "particularly good" choice here, Sam wondered how to move their conversation from the quality of food sourced locally, on to the identity of Julia's erstwhile husband.

"Have you ever thought of expanding the garden centre further into food, I mean like turning the café into a restaurant."

Julia almost shuddered as she shook her head. "No, no, I couldn't cope with that. Cakes and biscuits are fine because we buy them in, but once you start trying to cook on the premises, you run into all sorts of aggro."

Failure there, thought Sam. Somehow she must move on to Hector, so she ploughed on by asking whether Hector had any input into the affairs of his mother's business these days, finishing by saying, "Presumably he still has an investment in Peggy's Shack?"

"Yes, but he doesn't take any interest in the business. He handed the lot to me when we split up."

"Wouldn't you think of changing the name, now you've expanded so much?"

Julia laughed. "You're suggesting Julia's barn might sound more appropriate."

"Or Lady Bravo's Barn," said Sam in as jovial tone as she could muster. "That could sound upmarket."

"Yeah well, I might not always be Lady Bravo if I marry again."

"What about your children?"

"Our son is not remotely interested in this business."

That figured. Tabby, as Hector's current wife, said her stepson rarely came back to Hampshire.

"I suppose that's why Hector got Greg involved." Sam's heart pounded at the memory of the man.

"No, no." Jabbing her fork into the quiche, Julia sawed into it as she spoke. "Greg was at a loose end. He didn't know what to do with himself when he failed to get into MI5 and MI6, I believe, and then the Foreign Office,

261

so he just turned up here out of the blue. I hadn't a clue who he was. Nor did Hector. He hardly recognised him."

"Seems odd he should want to be involved in scrap metal."

"That was because he had a degree in languages and spoke Russian, so with Yuri Leonov putting a lot of money into the business, virtually owning it, Greg thought his Russian might be useful."

"And was it?"

Julia laughed. "Heavens no. Greg could quote poems and bits of Tolstoy but his knowledge of nuts and bolts was pretty limited, although," she finished sadly, "he was a nice boy."

"Sounds as though he didn't have the right temperament for the Home Office like his uncle. I suppose Greg changed his name from Guy because he wanted to work there and Guy Burgess might not have gone down well, especially if it was the secret services. Was that why Hector changed his name from Burgess to Bravo?"

Julia shrugged nonchalantly. She wrinkled her nose as she asked, "Who on earth told you that?"

"An old man in the scrap metal yard said something on those lines when I asked him about the history of the place."

"Oh Sid, he doesn't know what he's talking about most of the time. The old fellow's got a touch of dementia."

"He seemed pretty lucid and he was using a cutting machine. Is that safe if he's a bit nuts?"

"He can remember what to do all right. The muscle memory is okay, it's just people's names that get him confused. I expect he was thinking about some boyfriend of Peggy's. She was separated from Hector's father but she kept her maiden name for business anyway because it worked better for her. Her favourite song was 'In an English country garden' because her name was English."

Sam had finished her quiche and eaten as much of the salad as she wanted, but she started to pick at another bit of lettuce. She must prolong this meal to get the information she wanted. In desperation she tried to think of a different tack to try. Then it came to her.

"I know you said you didn't get on with her, but it must have been useful to have a mother-in-law in the flower business for special occasions like christenings or weddings, though I suppose you did the flowers yourself for your own wedding."

"No, as a matter of fact, she did them and though I don't like to admit it, she did make that beautiful old Selbourne church look glorious."

Caught you. At last she had the reference she wanted. As soon as she had dropped Julia back at Peggy's shack, she would go to Selbourne to see what name Hector had supplied for the registry. Now she could drop the awkward subjects and make polite social conversation for the rest of the meal to establish a friendly relationship.

This did not happen easily as Julia's hackles had been roused. She declined Sam's offer of a pudding, having previously said how much she enjoyed the café's deserts. Rather grudgingly agreed to have a coffee since

263

Sam said she thought she needed one and Sam was driving her back to work. Her suspicions of Sam seemed to have been roused again by Sam's sudden good humour.

However the ease with which Sam expected now to discover proof of Hector's name change proved to be a harder job that she anticipated. The vital information she needed, Julia Bravo's maiden name, she had omitted to get. Nor did she have the wedding date, she realised as she popped up the road to St Marys, the beautiful old church that afternoon.

Once inside the ancient church with its beautiful stained glass window featuring St Francis surrounded by beautiful depictions of every bird Sam had ever seen or heard, Sam realised it did not matter that the door to what might be the registry office was locked. When people signed the church register, as she had done, it was merely a tradition, marriages these days would be logged on line.

As she drove home with Monty dozing in the back, she groaned at the prospect of crunching through the number of Robert Burgesses who might be married to Julia someone.

26. A Shoplifting Incident

What a relief. Today was Tuesday, Sam's regular in store detection day. Often she thought of it as rather a boring, mundane duty day, but today she welcomed time without thinking about Elmsleigh Park. That included thoughts about Greg's and Yuri's death, which some instinct told her were connected. Today she would be free of it all. Or so she thought.

There was no Monty to distract her; he was with Crystal who enjoyed his company, saying he helped her adapt to the housewifely part of her current life style. She had to get him looked after because she was going to be out longer than usual. The town department store near Winchester where she was going to work was not one of her usual venues. It was, Laurie warned her, on high alert, because there was currently a spate of shop-lifting in the town. That was encouraging because it meant she would be busy, on the lookout all the time for wandering fingers moving things from shelves into capacious shopping bags.

To her surprise and consternation she might have missed something, her first few hours in the store were uneventful. The only people she saw looked like extremely respectable Hampshire matrons. They might have been golfers, she reflected. Thankfully she did not recognise any of them until, after her coffee break, she returned from the toilet to see Ekaterina.

There she stood, with a capacious shopping bag, looking rather bemused as an attractive young woman dashed up to speak to her. "I cannot find the tee shirt to put back on the shelf."

Help. Sam's first instinct was to hide before Ekaterina spotted her to ask for assistance, for that was what she was surely likely to do.

Already the situation was escalating. A short stocky man with a round face, whom Sam recognised as the store manager, stood behind the shop assistant. His mouth was pursed in a hard line as he concentrated on the dialogue between the two women.

"It was on the counter, no?" Asked Ekaterina.

"No," repeated the young shop assistant, speaking with a slight accent, which sounded possibly Eastern European. "It is not there. Have you got it?"

"I know not," said Ekaterina in a puzzled tone. Then, as the store manager stepped forward and the assistant eyed her carrier bag, Ekaterina opened it, to pull out the tee shirt in a transparent wrapping. She picked it out and handed it to the assistant.

At this juncture, the store manager stepped forward. "You are lucky you had not left the store or we would have called the police."

Ekaterina stared at him as he added, "You are banned from this store." Then, seeing Sam lurking nearby, he beckoned to her. "Take this woman's photo so we can put her on our list."

"I will," said Sam, "but I know this lady and I'm sure it is all an unfortunate accident."

"Do as you are asked," growled the store manager.

"Do you mind?" Sam asked Ekaterina with a sinking heart. "I'm afraid it is my job."

Before she could reply, Sam took a couple of photographs, then moved away, but remained within earshot.

Ekaterina pulled herself up straight, pulled her shoulders back. "I do not come back here," she said. Then she fished in her handbag to pull out a hard-backed wallet of the type it is impossible for thieves to photo through to copy cards. Out of it she pulled a glamourous shiny gold card with the store's logo on it. She thrust it at the store manager. "Here is your card."

He took it. "Yes, you will not need this."

"Niet, niet," Ekaterina shook her head, "that's not, not," then evidently lost for what she wanted to say added, "Zamanchivvy".

With that she stalked out of the store.

"What the hell do you think she meant?" The store manager asked the young shop assistant.

Blushing with embarrassment as she spoke, the Eastern European assistant replied, "She said she wouldn't be tempted to return."

"That's all right," said the manager. Turning to Sam with a contemptuous look, he added, "Forward those photos to me and I'll get them printed out to circulate."

With a heavy heart Sam did as he asked. Had Ekaterina been shop-lifting, she wondered? With Vladimir already under suspicion, it would not look good for her if her name with photograph was sent to the police to go on some suspects register. She had not wanted to get involved with the catalyst converter robberies again, but now she had, if not proof of Kyle's involvement, a positive suggestion. That was not something she wanted

267

either as Kyle was, though not a permanent employee of Elmsleigh Park, someone frequently called upon to help maintain the grounds, or even assist in the restaurant.

Later that afternoon as she crept upstairs to the café for a consoling cup of herbal tea, since she'd failed to apprehend any real shop-lifters, Sam began to worry that the store manager might complain about her too. That was Laurie's problem. She must not worry for she did have more information for him. The photo of Kyle in the scrap metal barn actually attempting to sell a catalyst converter must mean something.

Of course it does. She clapped her hands making enough noise for the half dozen elderly ladies sitting round a nearby table to turn round to look at her, thus breaking the cardinal rule of store detection, always to be discreet and never to draw attention to yourself. For a moment she did not care. The memory flooded into her mind of Kyle at the social evening after which the President's catalyst converter was taken. He was there in the kitchen helping; she had seen him. Naturally he would have watched with interest Jason's ejection of Vladimir from the clubhouse and heard his threats. Knowing of Vladimir's connection with the scrap metal business, he would have thought how safe he was. It would have appealed to Kyle's wicked sense of humour.

The club might have taken the Old Alresford agency off what she now thought of as the Cat case, but she must tell Laurie. He should also know about his important Elmsleigh Park contact, even if spies were not his remit. She did not want to discredit the Vice-Captain of her own golf club, but he was in touch with Laurie so she should tell him there was more than a little doubt whether Bravo was his real name. She had discovered no evidence anyone called Bravo had been married in Selbourne church in the appropriate time scale, but there was a Julia Masters who married a Robert Burgess.

Maybe Ekaterina could help put it all together which meant she had another good reason to visit her today, besides to give her the support she obviously needed. However when she knocked on the door of the terraced house in Alresford she had a sudden fear Ekaterina might refuse to speak to her. The look the Russian lady gave Sam, as she left the department store, her mouth slightly open with a suggestion her teeth were barred, hinted hostility.

Her fears were well founded for in answer to the ring of the doorbell, Ekaterina pulled her door open ajar to peer through the narrow gap with apprehension. Sam could almost read an anguished *Go Away* in what she could see of Ekaterina's tear-stained face through the available space. "I'm here to help," she said quickly, "Be your friend."

"So?" Ekaterina opened the door a little wider, but not enough to let Sam enter the house. She gulped emotionally as she spoke. "You pop up and go; you are not reliable."

"I know I haven't been much use to you, and I'm terribly sorry, but I think I have got something that might help now. I regret what happened in that shop. There was nothing I could do, getting drawn in at the end like that. I didn't know the full story, how you got landed with that tee shirt."

"I was going to buy it." Ekaterina sniffed as she pulled the door open wide enough for Sam to enter, but she did not stand aside to give her enough room to move inside. "The trouble was the woman in front at the till was taking ages, and it seemed the card machine was not working properly, or not being worked right so I said I would give cash since the tee-shirt was only fifteen pounds or so. Then I found I didn't have the money in my purse so I said to the cashier to put the tee-shirt on one side and I would go and get money from the cash machine opposite the shop. The trouble was I forgot, and so did the sales girl, that I had already put the tee-shirt in my bag. That nasty man was silly; I would have come back with the money."

"Yes, I'm sure you would." Sam bit back the obvious response that the manager was not to know that. "Anyway, I'm in trouble too for sticking up for you."

Ekaterina sniffed again. She looked doubtfully at Sam as if to suggest she had not noticed Sam's defence of her, but stood back to let Sam in saying, "I think you would like a cup of coffee?"

Sam nodded and followed Ekaterina into the house and along the hall into the kitchen, which despite it being a warm late summer day, seemed chilly. Was it the atmosphere here? Or had the row in the shop she battled with earlier, now got to her, or worse, her bereavement? As they entered the room, Ekaterina flopped down on a pine chair by the table, put her head on her hands and wept. "I cannot do anything; please you make it."

Sam looked round the kitchen shelves for the coffee machine. Everything else there was much as she remembered, except that a large photograph presumably of a much younger Yuri with a mass of surprisingly blond hair now hung on the wall, which made Sam stare at it in puzzlement, for the man she knew had strands of grey hair. Noticing her glance at the portrait, Ekaterina lifted her head to say with a sob, "Yes, I like that picture. I need it now that Vladimir is going back to Russia. He looks like his father don't you think? That is the photograph we have on the programme for his funeral."

"His funeral?" Sam queried, for there had been no notice of this at the club. She stood awkwardly beside her hostess, wondering if she should put her arm round her for comfort or go ahead with the coffee making. She compromised by patting Ekaterina on the shoulder before she walked over to the coffee machine which had a couple of cups nearby and fortunately clear instructions on it as to how to proceed.

Once the coffee, a double shot Americano, was in front of her, Ekaterina continued, "I am not sure how you call it, maybe memorial; he will not be buried here. Vladimir will take his ashes back to Russia after the inquest."

Suppressing a shudder at the thought of such a transport, Sam eyed the picture. She could not see much resemblance between the Yuri's big tough physique and his son's slimmer supple build, but she nodded. There was similarity in the broadness of their faces, but since she had only seen Vladimir's cheeks pulled in with anger as opposed to his father's usual cheerful smiling face, the resemblance was not striking, especially with that head of blond hair since Yuri's sparse hair had turned grey. So she simply mumbled, "How you will miss him", before she asked, "How will you manage the business without him. I didn't realise until recently that you're involved with the scrap metal business next o Peggy's Shack."

Ekaterina shrugged. Her wide mouth went down at the corners in a grimace as she smiled a rueful smile. "It was a little business, how do you say, 'on the side', to help out Hector Bravo, who is now your Vice-Captain." She took a breath and her eyes widened in what looked like real awe, although there was a slight sardonic touch to her tone. "He is not much use to me now, but I have other friends."

"Like Nicholas Roman?"

"Yes, he is society or party friend, but he does not have good business head like Ognyan Sokolov."

Not sure Laurie would like to hear that said about his sponsor, thought Sam. With the amount of time Yuri had spent at the club, she had thought his chums all revolved around golf, still she pressed on, "It's good you have some Russian friends here to help out.".

"No Oggi is not Russian. He is Bulgarian, but he has big share in our business now. He has just taken it to help Vladimir, which helps because he has what you call sideline in retail too, so good because he is EU citizen. You will know him; he is a member of your club."

"No, I don't think so." Sam racked her brains to think of anyone other than Yuri who had a Russian sounding name. She picked up her bag lying on the floor beside the table to delve into it for her club diary which she picked out and laid on the table. Flipping through the last couple of pages, she read the list of members. "His

272

name's not here. If he is a member, he must be ex-directory. Some people don't want their names listed."

Ekaterina walked over to the table with Sam's cup of coffee. "His name will be there, but he may not use his Bulgarian name. May I?" Not waiting for an answer, she picked up Sam's diary to read through the list of names. "No, I cannot see it. I cannot find Oggi."

Oggi? Of course. Sam tapped her forehead with three fingers. That figured. *Oggi the ogre.* That was what Crystal told her Ozzie was called him after she first saw him in the clubhouse. "You don't mean Ozzie Reynolds by any chance, do you?"

"He likes a posh name." Ekaterina nodded, giving a little choking laugh before, as she sat down, she put her elbows down, dropped her head into her cupped hands and wept again.

"Oh," Sam blew out through her lips. *Not another person who's changed their name. This is more than I can handle. Why do they do it? They can't all be spies. Or can they?* "Some British people seem to have changed their name too. I was told the other day that Hector Bravo started life as Robert Burgess."

She regretted the remark, which had meant to be anti-racist and consoling, the moment she let it drop from her mouth, when saw the expression on Ekaterina's face, the defensive way her forehead knitted in a frown and her lips pursed. "But he is a real gentleman. No?" Ekaterina asked with suspicion in her voice.

"He can put it on when he likes," replied Sam with a rueful shrug of her shoulders. Now was time she felt she must level with Ekaterina.

273

"Acting is what spies do." Ekaterina's suspicious tone resonated.

This is dangerous ground.

"Never mind that," said Sam. "The main point is that your name really is Leonov?"

Ekaterina's shoulders went back as she straightened up in her chair, obviously affronted. "We are proud of being Leonov. That is why we have called our oldest boy Alexei after the astronaut."

"Are you really related to him?" Asked Sam thinking of her ill-fated game.

"I do not know; it is my husband's family. We are not near relations so we never met him personally but we are proud that Yuri had and our boys have the same blond hair. We know all this from the book Alexei has written."

"I see. So that's how Hector knew about the drink that Alexei offered to the English astronauts when they met in space."

"Yes, they did that to please Vladimir, stop him saying bad things about your club."

Sam sipped her coffee. This was getting interesting. There was something about Ekaterina's tone of voice and the tension in her body language as she clutched her cup of coffee with both hands. "Was he reassured?"

Ekaterina shook her head. "Niet niet. He was angry about that man being there, the one Yuri used to call the Woolly Mammoth."

Sam's mouth dropped open. She nearly choked. "You mean Greg Burgess."

"I do not know his name, but he came to see me the day before you know. Suspicions, suspicions, always suspicions; you English are so suspicious you know. You think we are the spies, but it you who are always asking questions and worrying." Tears rolled down her face again as she spoke emotionally, mainly in English but interspersed with Russian

"No." Sam listened in enthralled disbelief at Ekaterina's garbled speech. Despite the interspersed sobs with mangled languages, she managed to gather that Greg had come to apologise to Ekaterina personally for believing her husband, Yuri Leonov was a spy. Once Yuri was dead, he realised this was not true, but he thought someone else at Elmsleigh Park was in secret intelligence, giving secrets away to the Russians. He had warned Ekaterina she might now be approached by them. His final tactless thrust was to ask her that, if she were approached, to please get in touch with him by leaving a message in the shed where he died.

27. Coffee with Hector

Thankful to get home Sam was greeted by an ecstatic Monty. He had, Sam picked up from a text Crystal sent her, been left there three hours previously because Crystal needed to drive miles to pick up Jason's children from some sports ground. With all their gear plus a friend in the car, there would be no room for Monty.

Feeling guilty about her other preoccupations, Sam immediately took him into the kitchen to feed him before she prepared her own supper. Sometimes she had an empty feeling eating alone in the evening, but tonight all she could think was how much better a place she was in than Ekaterina, even if Laurie had said she needed to clear her own name with regard to Greg Burgess.

Nevertheless, in bed she could not sleep. She would have to get up, somehow try to make sense of all the stuff churning around in her nightmarish doze. Looking at a computer screen before bedtime or during the night was not helpful to sleep, one of the older ladies at the golf club advised her, but Sam felt impelled to go downstairs to her desk where she could sort through all the information, to make a document to send to Laurie.

That would help her; even the thought was a comfort until she reached her desk to switch on the computer to see the envelope icon at the bottom of her screen blinking to indicate a message. Wearily she decided to look at it, wishing she hadn't the moment she saw it was from Hector Bravo.

Ostensibly friendly, there was an implicit threat in the tail.

"Dear Sam," he began.

"I hope you have had a good day. I appreciate your interest in me and understand you may wish to chat about plans I might have for the club. However, I ask that you liaise with me over any information you require about my work. As you are a journalist, I am sure you would not want to mislead people."

Mislead and sue: the words were connected. Sam shuddered as she read the ominous word mislead which somehow obscured the "Best wishes" at the end of the message.

Well she could not ring him at half past ten at night. Perhaps by morning the problem would have subsided, meaning she could forget about it. That was not to be. Whilst she resumed her write-up of the catalyst converter situation, the phone beside her rang. Not recognising the number, she answered to hear the strangely unctuous voice of Hector Bravo at the other end saying "We need to meet".

Wearily Sam agreed, refusing the offer of lunch, but suggesting they met for coffee. That's safer, she thought, until the picture of possible antimony disguised as sugar in the club's office filing cabinet flashed into her mind. Hector was at both the last meal Yuri ate at Elmsleigh Park as well as the drinks party he gave for Vladimir the night before Greg died. Since both events were at the club she would agree to go somewhere else, a neutral place where she could bring Monty.

They settled on the Hollybush, a dog friendly pub at Frensham in Surrey, over ten miles away from Elmsleigh Park. The inn had been a favourite haunt of

Sam's missing husband which made it feel safe for her. A place which he did not know, where he would not be recognised also appealed to Hector.

Sam thought she had made sure she would be there first by arriving ten minutes early, but as she reached the top of the stone steps up to the pub, through the large window of the lounge area she spied Hector. There he sat, waiting for her. Although he did not turn around to wave a greeting, she knew he had seen her because he stood up to walk to the bar where he stayed, doubtless waiting for her. She gritted her teeth; she wouldn't take any sugar in her coffee today, brown or white.

Monty stalked alongside her as she walked into the lower lounge area where there was a bar with a display of biscuits, buns, cakes and a coffee machine. At the sight of Hector, his fur almost bristled, whilst his lower lip curled showing his teeth.

"Thank you for agreeing to meet me; I'm sorry if you had to cancel a day's detective work." Hector greeted her.

Sam gaped at him. How did he know she was a detective? He was evidently not taking a day off himself, for although he wore a patterned open neck shirt, over his arm was his dark grey suit jacket matching the trousers that he wore.

Two can play at that game. "Thank you" she agreed with a nod and as friendly a smile as she could muster, "you are evidently going on to work later."

"No, I don't have to," he said, "I'm only going in because I've got a society club dinner in London tonight."

"Lucky for some," said Sam as they made their way to a pine table in the corner of the room. She sat down, pulling a chair out, then pushing Monty's backside to make him sit down beside her, in a jokey voice she added, "I suppose that's a men's only club."

"At the moment," agreed Hector in a similarly light-hearted tone, as he put the coffee with the large flapjack for her, down on the far side of the table before he sat down opposite with his cup of black Americano in front of himself. "No one's changed sex yet."

Sam cringed. She wanted to warn him such a jokey remark showed his age and he should be careful where he aired such humour. Instead she asked, "What is it you want to discuss with me out of earshot of Elmsleigh Park members."

With a quick glance round the table to make sure no one else was sitting within earshot, he leant forward to speak, his thick lips protruding. "You may for now be Lady Captain of a golf club, but it is completely unacceptable for you to gossip about me or question my former wife about me, let alone make malicious remarks about me to a foreign national."

Sam hoped her face was not colouring as she asked, "What do you mean?"

"I think you know." Hector squared his shoulders as he now leant back, but his head was bent forward so that he looked straight into her face, if not into her eyes.

Whilst Monty beside her gave a faint warning growl, Sam shrugged. She must not let this man with his authoritative manner make her feel guilty. She recalled the lawyer of a magazine she once worked for telling her

279

he would never put her in the witness box because she had a guilt complex. Now she felt it was only too true. Like it or not she was involved in Elmsleigh Park troubles, which included two deaths. She had a right to seek out the truth.

"What do you mean?" She repeated.

"Oh come on," his voice was impatient now. "You know what I'm referring to."

Sam took a bite out of the flapjack, frowned as she pretended to think, then shook her head. Thankfully the flapjack tasted all right but then she trusted the staff here. At that moment, it hit her. Her hand dropped to the table. It was Cynthia Reynolds who made the shortbread to go with the coffee machine her husband had provided. Some biscuits could have had antimony instead of sugar baked into them. How much easier it would have been for Ozzie to give Yuri contaminated biscuits to go with the coffee he drank, than tip fake sugar into it?

Her momentary reverie was interrupted by Hector. "Okay." His voice was hard now. "Perhaps you would like to explain why I have had two phone calls, one from my ex-wife saying you visited her to ask questions about me, even tried to bribe her by taking her out to lunch. Not content with that, you called on Ekaterina Leonov with further malicious insinuations."

Sam tried not to let her mouth drop open whilst she chewed the flapjack. It did not surprise her Julia had been in touch with Hector about their conversation, but how did he know about her subsequent meeting with Ekaterina? She pretended she still had a mouthful, chewing to give herself time to compose a reply. *Be strong,* she instructed herself, *attack is the best form of defence.* Beside her Monty nuzzled her legs in support.

"I'm surprised any informants you might have, who somehow know of my conversations with Ekaterina, do not appreciate my role in comforting the bereaved wife of a former loyal club member who was desperately upset because not only was her husband accused of spying but her son of stealing catalyst converters."

Hector shook his head whilst he breathed out between large white clenched teeth before he said, "You're right she was upset, but as far as I can discern it was you who upset her, helping catch her shop-lifting, before you explained to her I was a spy."

"I didn't." Hot with indignation, Sam spat the words out. "Whoever told you that was wrong."

"Yeah, well. It was Ekaterina herself who rang me last Tuesday evening. Immediately after the shop-lifting incident, where you played both sides against each other, as I have checked with the store. You went to her house using fake sympathy to question her. In that process you riled her enough with your mad implications about me, for her to ring me that night to pass them on. Apparently, you didn't actually elucidate whether I spy for Britain or Russia or both, as a double agent, but she intends to find out."

"How?" Sam asked intrigued.

"Through her son, not Vladimir, but the other one in Russia. He's got chums in the FSB, she says." He shook his head. "Heaven knows if it's true, but with that family anything's possible."

"That's very harsh," said Sam. *Come on. Attack. Go for the jugular.* "At least they haven't changed their name."

"We don't know that. You've only got her word for that."

"I'll get it checked."

"You've got facilities for that have you?" Hector asked sarcastically, "with your private detective work."

"I am a journalist mainly." Sam took a gulp of her coffee. "Anyway, I think we're out of time. Thank you for the flapjack, but I think I'll leave the rest; I don't think we've anything else to discuss." Picking up her handbag from the chair beside her, Sam stood up.

Hector waved his hand up and down in a signal for her to sit down again. "There's the possibly assisted death of my godson."

"Yes, after drinking a potion at a party you organised apparently to placate a man you now suggest is guilty of theft. And you provided the drink."

"He didn't imbibe much of what I provided. What he slurped back was the soup you recommended whilst you sat next him."

"What's that supposed to mean?"

"Well you're the one with sleight of hand, aren't you? Isn't that how you understand shop lifting so well?"

From where she was still standing, able to reach over the table, for a moment Sam was tempted to smash the cup of coffee over his head into his triumphant smirking face, but she managed to restrain herself. What a mistake it had been to do that conjuring act at a club Christmas charity event as a favour for Tabby last year, but she couldn't change that now any more than she could change what happened to Greg. She tapped her forehead with the long fingers of her right hand. The sudden realisation came to her: it could have been, no must have been, the borscht Greg drank that killed him.

"What I don't understand is why it didn't affect me." She said out loud. Then she nodded as she stepped away. Looking back at Hector she said, "Of course."

Words suddenly sounded in her mind. *What was it that Cynthia had said when she and Crystal visited the Reynolds to ask Ozzie to take part in her club entertainment?* Ozzie was good at magic. He could do a conjuring act. Well maybe that's what he did at the Leonov party? He dropped deadly nightshade berries into the bowls of borscht. She pictured him on that evening, helping pass things round, moving from place to place serving. Yet it was Hector who tried to escort Greg away from the club, supposedly back home. Suppose he followed after him later.

"Of course what?" Asked Hector. His wide mouth broke into an almost friendly smile of rapprochement as he added calmly, "Come on, sit down, have another coffee." He stood up, moved alongside her and patted her shoulder. "I'm going to get us both more coffee, so you can calm down before you drive back home."

Sam plonked her bag down on the chair again. She might as well acquiesce. He was the bereaved uncle. Yet, why on earth did he allow that sick man to go back to that ghastly shed to die when he could have taken him somewhere more savoury.

283

Back at the table Hector supplied the answer without her asking. The shed was where Greg wanted to go to check his recording equipment, the carefully disguised pieces of antimony, if that's what they were, or simply fake bits of some other rock.

"So Greg actually was in MI5?" Suggested Sam.

Hector gave a sad chuckle whilst he shook his head, confirming what Julia had told her. "That's what he wanted, but he was turned down."

"But I thought he was so brilliant, first class Cambridge degree and so on."

"Yeah but he sticks out like a sore thumb wherever he goes, or rather used to. Can't have someone so obvious in a secret service, but being Greg, he wanted to prove them wrong, thought if he could unearth a Soviet spy, they'd have to recruit him, so he went solo."

"And got the wrong man?" Sam watched Hector's face, studying it for any indication of angst about suspicions Greg might have had about his involvement with spying. As his expression went blank, she probed further. "More than once?"

His face still expressionless, Hector replied coldly. "We're not here to discuss a person's suspicions, right or wrong."

"Not even if they impinge on his death? He apologised to Ekaterina for thinking Yuri was a spy and asked her to get in touch with him if anyone approached her so he must have suspected someone. Maybe it was you, his own uncle he thought could be a spy for the wrong side. That's why he was so upset."

"Maybe," agreed Hector, now looking at her intently whilst Monty growled softly at his tone of voice. "But you're the one in the frame for his death. Because you fancied him; you wanted to help him but he turned you down. It's an old story."

"You're the one who changed your name," retorted Sam, glad to feel Monty's hackles rising alongside her.

"As you have," snorted Hector.

"I'm a married woman, or rather was; I've legally kept my husband's name."

"Yeah and I've legally kept my ex-wife's name."

Sam gaped at him. *That's a fib.* She would like to have got out her phone to point to the photographed entry from the register on line, which said a Robert Burgess had wed a Julia Masters and she didn't find a Bravo, male or female. Burgess was the only entry in the possible time frame for their marriage that she had found. Still she restrained the hand reaching down for her handbag.

No point in telling him what he knew, she thought. As she looked at the beaky nosed man opposite her, who would, were it not for his nose, have as Tabby always said, be handsome, it hit her: *Hector's mother got it wrong. Julia had not as she suggested, baby-snatched her son; she recruited him.* Had she not said she would not use the name Bravo for Peggy's Shack because she, Julia might marry again? Bravo wasn't her name either.

No point in mentioning the register either. He would be sure to deny that was him. Instead, thinking of Tabby's refusal to use the title Lady, she asked, "What? What about the title Sir?"

"Oh, I kept on with the baronetcy I inherited from my grandfather. Julia wanted to become Lady Bravo so I went along with it." Noting Sam's astounded expression, he continued, "Happy?"

"As Larry," she agreed. How bizarre other people's lives and relationships were. She certainly did not want to hear anything more about his and Julia's any more than she wanted his views on hers. All she could think now was that Crystal's first instinct was right. It was Ozzie Reynolds, or rather Oggi the Ogre, the man who somehow contaminated the borscht was the person she should have suspected all along. Hector might be fishy but maybe that was in the right way, or at least presumably on the right side. He was not the one with access to antimony or providing poisonous borscht.

"Funny thing is," she said, thinking aloud, "Cynthia Reynolds actually said the blackcurrants for the borscht came from his garden. Why would she admit that if they were actually deadly nightshade?"

Because the only berries in their garden are blackcurrants. If anyone searches their garden, she'll be proved right.

"Subtle. Surprising he would know about an English poisonous plant like deadly nightshade though, since he's Bulgarian."

Hector's mouth dropped open as he laughed. "You haven't done your research properly have you. Belladonna's rampant in Bulgaria. It was even pictured on a postage stamp in 1969."

"Really?" Sam's eyes widened. Finishing her coffee she stood up again to leave. "Thanks for the coffee but time to go I think. This is getting frightening."

Now Hector also stood up. "Yes, you need to watch it. That's one of the reasons I wanted to meet you here." He spoke in a neutral tone, following a couple of steps behind her as she made her way to the door.

There to her horror, as she descended the steps, she saw him.

Sitting in a car in the carpark was either his lookalike or Ozzie Reynolds himself. How did he know they would be there and what could be his purpose? It was not a coincidence; of that she was certain. Leaning backwards she nudged Hector who was walking, his head down with a frown on his face. "Look," she whispered. "There's Ozzie Reynolds, there in the carpark."

Hector looked to where she pointed at Ozzie's Jaguar car, parked next to hers, where the man sat in the front seat reading a newspaper. "Damn, he's come to spy on us?"

Sam's brow knitted whilst her hand tightened on Monty's lead, fear mingling with suspicion in her mind. "How he could know we were meeting, let alone here."

"Ekaterina would have been in touch with him. He's her business partner. Your mobile's on the club system as is mine. Pretty easy for him to track us."

"What shall we do?"

Hector put his arm over her shoulders. "Pretend we're having an affair. That's why we've come here to be out of the way of anyone."

Crumbs. This is the last thing I want. "How will that help?"

"He may try to blackmail one of us, show his true colours." He pulled her close to him, making Monty growl protectively.

Sam bent down to stroke him. "It's all right," she said, wondering if she actually believed it herself.

As the dog quietened down, Hector pulled Sam against his body, his lips against her face as though kissing her, he spoke in her ear in a low voice. "If he speaks to you down there, act out the situation. Beg him not to tell anyone he's seen us together."

Probably want to do that anyway. Certainly don't want Tabby getting the wrong impression. "Well I wouldn't want him talking to your wife."

"Precisely, and as long as he thinks he's got something to blackmail you with it'll be useful for him to keep you alive. Try to look grief stricken when I kiss you good bye on the bottom step."

Instead of relieved. "Where are you parked then?"

"Amongst other cars by the cricket ground, just down the road."

"You're no fool, are you?" She might have added that he knew what he what he was doing rather too well, as far as going undercover was concerned.

With the reluctant Monty by her side, she managed to kiss Hector chastely on the cheek, whilst she blinked hard trying to make tears come into her eyes.

"Be careful how you drive home though. Lose him as soon as you can," was Hector's final instruction. He did not have to say any more. Recently she had read of a formerly wealthy Russian who'd lost his money being suspiciously killed in a supposed car accident.

28. A battle in the shed.

As Sam walked alongside the window, by which Ozzie sat, to open her car's back door for Monty to jump on to the back seat, he pretended not to notice her. Or that was what she suspected, so turning around, she tapped on his window with her knuckles, wondering at the same time whether this was a sensible course of action.

"Hi," he greeted her in a normal friendly tone, "fancy meeting you here."

"Yes, it is odd," she agreed archly. "What brings you here?"

"Oh I arranged to meet a chum here who lives locally, but he doesn't seem to have turned up. You wouldn't like a bite of lunch instead, would you?"

"No thanks, I've just had coffee here with a friend. I need to get home."

She could not, would not play Hector's game of suggesting she was a guilty party in an affair since Ozzie was not looking at her with remote suspicion. He seemed so casually friendly her own suspicions began to seem absurd to her. Whatever nationality he might be originally, he spoke ordinary English you might hear on the proverbial omnibus without a shadow of any outside accent as he bade her goodbye.

Only driving home did fears surface inside her. For there he was, not exactly behind her in his black Rover, but three or four cars away. It was sheer luck she spotted him in the wing mirror on a corner. Yet was he following her? He would not need to if Hector was right and he could track her movements through her mobile. Damn it, she should have turned it off.

Was she was being ridiculous, neurotic, even hysterical? Why would an ordinary person like her be pursued by a Bulgarian spy? Her imagination must be working overtime. Yet there was the black Rover, if not the one Ozzie drove, a remarkable lookalike, keeping pace with her, a couple of cars away. She pressed her foot on the accelerator; from whomever was behind her, she would take evasive action.

Without indicating, she swept off left to Frensham Ponds, where she drove speedily into the large carpark, hiding her car behind other vehicles. Once her car was parked, she switched off her phone, got out and picked up a handful of dust which she splattered on her number plate, hoping if Ozzie did manage to get on to the right road, he might not identify her car. In the mean time she hid behind a tree near the entrance to see if he drove past.

Half an hour later, very bored not having seen nigh of him, she got back into her car to drive back to the road to pick up the A3 at Hindhead. Maybe she had over-reacted, but it did seem Hector was right. Ozzie wanted to keep tabs on her. She wished she could get off his radar by telling him he had nothing to fear from her, but that would not be true. The more she considered it, the more certain she became that Ozzie killed Greg.

There must have been deadly nightshade instead of blackcurrant in the sweet borscht which they drank. Thinking back as she drove, she remembered there had been more than one thermos. Greg must have been served from a different one from her and then given a poisoned one to take home. It would be a simple manoeuvre for a conjurer to swap thermos flasks at a party where everyone was handing things around to show goodwill. To the best of her recollection, Greg had a second helping and took a flask home; he must have put in in the old-fashioned bag on the back of his bike.

It might have been more difficult to drop enough fake sugar into Yuri's coffee the day before he died, but the obvious answer struck her again, making her take her hand off the wheel to bang her head with her fingers. Ozzie could have had some antimony-based shortbread to slip on to Yuri's saucer to supplement any fake sugar put in his coffee. Or it needn't have even been the sugar. Ozzie could have mixed up the ground up white stuff with the parmesan cheese Yuri sprinkled on his pasta sauce.

She must get away from him. As soon as she reached the A3, she pressed her foot on the accelerator.

Yet as far as Greg was concerned, she needed proof poison was in one of the thermoses? She must find an unwashed up one, but that would be impossible. Ozzie would have got rid of them. Yet if he was worried enough about it to follow her around, maybe he hadn't. Perhaps Greg had taken the thermos which Ozzie offered back to the shed? Maybe like Yuri, he realised he had been poisoned, that the Russian spy was not, as he feared, his uncle Hector but the Bulgarian, Ozzie Reynolds, or rather Oggi Sokolov. Surely Sokolov was a Russian name?

Sam decided she could not leave things as they were; she must go straight to Elmsleigh Park to search the shed. Although last time she went there it looked as if someone, presumably Vladimir, or maybe Simon had arranged for the ground staff to clear it. Yet they might not have found the thermos with remains of the borscht. If Greg suspected he had been poisoned, he might have hidden the thermos, hoping someone other than Oggi, like herself, would find it and realise what had happened before he died. It was a long shot, but having taken another day off from other work, she must investigate this, in the hope she might find something before the fold-up bed and cupboards were cleared, if not removed.

To her relief there were only a couple of other cars parked near the sheds. Nor were there any ground staff lurking about. She would not have wanted to see Kyle, whom she was now convinced was responsible for the catalyst converter robberies, if not at the behest of Ozzie.

Why had she not thought of it before? Kyle had been at the On My Family Tree party, working in the kitchen. She'd arranged for him to serve Ozzie because of the worry of Ozzie's wandering hands. Kyle would have known of Vladimir's threats against the club hierarchy and indignation with Jason. What an opportunity to let the members think Vladimir was responsible for the thefts, especially as he would soon be back off to Russia, out of contact to deny it.

Again, how was she to prove it? With that, as with the poisoning, she must find proof, she thought as she fished in the glove box of her car for the spare keys she had copied from Laurie's bunch. She could not worry about Kyle, your friend, she thought as she let Monty out of the car to go with her. He could be loose but she wrapped his lead round her waist in case he needed restraint. Her current urgent task was to find that thermos flask, which should have remnants of the borscht Greg drank at the reconciliation gathering Hector arranged, or rather in the flask Ozzie gave him to take home.

Thankfully the key she had still fitted the lock on the shed door, but she shuddered as she entered the shed to find, how much the same it looked as she remembered it when she had found Greg. It had been so unexpected to see him there. Why had she not realised he had another purpose, besides that of a gardener or scrap metal dealer. She shook herself as she started to look around with Monty sniffing at her heels behind her.

As she opened one of the cupboard doors which revealed mostly empty shelves, she reflected that if Greg came here to sleep, it was not surprising he looked dishevelled. Unless he came up to the clubhouse and sneaked into the men's changing rooms, there was nowhere for him to wash. Nor were there any cooking facilities, other than one calor gas ring. The shed was simply a place to doss down, as she had assumed it must be for David Charlie.

She was just bending down to the bottom, third shelf of the cupboard, when she spotted the thermos. There it was, exactly the same as the ones Ozzie had used to pour out the borscht. That was puzzling because she herself had experienced no symptoms of poisoning. If this were the answer to Greg's imbibing the poisonous stuff, somehow Ozzie must have distinguished between one thermos and another. *Sleight of hand.* She knew it since she could have done it herself, she thought ruefully. As she picked it out of the cupboard Monty gave a low growl.

"What is it?" She asked, turning around to see Ozzie standing in the shed's doorway.

"Hallo there," he said in a genial tone, shutting the door behind him. "I thought you'd be here."

You damn well knew it. Somehow he had found a way to trace her.

He smiled pleasantly as he strode towards her.

Though Monty growled and bared his teeth, he made no move to stop Ozzie as he reached out with both hands to pull Sam towards him.

"Get off me." She tried to wriggle out of his grasp, but to her horror, although he was only a few inches taller than her with a body that did not look toned to peak fitness, his grasp was firm.

"Let's have some fun before you go," he chuckled, "now we're here alone together."

"No. no. My dog's here," screamed Sam, hoping against hope there might be some ground staff around to hear her. If only she had not taught Monty not to jump up at people but how to attack.

"Nice boy," said Ozzie in a soothing tone.

Monty snarled back at him, but to Sam's disappointment did not try anything more aggressive.

"Yes, you'll miss your mistress, but it would be a bit suspicious if you died with her."

"You won't get away with this; people will guess if you kill me."

"Nah," he laughed as he nuzzled her neck. "What'll surprise them is that someone with a drug addiction can play reasonable golf."

"There's no way anyone's going to believe I'm a drug addict. People know me too well."

"True they'll be surprised to learn of your correspondence with dealers on the net and how it ties up with your medical records."

So that's how you did it with Greg, hacked into his medical records so when the autopsy showed atropine poisoning, it looked as though he had taken it deliberately. Her surprised moment of realisation made Sam relax, something she immediately regretted as Ozzie tightened his grasp on her, pushing her back hard against the cupboard.

Frantically as she tried, she could not release herself from him before he launched himself upon her. She tried to bring her knee up against his crotch, but somehow missed. This was awful. What could she do, trapped as she was by his large body as his hand started to pull down her trousers? Maybe she should bite him. No, he might take that as passion. *Scratch his eyes out.* Perhaps she could try that, but pinioned as she was, she could not get her hands up to his face She screamed and screamed again, "Help."

"Oh come on," he said in a sarcastic soothing tone, "you like it; I saw you with Hector."

His lips moved on to her mouth but she managed to jerk her head away to one side as she screamed again and again, "Help me. Help."

"I'm here," came a shout as the door opened.

Whilst Ozzie sniggered, looking over his shoulder, Sam saw David Charlie enter the shed.

"Do you want to die too?" With one hand still holding Sam, Ozzie pulled a gun from his pocket whilst he turned round to face the beggar.

"Not yet," snivelled David Charlie. "Can't we have a tune before we die." He gestured towards the guitar case lying on the table.

"Great. Nothing like a bit of music with sex." Ozzie thrust his groin against Sam's body making her gag as though about to vomit.

"No need for that," Ozzie admonished her, whilst David Charlie unzipped his guitar case to pull out the guitar.

A moment later, holding the guitar as a shield, he took a couple of steps towards Ozzie. Then with a quick, deft movement, with the strings forward, he smashed the instrument straight into Ozzie's face.

Whether from astonishment, or the pain of the strings cutting across his face, Ozzie dropped the gun to put his right hand up to his head, whilst he still clutched Sam firmly with his left.

"Fetch." Sam shouted instantly to Monty, nodding her head to point at the gun by Ozzie's feet.

Though Ozzie bent down to retrieve his weapon, the dog moved faster. In seconds he had the gun in his mouth.

"Think you're so clever," snarled Ozzie, turning his bruised and bleeding face towards David Charlie.

Both his hands now went around Sam's neck as he started to try to strangle her whilst David Charlie, still with the guitar in one hand, lent down to take the gun from Monty's mouth, which he slipped into his pocket.

"You won't want to be had up for my murder old man," snarled Ozzie.

"Too old to care." Now with the guitar sideways on, David Charlie raised it up and smashed it down on Ozzie's head.

At the same moment Sam brought her knee up to make a successful contact with Ozzie's groin. To her immense relief, as he groaned, his grasp on her slackened enough for her to punch him in what she hoped was his solar plexus.

After another bash on the head with the guitar, Ozzie slumped to the floor unconscious. At David Charlie's request, Sam handed him Monty's lead, strung round her waist, to tie Ozzie to the struts of the fold-up bed.

As they left the shed David Charlie explained he had seen Ozzie drive up to the carpark and get out without any golf clubs. to go towards the shed. This had aroused his curiosity, but it was only when he heard Sam scream that he realised something dire must be happening.

"He's pretty wily." Sam felt her bruised neck. "He may free himself and escape before we can get help."

David Charlie shook his head. He pulled a chain round his neck to reveal what looked like a large locket. "It's my emergency call thing" he explained. "It tells my son I've got a problem so he'll be along in a minute with the police."

"The police?"

"Yeah, I'd have come into the shed quicker, but I rang to tell him you were in the shed screaming before I came in."

Indeed, as he finished speaking a Land Rover roared up beside them and out jumped uniformed armed police officers who ordered them away, saying they'd be in touch later.

"The least I can do to thank you for saving my life is to give you a lift home," said Sam.

David Charlie thanked her. "A lift to Petersfield would be good".

"How come," he asked as he got into the car, "you let that bastard know you were going to the shed to investigate. I saw him following you."

"I don't know how he knew." Sam opened her handbag which she had left in the car. She lifted out her mobile. "Yes, he saw me this morning, and I realise he probably tracked me to the café where I had coffee through that, but I switched it off. How he knew where I went later mystifies me."

"That thing," said David Charlie pointing at her built in sat nav.

"I wasn't using it to drive here."

David Charlie felt around the Sat Nav until he found something. As Sam started the car, he pulled out a little silver disc that looked like a coin. "No, but he was. I bet this thing can pass some sort of message as to where your car is going."

"Crumbs," sighed Sam as she drove away. "I think I'll give up being a detective. It's far too complicated for me."

"Maybe it'll be a new job for me at last," chuckled David Charlie. "After all I did find that bag of antimony labelled sugar."

"You what?" Sam nearly drove into the club's gate in surprise.

Yes, David Charlie told her. He'd found the bag of supposed sugar in the shed and thought there was something odd about it, just as he realised one of the lumps of antimony was hollowed out to be used as a router for internet access. Deciding there was something odd about the bag with what looked like sugar granules, he gave it to Simon to investigate.

"But Simon didn't do anything about it," complained Sam.

"He did; he gave it to the police but because it was found in the shed, they assumed it belonged to Yuri. His prints were on the packet somewhere."

"Yours must be all over the shed, with your sleeping there."

He looked at her with distaste. "Not me. Plenty of better places for me."

"But your guitar's there?"

"Yes. There was a spate or thefts in the hostel so knowing Yuri rented a lockup shed, I asked him if I could use it for my guitar and he said yes; he was a genial kind of fellow."

"But why do you think Ozzie killed him? Surely Yuri was more use to him alive than dead."

"Don't know. Can only think Yuri was so upset about being thought a spy himself he'd spill the beans about Ozzie, accidently if not on purpose. Once Yuri was dead, Greg realised he'd made a mistake and the spy he was tracking must be Ozzie".

"I suppose you're right." Sam nodded. If he was so smart, she asked him when she dropped him at the hostel, how was it that David Charlie ended up as a homeless beggar.

That he told her, was another story.

Epilogue

The police took Ozzie into custody where he was charged under the name of Ognyan Sokolov with two counts of murder and one attempted murder. Although the post mortem after Yuri's death suggested his death was accidental through inadvertent imbibing of antimony, evidence of Ozzie being in the shed Yuri rented, where the bag of antimony purporting to be sugar was found, plus his presence at the club the day Yuri became ill, meant further investigations took place.

At Sam's instigation, through the Old Alresford Detective Agency, the police did a forensic search through all the Reynolds' kitchen equipment. The place had been industrially cleaned before they got there, which was suspicious in itself, but they did find traces of antimony in a baking tray possibly used to cook shortbread. Furthermore, it was established through searches on the internet that purchases of ground antimony were bought in the name of Oswald Reynolds.

The most conclusive evidence of surplus specs of antimony came from the glove box in the car Ozzie was driving at the time of Yuri's death. That vehicle, to Matthew Borden's alarm, was hired from his chain of garages, with whom an Oswald Reynolds, had a contract. To Matthew's further embarrassment, it arose that Simon invariably used his company cars to rescue visitors from whose cars' catalyst converters were stolen. Luckily no collusion could be found.

Again, in the light of Sam's lengthy statement to the police, there was an inquest into Greg's death. This took into account that his medical records, besides his social media, might have been hacked. With no other evidence anyone in the medical profession or otherwise had supplied Greg with any drugs, nor any indication until his death that he ever imbibed atropine, it was concluded he was poisoned. A subsequent search of the shed revealed a thermos with residue of borscht containing traces of deadly nightshade, referred to as Belladonna. Although there were no fingerprints on the thermos, Ozzie's prints were found inside the shed.

Sam's certainty Ozzie's motive for Greg's murder was the would-be investigator's discovery he was a spy caused scepticism amongst the police. Nonetheless, at Sam's suggestion, passed through Laurie, they took off the back of the portrait of Ozzie's supposed ancestor Joshua Reynolds. There, tucked in a large slim packet held in place by the ornate gold frame they found three passports, one Russian and two EU passports, one with a Bulgarian address and another with an English domicile. Only one had his English name. There was also a collection of international credit cards.

Ozzie, vigorously protests his innocence. Sentenced to a lengthy stay in prison, where he remains currently, he is appealing, both in the UK and, as a Bulgarian, to the European Court of Human rights. However a dossier of hacked emails recorded on discs by Greg, found hidden in flowerpots in Helen's bedroom, reveals the presence of a spy for Russia within the Elmsleigh Park environment.

On a happier note, Vladimir Leonov personally thanked Sam for her attention to his mother and her belief in his family. Stuck with Ozzie's investment in the antimony mine, he has managed to get the other directors of his company to insist Ozzie should have no involvement in any of his company's activities or a role on the board. He also says he will retain his father's investment in Elmsleigh Park and would himself take up the membership fee awarded to his father for the years it has left to run.

Vladimir is also grateful to Sam for pointing the finger at Kyle for the catalyst converter thefts. She persuaded a reluctant David Charlie to go into the witness box to admit he had seen Kyle frequently appearing and disappearing in the Visitors carpark, though he could not see what Kyle was actually doing around the cars or whether he might be underneath them. Kyle's assured friendly manner made David Charlie assume he worked for the club, whatever he might be doing.

Discovering his father Yuri had inadvertently assisted Kyle through staff at the scrap yard he owned purchasing converters to separate into various parts before being sent off to other dealers, mortified Vladimir, especially as Nicholas Roman, his father's good friend was a victim of the thefts. He told Sam it is a good job Kyle now awaiting trial is keeping his distance from Elmsleigh Park, otherwise he would be tempted to deal out rough justice himself. With mediation from Sam, Vladimir has become quite friendly with Jason who has invited him to join classes he gives in unarmed combat.

Golf would help him be patient, Sam told him as she encouraged Vladimir to take up the game again along with his renewed club membership. Along with Tabby, she is having to be patient herself over the rules query over the adder curled round Tabby's ball. That seems to be being passed from one authority to another. However to avoid further embarrassment to Elmsleigh, Tabby has scratched herself out of the tournament.

Better news, the best of all, as far as Sam is concerned, the club awarded honorary life membership to David Charlie for saving the life of the Lady Captain. To some extent it has assuaged Simon's embarrassment having to admit his connection to the former beggar.

His father, whom Simon explained, he adored as a child, had, as his musical career deteriorated, a midlife crisis when he left home with a beautiful seductive agent who promised him the world. She then squeezed every drop of money out of him before she ran off herself, leaving David Charlie too embarrassed to come home. Over ten years later when he turned up at the golf club, Simon initially did not recognise him.

Sam feels the club owes him more than a membership. However, her suggestion he should be allowed one of the former bedrooms in the clubhouse for his personal use was not greeted by enthusiasm by the club's management. At present, it is under the consideration of the Elmsleigh Park Cabinet.

Acknowledgements

I am indebted to my friend Cerina Nicamin who designed the cover of Outside Influence. For the beautiful photograph, I am grateful to Alresford Golf Club for allowing me to display their lovely chalkland course to give the impression of Elmsleigh Park. I must emphasise that though I have enjoyed playing at Alresford, I do not know any of their members so no one connected with that club is featured in this book.

I am also relieved to add that I am reliably told by a member that there is no man called Nicholas Roman, belonging to the splendid Royal Winchester golf club.

The substance antimony is however real and it is being mined in Russia. For current information about today's uses of that valuable mineral I am indebted to Jocelyn Waller, the mining expert and director of Far East Antimony Ltd., which was established to develop the Solonechen antimony mine in Eastern Russia. This exciting project is far removed from any sinister uses of antimony.

For knowledge about spies I have read too many books to list, but a major source are the works of Ben Macintyre besides Andrew Lownie's biography of Guy Burgess. Here I must mention my good friend and fellow club member, Diana Burgess, with whom I have played many games of golf is no relation of the late spy. Nor was her late husband Brian, although she did tell me with a smile that he worked in Russia as a diplomat for three years.

Thanks also to another friend and fellow golfer Gaye Regan for her in depth proof reading which has proved invaluable. She improved on the earlier proof reading done by my husband Rupert who has been the soul of patience listening to my endless talking about different aspects of the story.

The barring of Jews from certain golf clubs, also referred to in Leopoldstadt, Tom Stoppard's latest play in a scene set in 1955, should be something of the past. It was in the late 1930s that my parents, my British Church or England vicar's daughter mother met my Jewish father playing golf at the Wildernesse golf club where they were both members.

Nonetheless, Douglas Abelson, my uncle was refused membership of a club in the midlands, so he along with some fellow Jews started their own golf club, buying a race course and converting it into Shirley golf course actually in 1955. This parkland course still flourishes today for all comers. Although my uncle was subsequently invited to join the prestigious club that initially refused him, he stayed at Shirley so as not to desert his friends.

Whatever prejudices have arisen in the past, the game of golf which demands trust engenders great friendships. It also inspires romance otherwise I would never have been born.